ON SCREEN
& OFF AGAIN

ON SCREEN
& OFF AGAIN

CAITLIN CROSS

Published by 8th Note Press
Text Copyright © 2024 by Caitlin Cross
All rights reserved.

ISBN: 978-1-961795-44-0

Cover art by Michelle Kwon
Typeset by Typo•glyphix

For Andrew, my forever leading man

ON SCREEN
& OFF AGAIN

Now

DAXON

❧

Out the window of this coffee shop is a billboard with my humungous face on it.

I see it as soon as I sit down. It's looming over Sepulveda, an ad for the limited series thriller I managed to sneak my way onto. Nobody's gonna look up at that thing and see me, though, not with an ensemble like that. The lead is Daniel Craig. And, really, I should probably be Andrew Garfield, but he must have been poisoned or in hiding or something, so they wound up with me.

My hand shakes a little as I raise the coffee to my lips. My glasses slip down my nose.

The only reason I'm up there on the side of a building is because of Greg Edgeway. He's inexplicably been in my corner since that first screen test. Pushed me all the way through the casting process until I got to spend six months in front of the camera while he sat behind, feeding me magic.

I owe him everything.

And today, he wants to meet me for coffee. To discuss a leading role in a film he'll be directing.

Even *thinking* those words, I get giddy and fluttery and nervous, like I used to get about a girl when I was seventeen. Greg wants me to play the *lead*. As in, my name comes first on the call sheet. My name comes first in the fucking *credits*. That is not the reality that I've been orbiting—ever.

I've built a career on sidekicks and comic relief. But I'd be lying if I said I didn't want more.

A bell above the door chimes and I almost jump out of my skin in anticipation. Greg comes striding in, shoulders back, ball cap just so, over to my table.

"Dax." He throws out his powerful hand.

I get up too fast and almost send my chair crashing to the floor before throwing my increasingly clammy hand into his crushing grip and grinning, breathless. "Greg. How are you?"

"Not as good as you are. Jesus. Look at you up there." He points to the billboard and sits down across from me, signaling to a passing server for coffee.

Greg has this bad-ass old Hollywood vibe to him. He used to run in the same circles as Spielberg, Lucas, Cameron. They all were young dudes in the seventies, set loose on some of the greatest films of all time, and they have the Oscars to show for it. Including Greg.

"Have I thanked you lately?" I say.

"At least eight hundred times," says Greg. We laugh. "I brought you this." He digs in his computer bag and pulls out a bound script and a paperback book. He hands them to me.

"*To the Stars*," I read off the book's front cover.

"Heard of it?"

"Yeah, actually." It's one of those books that sweeps bestseller lists like wildfire. "I saw something about it yesterday, I think. They said it's been the number-one bestseller for twenty-five weeks."

"That's it," says Greg. "And I've got the film rights."

My breathing quickens. I keep my face neutral, professional, normal, but if I was Daffy Duck, my beak would be falling off in surprise. *This* is the film he wants me to star in?

"And you want me to . . . star?"

The waiter arrives with Greg's coffee and he takes his time stirring in the sugar, adding a splash of milk. He clinks his spoon softly on the mug's edge, then lays it down, folds his hands beneath his chin and looks at me.

"I read that book in one night. Gorgeous story. The male lead is Nick. Young kid, bright, ambitious, dirt poor. Falls for a beautiful girl just extremely out of his league. And she falls for him. Daxon, I closed the cover when it was over and the only person I had in my head as Nick was you."

I blink at him. "Did you leave the gas on, or something?"

"Don't be a smart-ass," says Greg, laughing. "This part is yours."

The moon could fall out of the sky and crash into the parking lot outside and I wouldn't see it. "It's mine. Just like that? No audition?"

"That was your audition," he says, and gestures out the window to the billboard. "Now I just gotta find a Lila."

"A what?"

"The female lead. Lila. I want someone unexpected, like you. Someone who feels real."

He nods. I nod. I may have forgotten how to speak. "We start auditions next week," says Greg. "I want you there for chemistry reads. What do you say?" He holds out his hand to me again.

Numb, trembling, full of lightning bolts, I stretch out my hand and we shake on it.

I read the book in an afternoon and wander around my apartment in a haze for hours afterwards, my eyes puffy. This is the saddest fucking thing I've ever read. The story's breathtaking. The characters are alive and full of hope and softness, right on the cusp of World War II, where life has nothing but shit to throw at them.

And if I thought the book was good, Greg's script is better.

The hard thing, I realize as we head into auditions, is that finding someone for Lila who not only is gorgeous, feels like a real person, is funny in a way you wouldn't expect, and looks timeless, but can also act and do it well, may be almost impossible.

That first week, I think we see forty-five women.

The next week, forty-five more.

Some auditions are short. Not a fit, the scene goes by, no sparks, a name is crossed off a list and they send in the next. Some, however, are long, with actresses who want to spend twenty minutes talking through the dynamic of Nick and Lila, creating off-the-page backstory to increase our on-screen chemistry.

And there are a handful that are really good. Collectively, they have everything you'd need to bring Lila to life. But individually, something is always lacking.

Greg takes me and the casting team to dinner late on Friday after an endless callback session where no actual decision is made. He massages the place between his brows, stares at the table for a while, then looks up at me.

"Know anyone who might be good?" he asks.

I'm about to tell him no, when a name comes flying out of the past, straight out of my heart, and kicks me in the face: Wilhelmina Chase.

Okay, so we haven't spoken in probably seven years. That's problem number one. Problem number two is I have absolutely no idea how to get back in touch with her.

There's no how-to for reconnecting with your estranged ex-childhood best friend and first girlfriend—first *everything*. Really, there's not a whole lot of my early life that Wil wasn't part of. It used to be so easy with her, like opening the blinds and letting the sun in. But I'm imagining myself texting her now and coming up short.

Does she even have the same number?

Focus, Daxon, she used to say to me. I can hear her voice now, clanging off the walls of my skull.

I'll text her. Maybe. If I take enough deep breaths first. Or, no, I'll call her. I'll be really casual and normal and calm and . . . who the hell am I kidding? I know the first thing to fall out of my mouth the moment she says "Hello?" will be nervous gibberish.

Point is, there's no easy way to do this.

I'll just have to jump, and hope I land on something solid.

Here goes nothing.

Literally.

I have no ideas.

Please send help.

Then

WILHELMINA

G olden light in my eyes, tiny voices screaming out in the shadowed audience, and an iconic purple wig pinned to my head, I take a bow, and season six is a couple episodes away from done.

A bell rings. The stage lights fade and the work lights take over. Our soundstage is just a box full of seats again—not a Baldovian palace.

"That's a wrap on *Marnie, Maybe,* episode seventeen, season six, folks."

I'm expecting it to be our director. His voice, warm and patient, has pushed me gently through these last five years of glittering chaos. He's made me feel calm.

But the voice slithering through our speaker system is that of Harris Bastian, our executive producer. The phony, impatient sound of it prickles the hair at the back of my neck. I hate Harris Bastian.

"How about another big hand for our cast and crew."

That's my cue. Smile. Wave. Tune him out.

Little starry eyes blink excitedly at me from the audience bleachers and I head over, signing lunch boxes and spiral notebooks with my face on them. I don't know why, but lately, I feel my stomach dropping low inside me any time I see a Marnie poster or a (hideous) Marnie doll. I want more than this, and I'm also scared to let it go.

"Wil, production wants you backstage," an assistant tells me mid-autograph. I wave goodbye to the crowd, letting her lead me off.

Sometimes, after tapings we get notes. I head into our director Bill's office, but I see he's not alone.

Harris stands behind him to the left, arms folded, expression blank. Our showrunner sits on a chair to my right. It's her face that tells me to start worrying.

"Hey, Wil, take a seat," says Bill.

"What's going on?" I ask.

Harris snorts. "I don't know what this production is for, Bill, let's just lay it out there."

If my stomach could fall out of my butt, it would. I wish they'd waited until I could get changed. In a room full of adults wearing normal clothes, I look like someone who just won a competition where you try to put on as many outfits as you can in thirty seconds. Plus—the purple wig. I hate the purple wig, but it's my character's identity in a way that nothing else is.

"Should I get Daxon?" I ask. My voice is tremulous and small, like a child on timeout. The empty chair next to me looks especially lonely without my best friend and co-star sitting there.

I can't really remember a time that he wasn't there with me. We auditioned for the Magicworks network, for our show, as twelve-year-old child actor monsters, seated side-by-side. I remember seeing him in the waiting room. He was shorter than me. A little pudgy. Brown curls that could probably stand to be trimmed. And friendly, funny eyes. A soft face with a prankster's smile.

We were instant friends.

Bill's soft frown tells me that, whatever this is, it's bad news.

"You've worked really hard the past five years and I want you to know we've seen that, we appreciate it, we love you for it," Bill says.

Harris pulls the ball cap from his head and ruffles his thinning hair with an impatient, shallow breath. "Today, Bill."

Bill's eyes hit the desk. He chews his lip. "We just received word that we've been canceled. No final season. We'll film just these last couple episodes coming down the pike, and that'll be it."

I stare at him.

My entire world is crumbling, cracking, giving way. Since I could stand, since the first word out of my mouth, I've wanted to be a performer. I worked so fucking hard for it. And, five years ago, I got it. Not only that, I really rolled around in it. Covered myself in glittering stardust and, for a little while there, I could fly if I wanted to.

And now . . .

"What?" I say.

"Look, it's a network decision. It happens. We'll go live with the news tonight. 'Til then, don't say anything to anyone about it." The way Harris says it is like he's sweeping something gross into a dustpan and dumping it into the trash. "I gotta make a call." He leaves the room.

"I'll give you a moment," says Bill, and the room empties.

But the last thing I want is to be alone. I bolt up off the chair and crash through the door with my sights set on our stage. Maybe Dax is still there.

We're canceled.

There's only one reason why a hit show like *Marnie, Maybe* gets canceled—because its star isn't the brightest in the sky anymore.

I walk as far and as fast as I can, out the door of this row of offices, across the lot where our neat line of trailers has sat since day one. It's started raining. I hurry past teamsters moving set pieces, and hair and makeup assistants sharing a cigarette under a tree to keep dry.

Can't find Daxon Avery? Usually, it's not hard. Follow the sound of people laughing, and he'll be in the middle, glowing and magnificent like a bonfire on a cold night.

Benny from Security is monitoring the stage door for Studio 7B. When he sees me, damp from the rain, he opens the door without asking any questions.

"Thanks, Benny," I murmur with a wave, and head inside.

It's cleared out by now. No more audience, no more crew. It's quiet. Dark.

Above the seats, up high, there are posters for shows that have filmed here. My face is enormous, hanging up along the back wall, smiling, glittering. I'm young in that picture. I mean, younger than I am now. Thirteen, probably. From our first season.

I feel a responsibility to tell her—that little girl who had just lost her mother, and lost herself until she found it on this stage—that it's all over now. And it's her fault.

"Wil!"

I shut my eyes, my back to him. "Did they tell you?"

Dax's feet come to a squeaky stop. "I just heard."

I can't think of anything else to say. My fingers fish in my wig for the pins, pulling them roughly out. One snags painfully on my hair, so I growl and throw it across the dark stage.

"Want help?" Dax asks.

"No," I say sharply. I turn to look at him. And it's funny how lately, when our eyes connect, my stomach bottoms out. My face goes suddenly hot. There are so many new things that stand out to me now when Daxon Avery looks down into my face. For one, he's never been taller than me—that's new. The angles in his jaw? New. The nearly-there stubble across his chin? New.

Forever, he's been just Dax. Next to me in the makeup chair doing silly impressions. Discreetly ripping the corners off of his script pages at our table reads, balling them up and tossing them at Harris's coffee mug until he lands one. My best friend in the world.

Now he's seventeen, and tall, and gorgeous. And when I'm not expecting him, when he sneaks up on me or comes around a corner and we're suddenly face-to-face, my heart starts hammering.

"Come here," he says.

"Dax, I'm fine."

"Come here."

I close the distance between us, coming to stand right in front of him, then turning so he can pull out the last pins. My eyes fill with tears.

This set built us. And all of the people around it, our writers, director, crew, they took us from chatty, over-confident little shitheads to actors. From here, we were supposed to keep rising. Moving forward. Riding high into our last season and on to the next big thing, a project where I wasn't a princess-turned-pop-star in disguise. But what now?

"This is so fucked," I breathe.

"Extremely," says Dax. He pulls away the last pins with gentle fingers and peels off the wig. I turn around once it's off, removing the wig cap.

"Feels good to get that off," I say, but instantly start to cry.

Dax folds me into a hug, just us two alone in the dark in the middle of Studio 7B. He pulls back a little, looking down into my face, and brushes the tears off my cheeks with his thumb. "It's not over," he says quietly. "Not yet."

Our show? Me? This warm, fluttering thing between us now that I can't name?

Benny calls for us to clear out.

"You're pretty optimistic for someone who just got canceled," I say.

"Honestly, let's blame Dougie. He's a smug little asshole. He had it coming." He's grinning, but there's something shadowy circling beneath the surface. Like maybe he really does blame his character.

Dougie is Marnie's best friend. Her partner in crime, the one person who knows her secret—that she's moonlighting as a pop star.

The show started with Dougie. His ordinary world getting flipped on its axis by the new girl in town, a princess—Marnie—and their clunky misadventures through school, friends, life in general, plus the added wackiness of Marnie's duties as a royal and her secret singing career.

But it's surely not Dougie who ended everything for us. Sweet, goofy Dougie, cuter and cuter as the seasons trickled on. The grounded foundation every show needs in order to let the audience fly away with the purple hurricane that is a character like Marnie.

It's my name in the title. This is because of me.

"You know what," I say, "I think you're right. It's definitely Dougie's fault." I wrinkle my nose at him and Dax glares playfully back. "Come over tonight," I say. We make our way to our trailers, parked across from each other. The way they've been since we were thirteen. "Dad's cooking."

⁓

"It's me!" Daxon's voice calls from the foyer.

"Dining room!" I say. One of my favorite rooms. There are pictures of me as a little girl with Mom and Dad together. A few with just Dad. And even some with Dax are framed along the walls.

One leaps out at me as I pass it. Dad and me on set sometime in the first season, laughing into the lens. Having him play Marnie's dad has been everything. My safety net. He wasn't on set tonight when the news broke, but by the time I got home, he'd heard.

"What's he making?" Dax asks. We take placemats from the pile at the edge of the table and set them at each place setting.

"Pot pie."

"Daxon!" Dad booms. They shake and Dad claps his hand to Dax's shoulder. For the first few years, it was just Dad and me. And then there was Dax, and in some weird way, it's like he got a son. "Jesus Christ, save some bone structure for the rest of us."

Oh my god. I have a hard enough time pretending I don't notice things like Daxon's jaw. The space from his throat up to his ears. How it's angular and taut now. Regardless, I don't need it pointed out. "*Dad.*"

"I'll see what I can do." Dax plays along.

"Good man," Dad says, taking a seat. He pours himself a glass of wine and clears his throat. "So, I have some news."

It's in the way that his mouth twitches downwards a fraction of an inch, like he's bracing for my reaction, that tells my stomach to flush suddenly cold. Something's wrong. Something other than *Marnie* being canceled. "What's going on?" I say.

Dad sips his wine and pulls a face, ignoring me. "Daxon, word of advice for you, don't bother with the fancy shit. All wine tastes the same: like disappointment pissed in your grape juice. Write that down."

"*Dad,*" I say, my voice sharp. I set my fork down. Lean forward in my seat.

Dad looks from Daxon to me, then smiles slowly at his plate. My heartbeat is loud in my ears. But if it's bad news, he doesn't think so. "I met someone."

Now

WILHELMINA

work the fabric of my dad's bow tie, pulling and wiggling it into place until it's perfect. He asks me what my plans are for tonight.

"Might go out with Cassie and Margot." This is half-true. I turn him by the shoulders to face the mirror. "Looking sharp, Chase."

He adjusts the lapels of his jacket. Fiddles with the cufflinks. Gives his reflection a slow, shy smile that tells me he believes me in a way that makes my heart go soft.

"Do you think she'll be there?" he asks his reflection. All my organs squeeze tight with anger. I want to fling out my arms and hold him tight. Protect him from her: Katrina Tyson-Taylor, his ex-fiancée. Or Satan, as she's known in some circles. Okay, *my* circles.

"Where, Hell?"

"Wil."

Even though I'm twenty-four and haven't lived here in years, his voice takes on a scolding edge like I've overstepped and he's trying to course-correct. It pisses me off that he's still sensitive about her. That he lets her stay under his skin.

"Tell me I'm wrong," I challenge, an eyebrow raised.

Dad turns to face me. At first, he's stern. Then he goes soft and tired, leaning forward to press a kiss to my forehead. "I look okay?"

I nod. "Very debonair."

"Thanks, kid." He sits on the cushioned bench at the end of his bed and pulls on his socks and shoes. "You sure you don't want to come with?"

"Yep." I say it fast. Certain. Final. The thought of camera flashes, of men screaming at me to look this way and that way, of being interviewed about what it's like to have been famous—and what I'm up to now that I'm obsolete—sends a chill screaming down my spine.

Dad gets this look like maybe he wants to say something to convince me, but the hardness across my face and in my eyes makes him drop it. "I gotta get going. Walk me out?"

∞

"Do you know the code?" Margot asks.

Katrina Tyson-Taylor's locked front gates stand tall beside a sloping hillside full of ivy. A brick wall at hip height runs the length of the hill, and I know how we'll get in. "Don't need it," I say.

"Oh, no way," Cassie whines, taking in our route. "These are Louboutins."

I'd be faster alone. But two extra pairs of eyes are crucial for a hit like this one.

"Wait in the car if you don't want to come in." I glance back at Margot's car, parked inconspicuously in the dark space between streetlights.

"I didn't say that," says Cassie, pouting in the dark.

"Let's go," says Margot seriously. She's always like that—all business. "Stay to the right. There's a camera on the left."

Sure enough, Katrina's got a security camera perched on the left-most gate, aimed at the driveway.

"Hoods up," I say, pulling my black hoodie close around me. It hangs low over my eyes. Margot and Cassie do the same. We're almost invisible in the darkness, save for Cassie's annoying shoes, covered in rhinestones.

Up and over the brick wall we go, until we're wading through tangled black ivy, disappearing away from the street-lights' orange glow into the dark.

"My heel keeps getting stuck," Cassie says. Margot and I shush her.

At the crest of the ivy slope, soft, wild grass takes over. We scoot down on our asses and hit the cobblestone of the driveway.

"Alarm system?" whispers Margot at my left shoulder.

"No," I say. "Not since I was here last." Weeks ago, when this house was a "real estate investment opportunity," not just the place she'd sneak men into behind my dad's back.

"How do we get in?" Cassie asks.

I lead them around the perimeter of the mansion towards a back door, and then I point at the doggy door's rubber flap. "Margot, you're first."

"On it."

A Nigerian supermodel mother and a Mexican rock star father brought tall, gorgeous Margot Martinez into the world, so slight and willowy that I get nervous the Santa Ana winds will blow her away. But she's perfect for this.

"Wait," says Cassie. "Does she have a dog?" I can't tell if she's freaked or excited.

White, blonde-haired, blue-eyed Cassie Levy is Margot's best childhood friend, an heiress whose full-time job is spending money, and she's growing on me.

I snort. "Yeah, Toby." An ancient Lab that's long gone deaf. "He won't get in the way. Let's go."

From the other side, Margot unlocks the front door and holds it open for us. "Entrez-vous."

Now I take the lead, the lifeless marble hall stretching ahead of us. No paintings. No pictures. It's like nobody lives here. And for whatever reason, that gives me a chill down my spine. I smell the adrenaline radiating off my own skin.

In my peripheral, I only just make out Cassie's hand rising towards a light switch. I grab at it, fierce and fast.

"Ow! Wil. What the fuck?"

"Keep the light off," I hiss.

This isn't our first hit. I mean, we're not career criminals, it was just the once. And I never thought I'd be doing this again.

On my thirteenth birthday, Harris Bastian, the executive producer on *Marnie*, came into the wardrobe trailer while I was dressing—without knocking—and told our costumer, Janet, one of my favorite people of all time, that *we decided Marnie shouldn't have tits yet*. And I don't know if it was the shame of doubling up on sports bras under my costume that day, or the white-hot humiliation of being made to model my costumes the rest of that season for Harris, turning sideways for his approval, that put me over the edge, but bitches never forget a misogynistic, predatory dick.

I'm bitches.

It won't be a free-for-all. I'm going to take one thing, something Katrina can't replace. Like the years of my dad's life she wasted cheating on him. For Harris, it was an original *Playboy* from the seventies with Barbi Benton smoldering on the cover, a personalized autograph scrawled across her chest.

Katrina's bedroom is upstairs. Single-file, we go in, Margot lingering in the doorframe, playing lookout.

"Where does she keep it?" Cassie whispers.

"Don't know. Check the dresser."

I go for the colorless nightstand, starting with the bottom of three drawers. The first is silky underwear rolled up perfect and neat. Carefully, I sink my hand between a row, feeling nausea creep its way up my esophagus. But where do you keep something you don't want to look at? Tucked away under something else.

Next drawer, I'm not as careful, pushing loose bracelets and pearl necklaces aside as my fingers plunge hungrily towards the bottom. Not here, either. I growl under my breath and rip open the top drawer.

She has a journal in here and *oh holy Jesus* do I want to shove it into my hoodie so I can take it home with me and stay up the rest of the night reading all the petty bullshit she's filled it with. Except I already know what's going to be in it—Ben Cooper.

Fuck Ben Cooper, his Best Actor Oscar, and his chiseled jaw.

The rest of the top drawer is full of knick-knacks. I slam it shut and sit on the edge of the bed. *Where the hell is it?*

"Anything?" I see Cassie trying on a Burberry scarf and sunglasses.

"Would she miss these?"

"No," I sigh. "But keep looking, Cass."

"Ten minutes," says Margot from the doorway, "and we should go."

I use every bit of that ten minutes going through every drawer, every basket, every shelf. I'm being much less careful now; my sweating hands dump thousand-dollar purses to the floor, scatter shoes and jewelry. Cassie stands back, watching me like I'm a landmine she's afraid might go off if she takes a step.

"Wil, let's forget it."

"*No*." My chest rises and falls. Sweat beads along the back of my neck. I go for the last place I can think of: the bed. I pull up the king-sized mattress and feel around. Nothing. I pull back the gaudy silk sheets. Nothing. I slide my hand under her pillow and feel myself go rigid.

It's here.

Margot whistles from the doorframe that it's time to go. I know I should plunge the tiny, velvet box into my pocket and run. But I undo the catch and let the cool diamond fall onto my sweating palm.

Suddenly, a floorboard in the hall creaks. Every drop of my blood turns to ice.

I hear the soft shuffling of heavy boots. The click of a flashlight. My heart sinks like an anchor to the bottom of the ocean as the light hits me in the face.

"Hands up! Don't move!"

∞

I smile pretty for my mug shot.

It's bound for the tabloids and countless articles on has-been child actresses and the ultra-depressing lives they're living now. Might as well work it.

An officer guides me roughly by the shoulder towards a holding cell.

"Oh shit. Are you Marnie?" A girl my age. She's lying on a cement bench in the cell, blood staining her shirt and nose and knuckles.

Oh good. A fan. "Yup."

"Girl, what happened to you?"

"Drugs," I lie. "Lotta drugs."

"Shit. That's sad."

"Yup."

The door to the holding cell buzzes as Margot is led back in from making her one phone call. I reach for her. I feel like shit; it's my fault she's here. But the guard shouts, "No touching!" so I let my hands fall limp to my sides.

"Who'd you call?" I ask her.

"My brother." Margot sighs. "He didn't pick up."

The guard turns to me. "Wilhelmina Chase. One phone call. Let's go."

"Tell Dougie I said *what's up*," says my blood-stained prison bestie.

Dougie Miles, she means. Marnie's best friend on the show.

The guard leads me to the phone hanging from the wall and waits for me to pick up the receiver. I run my tongue across my teeth, thinking. The people who are first on my list to call from jail are in here with me. Dad? No, he'll still be at the Emmys, looking at his knees as Katrina Tyson-Taylor accepts her little gold statue for Best Actress in a Comedy Series and thanks everyone but him. Besides, I don't have his new number memorized.

Shit, I don't think I have anyone's memorized.

Then a phone number lights up inside my memory, and it's one I haven't called in years.

Tell Dougie . . .

My fingers are quick on the buttons, hoping it's still the same. There's a click, a breath, and his voice comes into my ear, low, concerned. So familiar, my heart rises.

"Hello?"

"Dax," I breathe into the phone. The guard beside me clears his throat pointedly, telling me to keep it brief. "It's Wil."

"Wil . . . what're you—what's this number? Where are you calling me from?"

"Jail." I make the word sound casual. Like I'm out for a cup of coffee and called him simply to shoot the shit. "You busy?"

Now

DAXON

Hearing Wil's voice through the phone is like teleporting to a place I haven't been in forever.

I hear the sound of my name dropping off her tongue in a desperate breath, and it brings me right back to seventeen. My lungs stop functioning. I'm like a goldfish that's just jumped out of the tank, flopping useless as it suffocates on the counter.

I can picture her so clearly, or at least the way my teenage heart saw her, wild and haunted. The image is inside my bones.

But wait—she's in *jail*? Suddenly, I've got six thousand questions and a few million concerns. My stomach twists. I haven't heard her voice in so long, haven't texted her, haven't seen her at all.

Which'll never stop being weird considering there was a time when she was my night sky, every star.

"You busy?"

Her question hangs there a second while I evaluate my situation. I'm at home, building the Millennium Falcon out of Legos. In my underwear. "Uh—no, I'm just hanging out." *There you go, Daxon, keep it casual.*

"Okay," she says. "Could you, um, would you mind . . . bailing me out?" She relays the location.

"Okay. Yeah. Sure. Okay."

"Like, now?"

"Oh, like, *now*? Like, right now. Okay." I get up and fish one-handed for a T-shirt and some jeans.

"Dax?"

"Yeah?"

There's a stretch of silence so long I think, by the time it ends, I'll be forty. I wait for her to say whatever it is she wants to say, my bruised imagination inventing words I know I'm not about to hear again, words I'd step on a thousand Legos to hear again.

"Please hurry."

I hear myself telling the officer behind the bulletproof glass that I'm here to bail out Wilhelmina Chase.

I watch my hand sign the bail receipt in my dopey scrawl, and then I sit, waiting, my knee jiggling as I try to think of something to say to her. *Does your dad still make pot pie?* comes to mind. *Arrests aside, how about coming in to audition for this movie?* is all I got.

"Is this what our tax dollars pay for? There are guinea pig pens cleaner than this place. And why are all the toilets clogged?"

I hear her before I see her, and immediately I stand. The officer she's talking to rolls his eyes as he removes her handcuffs, and I catch the two-inch, jagged scar on her left wrist from the summer she learned to climb the trellis leading up to my bedroom window.

She rubs at her hands and waits, scowling, as the officer behind the desk gathers her effects. And then Wil turns and looks into my face. The expression there is one that used to mean *shut up and don't tell my dad*. Except we're not kids anymore, so it's probably taken on new layers in the years of not knowing her.

"Ready?" I ask. This half-laugh, half-air sound comes falling out of my mouth as I try to figure out whether I'm going to smile or not—whether I *should*.

Given the things we said to each other, the way we broke up, maybe I should turn and go. But I feel it happen, feel the edge of my lips starting to rise.

"This is a three-for-one sale," Wil says, all business. She turns to the desk. "He's bailing out Margot Martinez and Cassie Levy, too." The officer nods and calls in the order through the walkie-talkie attached at his shoulder.

"I—am?"

"Get your wallet out," says Wil, pivoting back to me. I do what she says, because that's what you do with Wil, and I hand it over.

"Are they coming right out? What's the ETA?" she asks the officer.

I imagine having the confidence to tell a cop—or literally, anyone—what to do and how to do it. To take over any situation and drive.

This is something that clearly hasn't changed in Wil. Her tenacity. Her *audacity*.

Man. Seven years. How the hell does it feel like a blip and an eon at the same time? Like all I did was turn around for a moment, and we were nothing.

Two more bails are posted, and we're joined by two girls dressed all in dark colors. One, extremely pretty and Black, tall with long hair, wears an oversized hoodie and black jeans. The other, white with choppy, shoulder-length blonde hair, wears a black dress, her black tights full of rips and snags.

I remember the tall model girl from years back, and she smiles at me like she remembers me, too, but I don't smile back. Last time I saw her, she was helping Wil walk out of my life forever.

"Drive us home?" Wil asks me, shoving the sleeves of her black jacket to her elbows.

I reach for the door, but she beats me there, pushing out into the night. "Uh, yeah. Sure," I say to her back.

Cassie and Margot clutch each other by the arm and head down the jail steps towards the parking lot, whispering and laughing. But Wil stops at the top step, waiting for me. Our eyes meet, brown on hazel, and I'm filled with butterflies that I was sure had forgotten how to take flight.

She's here. She's standing right in front of me, and it feels like, if I blink, I'll lose her again. I think for a second she's about to say something, but Margot and Cassie call her name harshly from the lot and she hurries down the steps after them, saying, "Let's go, Daxon," over her shoulder. I've never had a choice, so I go.

The route to Wil's dad's place is written neatly across the part of my brain that knows her favorite color, and the way she has a different laugh depending on the situation or the lie she's getting away with. Things I know better than parts of myself. I can't help but wonder if any of them have changed.

"No, not east. Take the west. We're going to my place," Wil tells me from the passenger seat, all but taking the wheel.

Her place. She would have her own place by now. "What's the exit?" I ask.

"Topanga."

Margot and Cassie are glued to the glow of a cell phone in the back seat. They speculate loudly about a text from someone, and Wil is turned almost all the way around in her seat to participate, leaving me somehow alone up front, even with her arm, her breath, the familiar homey smell of her clothes and perfume five inches away.

I can't help myself from asking it. "What—uh, what did you guys do?" I'm afraid of the answer.

"Do you know Timothée Chalomet?" Cassie asks. I glance at her and Margot in the rearview, their faces eager in the dark, and I'm about to tell them no, unfortunately, I don't, when a text comes in and they're back to the phone.

"Wil," I say. But Wil is laughing. Snorting and silly, draped over the seat with her chin on her arm, poking at the phone screen. "*Wil.*" No answer. I should pull over, maybe, figure out what happened and go from there. But I let myself play chauffeur while Wil tosses directions to me, dissecting the idea that, out of everyone cool and important that I'm sure her life is filled with now—she called *me*.

Up in the dark hills, along sloped, curving roadways where ivy and bougainvillea overflow against walls and rooftops, is Wil's place. Spanish-style and taller rather than wider. Black awnings trumpet from the second-story windows.

I park in the driveway and Margot and Cassie burst out of the back seat, talking a mile a minute like they're coming back from a night out at a club, not jail. The crickets chorus. Wil takes her time closing the passenger door, running a hand through her hair—so much shorter than I've ever seen it, sharp and straight to her chin, but still the same copper color.

"You still drive like someone's grandmother," she says to me over the hood of the car.

I let out a tired laugh and run my hand down my face. "Thank you?" The moon hits her just right, the corners of her lips beginning to lift. "It's a nice house," I say.

"Walk me to the door?"

I nod like I'm a bobblehead, but grin and say okay, letting her lead the way up to the front door. "So . . . what'd you do?"

"Why?" Wil's eyes narrow a little as they scrutinize my face.

Part of me doesn't want to know. Not really. Wil chose this wild, out-all-night, Hollywood tabloid life that I never wanted a piece of.

If I think about it, my life has been a puzzle, every piece pushed together with precision and intention. Damn it, my life is one big Lego set, coming together brick by brick, and now I'm hoping I have a foundation big enough to stand on.

But there will always be one piece missing.

"Because . . . I don't know. You're—we haven't . . . You called me. I gotta know."

As Wil crosses her arms across her chest, tips her chin at me and examines the tiled archway above her front door, I'm hit with the reality of us. A thousand years apart could never pull her from my life completely. Her heart-shaped face, her unscrupulous hazel glare. These things are burned into my brain—my soul—forever.

"I went to get it back," she says.

"Get what back?"

"My dad's ring. From Katrina."

The tabloids ate that story up, Katrina's indiscretions just before their wedding, Bob's shattered heart. It's not hard to see how it could've lit a fuse under Wil. My eyebrows furrow. "You mean, you went to steal it? What did you do, break in?"

"I went to get what belongs to my dad."

"Jesus, Wil." I shake my head. She was always good at pushing boundaries, but this one she clearly took a flying leap over.

Wil rolls her eyes at me and, for a flash of a millisecond, she's seventeen again. "It's not a big deal," she says, waving her hand lazily into the night air like she's dismissing smoke from a cigarette.

"Getting arrested?" I scoff. "It's actually a pretty big deal, yeah."

"I don't need a lecture." Wil holds her hand up to me like she's pressing pause. Her other hand drifts towards the doorknob, her shoulders pivoting to dismiss me. My stomach leaps. This is it, she's about to disappear. How many years will it be this time? Ten? Forty?

"Why did you call me?" I ask, the question leaping out of my chest.

Wil's hand hesitates over the knob. Then, slowly, it drops to her side, swinging. Her eyes sweep sideways to meet mine. "You get one call. Yours is the only number I could remember."

I blink at her. "You remembered it?" We felt so important and grown-up the day we got our own phones. Spent hours learning the numbers by heart.

"You didn't change it?" Wil asks, her smile lopsided and challenging and so frustratingly sexy it's like a poison dart to the chest.

"Well," I start, my voice sing-song and throwaway, shoving my hands into the front pockets of my jeans, "you never know when Wilhelmina Chase is gonna call you from the big house." I say it to my shoes, then let my eyes rise to meet hers.

Wil chews her lip, appraising me, and she's not smiling anymore. Actually, she looks kind of ashen, sober—sad. She takes two steps forward and, with no warning, wraps me in a hug. Before I can release the startled breath that fills my lungs as her small arms wrap firmly around my torso, she's already gone, retracted her embrace and crossed her arms.

"Thank you," she says. "For answering."

I breathe into the night air, drinking her in, trying to memorize the moonlight on her shoulders, the porch light in her eyes. "Thanks for remembering my number."

"I remember everything."

Now

WILHELMINA

Trending in Celebrity

#WilChaseArrest

Trending in News

Wilhelmina Chase

Trending

#MarnieMaybe

#childhoodruined

Kira Winston @kdub3473 2h

Who had Wilhelmina Chase getting arrested on their 2025 bingo card??

Brenda Morales @morales95 1h

Marnie wtfffff #childhoodruined

Benjy Zhang @benjybyrihanna93 1h

Okay but marnie's mugshot is a lowkey slay

Kat Brown @xxkittykat7878 2h

MARNIE MAYBE U SHOULD RE-EVALUATE LMAO

The gavel slams and, just like that, one hundred hours of community service is staring me down.

Among "serve the community you've harmed" and "irresponsible disregard for private property," the words "first-time offender" and "upstanding public figure" were thrown around.

"What about me is upstanding?" I ask my lawyer, Paula.

She slaps me with a look that says *shut up, please* as we exit the courthouse doors and descend the steps into a sea of cameras and flashbulbs. Reflexively, I push my sunglasses higher on my nose, like they're my shield against a dragon. Or thirty dragons pushing into each other and breathing fire as they try to get the perfect shot of me cannonballing into a quarter-life crisis.

"Wil! Was it a fair sentence?"

"Wilhelmina! Over here! Comment?"

"Do you think you got off easy?"

I'm not sure what's worse: grown men yelling hungrily in my face, or the social media hashtag *childhood ruined* that I catch as I scroll briefly through my phone. There are hundreds of posts. People laughing at me, people pulling me from the trash pile in the back of their minds to lament my loss of innocence. Marnie was a constant for so many of these fans growing up. And I'm sorry they have to see her spiraling.

I'm sorry *I* have to see it.

I pick a spot at the hem of Paula's tasteful skirt-suit to zero in on, as she carves a path for us through the chaos, and try to tune them all out. Try to turn their shouts into ordinary city sounds. A bus rumbling by. A plane roaring overhead. A car honking in the distance.

But each of their questions, each of the ways my name comes shooting from their mouths, pierces me in the chest. I push down the urge to look around for a tourniquet.

In the car, I trace the outline of my phone, willing it to ring or sing out with an incoming text. From Margot or Cassie, but mostly from Dad. Except, hey, it turns out that when you attempt to burglarize your father's ex-fiancée, he doesn't pop bottles of champagne. He closes himself off to you. When he looks at you, as you tell him what you've done, it's with quiet disbelief. With a touch of shame.

We were just starting to heal, too.

I chew my thumbnail until it's short on one side, the skin raw pink. My knee bounces against the black leather seats of the SUV. And as we merge onto the freeway, I see a group of people in orange vests spearing stray pieces of garbage along the side of the road and shoving them into sacks.

Oh, holy fuck. This is my future.

Awesome.

My heart kicks into overdrive, pounding inside my chest as I realize that this may never go away for me. The social media posts are one thing, but I'd forgotten about tabloids and magazines. FORMER CHILD STAR 'STICKS' IT TO HOLLYWOOD. It'll run next to a terrible picture of me squinting in the sun, or sneezing, or, I don't know, sobbing, probably, on the side of the 101 with a trash-stabbing pole in hand.

I need a distraction. And pulling up his contact is too easy, too natural.

Are you busy tonight? Dinner?

Hitting send takes about four seconds. It's the waiting for Dax to reply part that starts eating at me. Like those tiny green dinosaurs in Jurassic Park—slow and tame at first, then merciless.

But, in my hand, my phone vibrates, and a little bell eases the tension in my chest at the reply sitting right there on my screen.

Love to. Mexican?

And that's how I dip back into the sweet, sun-drenched sea of all the good things we used to be—over margaritas and chips and guac.

There's a booth in the back, black rounded leather beneath a neon sombrero. Through the nearest window, I watch dusk slip its fingers between the distant skyscrapers, brushing calm, beautiful, encroaching dark across Los Angeles.

Somewhere between me shoveling guacamole in my mouth and raising my hand in the air for a refill on my margarita, Dax and I ease our way into a normal conversation.

"So, you graduated."

"Barely," he says.

"And you loved Yale?" I ask. The word *loved* sends wings fluttering up through my ribs. He used to love me.

"Yale was cool," says Dax vaguely. He sips his margarita.

My eyebrows jump up. "Yale was cool?"

"What?" He frowns. I snort. "It was. They brought in guest directors and professors all the time. It's constant improv and Shakespeare and moving through the space like a goose and—" He peeks at my expression and I see pink creeping across his cheeks, drifting to the tips of his ears. "All of that is cool, by the way."

I stir my cup of leftover ice with my straw and make bug eyes at the tabletop. He's so incredibly, spectacularly dorky. "Did you say 'like a goose'?" I squint at him.

Dax's fingers plunge into his warm brown hair, leaving it spiked and chaotic by the time he's dragging his hands down his face in exasperation. Damn it, the last seven years have been kind to him. "See, this is why I didn't tell you about it."

"I thought it was because I was pissed at you." I'll always have the instinct in me to quip, to slap a button on the last thing someone said. I say it with a smile, but the weight of it, heavy enough to snap our table in half, is absolutely and completely unfunny.

When I let myself look at him, Dax is scratching at his chin. "Uh, well, sure. Yeah. Could be."

"I'm over it," I say quickly. And I shake my head for good measure, smiling right through that lie. It's a lie, isn't it? That the way we ended is something I'm over. For so many years now, I've pinned that notion to the back of my brain.

It was the right choice for him.

Maybe I wish it hadn't been so easy for him to make.

"Okay," he says, nibbling his bottom lip. Dax's eyes dip towards his lap for a beat, then they're on me and the frozen-over look is gone. His expression is bright, friendly, interested, a little funny like he always is without trying. I can feel the twitch of muscles around my lips, making my fake-ass, totally-over-it smile turn real. "So, Wilhelmina."

"So, Daxonius."

His laugh is spluttering and goofy and full-bodied. He thumps his fist against his chest, grinning wide, and says to the ceiling, "Oh my god." Then his eyes are on me again, his head shaking side to side. "How ya been?"

It's the silly Midwestern accent he's using that rips my first sip of a third margarita up and out through my nasal passage. I splutter and cough and laugh, flipping him off as I wipe down my face with my red cloth napkin. "Oh, you know," I play along. My fingers fold the napkin into a tiny, neat square. "Keeping busy. Little of this, little of that."

"Ya don't say," he Midwesterns again. Then he makes eye contact with our waiter and orders a Coke. When we're alone, I watch his smile get smaller. "I booked something big." He's chewing his lip again. "A movie. *To the Stars*. Based on the book. I'm the lead."

"Shit." That sobers me up. "That's huge." A bestseller. An in-your-face bestseller. Reese's Book Club. The buzz around this book is like pressing your ear to a hive. For a moment, I let myself imagine that buzz around Daxon, and I want to shield him from thirsty women, from scrutiny, from the kind of fame you can't shake yourself free from.

Another part of me wants to tell him how proud I am. He really did it. Which is good, it's so good, that these years away have given him fame and reach and the kind of notoriety I was sure would be mine instead. I know it's good. But I can't shake the gnawing jealousy.

He nods. "Filming in South Carolina."

"When?"

"Four weeks."

"Who's starring?" I ask. Dax scratches at his chest and rattles off what they have of the cast so far. A few bigger names, a few I don't recognize. "Who's the other lead?"

"That's the thing," he says. "Can't find one."

My eyebrows collapse into a thick, doubtful line. "Can't find one? You need a romantic lead and you can't find one? Throw a rock, Dax." I gesture towards the window, incredulous.

"We've auditioned, like, eight trillion women," he says. I realize how tired he looks. "Nobody . . . fits."

"Oh, come on," I scoff at him.

"It's true. Swear to god. I've been reading audition sides since eight this morning. Nothing's clicking."

"You'll find someone," I say, because it's true.

He sits forward, leaning his forearms on the table. Then his eyes zero in on me. I want to look away, but I can't. He's got his long-sleeved shirt rolled to his elbows, a vein from the top of his hand snaking around his forearm. The fucking audacity. Finally, he opens his mouth.

"How about . . . you?"

Now

DAXON

⌒∞⌒

My lungs still while I wait for her reaction, but I know it's not far off. Wil can't hide her feelings to save her life—they're written right there on her face, plainly in all-caps, permanent marker.

And when I see what it is she's feeling, my stomach lurches. She's *freaked*.

"W-what?" Wil's eyes are huge. They flit wildly around her lap, then up at me, then down again.

"I know you're busy committing felonies, but think about it."

Suddenly she laughs and glares playfully at me, like she's in on a joke. "You're shitting me, right?"

"No. Zero shit." I shake my head.

"Oh." Wil's smile fades immediately. She screws up her face, her eyebrows furrowed and tight, and squints at me. "Why are you asking me this?"

"You're right for the part."

"So . . . it's a 'type' thing?"

I give a big, animated sigh and let my hand drag its way heavily down my face. "Just say you'll audition."

Wil blinks. "No."

"Wil." I sit up straighter in my seat, leaning forward and locking my eyes on her terrified gaze. It's a look all too similar to the one she wore the day I left.

"I can't."

"Why?"

"I . . . I'm starting community service soon. A hundred hours."

"We don't start filming for a month. You have time."

But that's not it. I know with one glance at her face, pale and wooden with agonizing self-doubt, with fear.

"No," says Wil, and it's a curt, crisp, terrified sound that falls out of her mouth. "Thanks. But no."

"Come on." My voice comes out soft and quiet, barely audible over the hum of conversation around us. I can see her clear as day in this role. Her vibrancy, her willingness to go there and be loud and emotionally raw. "You'd be great."

For a second time, Wil laughs. Only, there's nothing funny about this one. It's a choking sound, a shield but a really poor one. "You know what, I'm gonna go."

"I'll come with you."

"No. I'm fine."

"Hang on a sec." I dig in my pocket, pull out my wallet and leave more than enough cash for the meal and the tip beneath the lip of my plate.

Wil's back is to me, but she waits. When I'm right behind her, she starts up again, head down, plowing through the restaurant until a blast of warm night air hits us.

And then come the flashes. Strobing and constant, bobbing in the darkness in the hands of three paparazzi.

"Daxon, Wilhelmina, is there a *Marnie, Maybe* reunion in the works?"

"Wil, do you think you deserved jail time?"

In front of me, Wil turns to stone. Her shoulders are rising and falling too fast, and in the glow of the camera flashes and the city lights, I make a decision. I reach out and take her hand in mine, firmly, and all but pull her down the sidewalk behind me, ignoring the photographers.

"I'll drive you home," I say softly when we're alone, loosening my grip on her hand.

Wil doesn't let go, though. She doesn't say anything until we're standing in front of my car. I go to open the door for her. An ambulance whizzes by, screaming into the darkness, and Wil stops and looks up into my face.

"I'll come in for it. I'll read." Her voice is barely a whisper over the traffic passing us and the distant calls of the photographers, but I hear it loud and perfect and clear.

"You will?" I say, my hopes rising.

"I will." Her hazel eyes, lined in black and wide as the moon, trace mine with a desperation I haven't seen there in what feels like a thousand years. It's the same look she had the day *Marnie* was canceled.

It's when she lets go of my hand that I remember she was still holding it, that I remember my name. How to inhale and exhale. Wil dips into the passenger seat and I shut the door behind her, my fingers cool and free without her clutching grasp.

But I miss the feeling as soon as it's gone, and in the darkness, I flex my hand wide and back in again, remembering.

The purring sound of wheels on road fills the silence. Wil looks out the passenger-side window at the lights going by. Halfway to her house, she draws in a huge breath and looks to me.

"I've been auditioning," she says. "For everything."

I glance at her, then back to the road. This is news. I haven't read her name in years, haven't seen her in anything coming out. "And?"

"Not one."

"Callbacks, at least?"

"Not one."

I can hear the place where her voice snaps clean in half. She takes in a huge gulp of air and presses her hands to her cheeks, fingers turning claw-like as they grip her skin.

"That doesn't—" I start, but she cuts across me.

"Not *one*, Dax."

I catch my tongue between my teeth and bite down. A couple seconds tick by and then I hear her give a small sniff, catch the flash of her knocking something off her cheek. In the center console, I have a box of tissues, and I dig around for it and pass it over without words, my eyes on the road.

Really, when it comes down to it, I'm not good at comforting. I mean, I try. But I'm awkward and fumbling and never wind up saying the thing that would help. The most I can typically pull off is offering a little bit of *Star Wars* trivia in the hope of a decent distraction. It's not usually well-received.

Ten minutes roll by in silence and we pull up to her front gate, gravel crunching under the tires as I navigate the driveway. I kill the engine and sneak a glance at Wil. The look on her face as she stares up at her house, empty in the eyes, doesn't let me look away.

"You scared?" I ask her gently.

She nods. "Yep."

I don't know what to say to this. I know what I *used* to say. How easy it would have been a handful of years ago to reach across the seat and pull her close to me, my fingertips in her hair, her lips on mine. But now? I glance at the steering wheel then back at her.

"I have the script in the trunk. You wanna read with me?"

∽

We shift in the shadows of Wil's dark kitchen until she flips on the light, setting her bag on the island. I curl the script into a tube and hit it softly, absently, against my open palm, staring around at the way Adult Wil decorates a house.

Colorful is the first word that comes to me. No, scratch that. Wil's kitchen is a chaotic *storm* of color and print. Exotic blue tile around the stove, hot pink swirling marble countertops. Kitchen chairs with chrome frames and electric-green, faux-snakeskin cushions.

If I didn't know Wil, I might get the feeling somebody blindfolded her, held up a bunch of samples, she pointed at random, and here we are.

Except I do know her. Or *did*. And every inch of this kitchen is Wilhelmina Chase. Gregarious and wild, a whirlwind of color and life, a testament to the living piece of art calling this place home.

Wil goes to the fridge and pulls out a White Claw. "Want one?" she asks me. I nod, thank her, and catch it as she tosses it to me, the way she'd do with Cokes from the mini fridge in her trailer a thousand years ago.

Plopping the script on the island, I pull out one of the bar chairs (leopard-print bamboo) and sit. When I take a deep breath, I realize that the room smells like her. Like childhood, like dinners with her dad. Like summer. Our last summer. Inside my chest, my heart kicks and tightens, a grenade ready to blow.

She pulls up the chair next to mine and reaches across me for the script, her arm brushing my chest.

"Which scene?" asks Wil.

"Page twenty-seven." I watch her flip through my high-lighted, crinkled pages, finding the audition scene I have cattle-branded on my brain from a week of reading through it with hopefuls.

"I didn't read the book," says Wil after a silent few seconds of scanning the page. She glances at me. "Give me the SparkNotes version."

I lean back a little in my chair and think how best to explain. "Well, uh—"

"Ooh, no, wait. Let me guess first," says Wil, scrunching up her face in faux concentration. "Boy meets girl. Boy loses girl. Boy gets girl back?"

A snort comes barreling out of my chest and I shake my head at her slowly, eyes narrowing in disbelief. "Does Hollywood know about you?"

"Har-har," says Wil dryly.

We share a grin for a second too long—long enough to create that feeling in my gut like I missed a step—and then I take a long drink from the white can in front of me and clear my throat. "It's set in the forties, during World War II. Lila and Nick fall in love one summer before the war starts—as teenagers—and reunite on the battlefield as young adults, towards the end of the war when he's wounded and she's the nurse assigned to his unit."

Next to me, Wil seems to melt a little. Her elbow's resting on the counter, her chin in her hand, and she's slouching forward slightly, her lips pulled into a faraway kind of smile. "Oh," she says softly.

"Yeah," I say.

God, it's familiar, isn't it? I feel like I'm reading from the back of our own book, Wil's and mine.

Then

DAXON

∞

I met someone.

This is not the plot twist I was expecting. And holy shit, it has the worst timing, literally, ever.

I know those three words are like a giant foot stomping on the secret clubhouse Wil and her dad have built, just the two of them. And it's weird to me that Bob doesn't see that.

"Who?" says Wil. I can tell by the sound of her voice, low and curt, that she's holding back a shout. I stare at my fork.

Bob Chase is the kind of talent that comes along every six lifetimes. A stand-up comedy veteran turned TV actor, he's probably the most famous person I've ever met. Or, let me rephrase that: the most famous person I've ever *cared* about meeting. A chunk of the stuff I do—well, *did*, I guess—on *Marnie* is mostly a really sorry impression of him. It takes a lot of self-restraint and willpower not to fall to my knees and kiss his ring on a daily basis.

He's great, but subtlety is not his game.

"She's an actress. You probably know her," says Bob. He smiles at Wil, but the look on her face makes that smile disappear.

"Who," she says.

"Katrina Tyson-Taylor."

"Oh," I say, recognizing the name. "She's funny."

"Yep," Bob says. Wil glares between us and I go back to looking pointedly at the fork. "We've had a few dates. Couple dinners. I want you to meet her, Wil."

"Excuse me," Wil says. She jerks her chair back and the legs screech across the hardwood. Bob and I listen to the sound of her quickly disappearing footsteps as they climb the stairs to her room.

Above our heads, Wil's door slams.

"I got it," I tell him and fold my napkin.

I knock at Wil's closed door.

"Yeah?"

I shuffle in and shut the door gently behind me. Wil is fetal on the bed and I sink myself down onto the corner of the mattress. "You good?"

"Everything's ending," Wil says.

I want to hold out my hand for her, or maybe just take hers in mine and stay like that a while. Anything to keep my stomach from flinging itself out of my mouth, because she's right. It is. But not every part. "Not everything," I say.

Wil lifts her head and squints at me. "You were at that table, right? Just now? And tonight, on set? *Everything* is ending."

I twist a tassel from the blanket draped along the edge of her bed around my finger, staring down at the comforter. I know that *everything* includes the life Wil's shared with her dad up until now, just the two of them, recovering from the years before I knew her when her mom passed away.

Unsurprisingly, that's something that's really stuck around for her, even years later. The pain of losing her mom.

Two Christmases ago, Wil and I climbed onto the roof

of my dads' place and shared a cigarette, coughing and choking in the freezing night air. She was wearing red lipstick and missing her mother the way she always does on the holidays. We smoked that thing down to the filter, me gagging, and when Wil went to chuck it off the roof, I stopped her and tucked it into my pocket, saying we shouldn't litter.

It's inside my bedside-table drawer still, rolling loose.

I should tell her how I feel. How I've always felt.

There isn't a day, or hour, or minute I can pinpoint my feelings for Wil back to. No one glance, no single smile—it was everything, slowly, over time, better and better as the years rolled on, that helped me realize it.

I lift my eyes to hers. But immediately, I have to look away, across the room, anywhere but into the turbulent water of her stare.

When I've forced my eyes back to hers, I swallow. Wil's teeth catch her bottom lip. The only sound is our breathing, soft and steady in the quiet, but I'm sure that my nervous heart slamming around my rib cage is making enough noise for her to hear.

This feels like my one chance. Right at the brink of a huge change, before everything we've ever known ends.

"Wil, I wanna tell you something."

"What?"

Bob opens the door, pulling it wide. "Wil, let's talk about this. With the door open, please." He casts me a faux-accusatory look.

"Oh my god, like anything's gonna happen," Wil snaps automatically. "It's *Daxon*."

I clench my jaw so tightly, I can feel a muscle begin to twitch there. My moment's gone. "I'll get going," I say.

"No, stay," Wil says.

I shake my head. Really, I'm convinced that if I stay, the anxiety of what I was about to let slip will unhinge its jaw and eat me whole like an anaconda. "Uh, no, that's okay. I'll text you."

"Night, Daxon," says Bob as I disappear through the door. I can hear them plainly as I take the stairs.

"You're pissed," Bob says to Wil.

"Duh," she says.

"I don't want you to be pissed. I thought maybe you'd be . . . I don't know, happy for me?"

"You picked, like, the worst time ever to tell me this news, you know that, right?"

"Kid, shows get canceled. Happens all the time. First thing tomorrow, I'll call Sherrie, we'll get some auditions lined up. On to the next."

"I don't want auditions; I want *my* show. I want everything to stay the same."

"Wil."

"No," she chokes out.

My throat constricts. I reach the bottom of the staircase and cross the foyer to the front door, my hand on the knob. Outside, it's warm and dark, stars coming alive, the moon rising. Wind in the trees.

Ever since a growth spurt last summer, my legs are finally useful, and they stride long and quickly across the driveway towards my car. I can't believe I almost told her.

"Dax!"

I stop and turn towards the sound of her voice. Wil is running out the front door, jogging towards me. The look on her face could snap me in two. "You okay?"

She's panting, searching my eyes as she stops in front of me, closer than usual. So close I can feel the heat from her skin radiating. "No," says Wil. "I don't want this to end. I don't want *us* to end."

I let my eyes trace hers, stopping at her lips, then back up and around again. My stomach is on a hamster wheel, running for its life. I'm transfixed, and completely helpless to do anything about it, like she's just waved her hand in front of my face Obi-Wan-style and said *you will fall so hard for me you won't know which way is up.*

"We won't," I say. I swallow. "Wil, I—"

But she beats me there. Before I can say it, Wil closes the gap between us, pulling herself onto her tiptoes to kiss me, sweet and lingering in the moonlight. My arms fold carefully around her, at first, like she's something breakable, and then firm and sure and wanting, tight. Her hips brush mine. Our stomachs press together and I'm melting here, holding fast to her. We're walking the thinnest line at the edge of uncertainty, burning, ready to fall.

Now

WILHELMINA

∞

TO THE STARS - OFFICIAL SCRIPT

INT. LILA'S BEDROOM - EVENING

LILA sits before a mirror, lit only by flickering candlelight, staring at her reflection. We see by the look in her eyes that she's made a decision. In the background a door opens. NICK comes in.

> NICK
> *(quietly, on edge)*
>
> I looked for you after dinner.
> Mom was worried.

> LILA
> *(to her reflection)*
>
> I didn't want to be rude.

(a beat)

But I couldn't—*didn't* want to overstay
my welcome.

NICK

My parents didn't mean that stuff.
About you and me. About your father.
Your family being who they are.
They don't understand, is all.

LILA

Maybe not.

(she turns from the mirror)

But they're right about one thing:
summer's almost gone. We never talked
about what comes next.

NICK

You and me, that's what comes next.

(reacting to her wilting expression)

Right?

LILA

I'm leaving. Going to school.
I got my letter last week.

NICK

You got in?

LILA

I was gonna tell you. I got the letter
a couple days ago and . . .

NICK's expression falls. This is the news
he's been dreading.

LILA

Don't look at me like that, please.

NICK

Days ago? You should've told me.

LILA

I know.

NICK

So, you're going to school. We can do
long-distance. I'll write you. You can
come back on breaks, or I'll visit you.
I'll save up for it. It'll be just
like it is now.

LILA
(angry)

Stop it. Stop it. No, it won't. It won't.
I'll be thousands of miles away and you'll
be here, hating me for leaving, hating me
just like your family.

We're only cold reading—well, I am, at least. But the boiling feeling in my chest makes me want to close the script and tell Dax I can't do it.

Because when I say these words, I'm seventeen. Right before I shattered and blew off with the breeze, forgotten, not just by Hollywood, but by myself.

But one look at Daxon and I know I can't quit this.

He's *great*. He's emotional and present in a way I've never seen him act before, and we're only sitting in my kitchen. No cameras. No director. I can see the years he's worked at this radiating off his skin like a glow.

I glance back at the lines. Dax *is* Nick. He's transformed.

Or, maybe—am *I* Nick?

"This sounds kinda familiar." I try to add an airy laugh to this, but it dies on my tongue.

"Stay in it," Dax urges me. There's that technique, that dedication, rearing its gorgeous head. I pull myself closer to the script and wait for Dax's next line.

```
                        NICK


        Who'll be hating you? Who, Lila?
        'Cause it won't be me. Couldn't be.



                        LILA
                    (impatiently)


        Yes, you. You will. I'll go and it'll
        start growing on you. Slow, at first. Then
```

more and more and more until you can't
think of me anymore without wanting to
scream out.

A beat. She's emotional now, imagining it.
What her life would be without Nick.
Paying calls to other people's wealthy
families. Attending banquets and balls.
Settling for a fixed-up marriage to some
industrial tycoon's promising son. No
choices, no freedom. No happiness.

LILA

And you won't remember us. Or this summer.
Holding my hand. Rowing me out past the
tall grass just as the sun's going down.
Daring me to jump in, and when I don't,
you do, so of course I do, too.

My throat gets tighter as I read through it aloud. It's like
we're walking down a muddy road, stepping in our old footprints. I steal a glance at Dax and he's looking at me. His dark
eyes search my face and I can't tell if he's Nick or Daxon.

                         NICK

        How the hell am I going to forget you?
                Huh? Tell me just how.

                         LILA
                       (crying)

        I don't know just how. All I know is you
            will. I'll be gone, and you will.
                    You'll forget.

                         NICK

        Can't forget what's carved on your goddamn
        soul, Lila. You think you'll be easy to
        get rid of? You'll take me eight hundred
        years just to stop thinking about, let
        alone forget. I will love you forever.

"Oopsie."

It's Margot. Standing in the kitchen doorway, shopping bags in her hands, a wide-eyed expression painting her face. She's come in smack on Dax as Nick saying *I will love you forever*, which wins the award for Most Awkward Thing To Walk In On Ever. Especially given the fact that she was front and center for our catastrophic breakup.

"I'll go," she adds, turning.

"No, no, you're fine," I tell her. My voice comes out squeaky and high and I swallow, blood rising to my cheeks. "Dax just booked a big movie. I'm auditioning for it," I say. And I wave my hand around in a big show of *it's no big deal.* "We were just running lines. That's all." Why did I need to say that? I force my still wildly gesticulating hand under my knee and throw the island countertop a look, then fix my face.

Daxon raises a hand in greeting. "Hey, Margot."

Margot's eyes are still dinner plates. "Shut up, are you serious?" she asks.

"I mean, it's just an audition," I say, shaking my head. If I can downplay it low enough that it sinks through the floor and can't bite me, my churning stomach might be happy.

"Still," she argues. "That's big. Yay!"

Dax looks between us.

"I'm gonna get going," he says. "Wil, can you come in tomorrow?" He checks his phone. "Ten, if you can."

"Ten's fine," I say. I reach for the script where it lies forgotten on the island and hand it to Dax. "I'll see you tomorrow."

"Keep it," he says, then smiles. "I'll text you the address."

"Lemme walk you out," I offer. But he waves me down.

"I'll be fine. See you tomorrow."

Once the front door has clicked gently closed and all that's left of him is the spiced smell of comfort and home, I stand up. Margot's setting her shopping bags on the counter and pretending to look through them. But I know she wants to start questioning me.

"What'd you get?" I say. If I cut her off before she starts, maybe I can avoid the truth.

"A new Louis. What'd you get?" Her eyes are dancing with double entendre.

"Nothing," I tell her sharply. "Dinner. That's all."

"Mmhm," says Margot. Her eyes are spewing disbelief like laser vision. "And what else?"

I laugh, because if I don't, I'm going to vomit spectacularly across the kitchen tile. I wave my hand around again, feeling slightly like a lunatic. "It's not like that."

Margot's head tilts. "You're a terrible liar."

"I'm completely serious! It's not . . . Dax and I . . . we . . . no, we didn't, we *wouldn't*, we . . ." I let myself peter out and lick my lip with a tongue dry as sand. "That was a hundred years ago. Ya know? It's . . . it's over. It's not gonna . . . we . . ." But clearly, the words won't come. And I can't decide if it's because I don't know what to say or if I don't believe them. "Lemme see the Louis," I say, holding my hand out.

Margot laughs and hands it over. "What if you get this part?"

The air hisses slowly out of my lungs like they're deflating balloons. A couple minutes ago, Daxon was right here in this kitchen. My kitchen. And he was looking at me and saying things that I have dreams about at night. Things we used to say to each other. When the sun was low in the sky and the birds were quieting and it was him and me and the back seat of his car, or out in the pool as the stars came out. Declarations of longing and forever and everything so perfect it can never last.

"I don't know," I say, because it's the truth. "I really don't know."

Later, when I slip into bed, I reach for the script on my bedside table, and I read.

The curling edges of it tickle my thigh as I balance it in my lap, reading by lamplight. And I don't just read, I *devour*. From page two, my eyes well with tears, and they stay there for two hundred more pages.

I read until soft pink light filters through the window beside my bed. I barely notice that I didn't sleep by the time my trembling hands close the script and set it gently aside, like it's made of porcelain.

In the semi-darkness, I wipe at my puffy, itching eyes. That was the absolute, single-most beautiful thing I have ever read in my life. In those pages are living, aching people. I *know* that hurt, I *know* what it's like to feel that way.

And I know for sure that there's no room for us to open up our rusted cage of tiny, precious memories.

There's no way I can let us slip back into what we used to be if I'm going to put my soul into this audition, this role, this chance. If I don't get this part, I will never forgive myself.

Now

DAXON

∞

The first thing I notice about Wil when she comes into the studio is that her eyes are puffy. Her face is flushed.

She wears a black tank top and jeans, her short, auburn hair tucked behind her ears. And she's so pretty, frowning because it's early or because she's nervous, that I can almost forget about the stakes here.

If this doesn't work, we're back to square one, and whatever pieces of our past selves we excavated last night could turn to dust.

"Hi?" she breathes from the doorway. "They said you were ready for me?"

"Hey, come on in," I say. "Greg, this is Wil Chase."

Greg, our director, extends a hand to Wil and she takes it, giving a comparatively softer shake than the sturdy, no-bullshit one I know from years ago. She's clutching her script and headshot to her chest like a new kid on the first day of school—like they're her lifeline.

"Daxon says you're something else," says Greg. A nervous breath of laughter falls out of Wil's mouth, but she doesn't say anything else.

"She's incredible," I add. Her eyes hit mine, grateful and nervous, before they drop to the carpet.

"You ready?" Greg is looking at Wil, and she can only nod.

"Let's go," I say.

Our casting director, Nancy, has Wil stand on two crossed pieces of neon tape stuck to the carpet in front of the camera. "Let's start with a slate." Nancy's got this inviting, easy way about everything she says and does. She's rooting for you before you've even opened your mouth.

Wil licks her lip. I watch her through the monitor. And it's not the most high-def feed or anything, but it's clearer to me than ever that the camera loves her.

"Hi, I'm Wilhelmina Chase," she says to camera.

I remember Wil's slate from our *Marnie* audition. Not that I was there in the room watching her or anything, but I was sitting out in the waiting room, and her voice was so strong, so loud, so completely confident, that it bled through the walls and filled up the place. Today, it's so soft, I'm worried the camera won't catch it.

"Okay, let's start with the breakup scene. Wil, do you have the sides?" asks Nancy. She reaches around to open up a binder and picks through until she finds a couple of stapled pages.

"I'm off-book," says Wil.

Nancy's eyebrows hit the ceiling. "Okay," she says like she's game. "Dax." She turns to me. "Come here and stand off-camera. We'll do a tight in on Wil."

"Wil, when you're ready," says Greg.

I meet Wil's gaze, and as she looks back at me, something in her eyes catches fire.

                    LILA
              (emotional, hurt)

        Don't look at me like that.

   A three-freaking-second-long line and I already have full-body chills. The room is ghostly quiet around us. My heart slams into my ribs. Wil's eyes bore into mine, and as I look back, the room empties and it's only us two, Nick and Lila, circling goodbye.

                    NICK

      Like what, Li? Like I'm mad at you?
         I am. Can't change that.

                    LILA

   I know I can't. I'm not trying to. I'm just—

My line cuts her off, with my voice rising in volume.

                    NICK

      Just getting out while you still can.
    Hell, I don't blame you for that. Go on.
         Nothing left for you here.

LILA

Would you just listen to me?

Wil's voice pours over the words like cream into coffee, settling comfortably around Lila's southern accent. And the crescendo of her question, the way her voice peaks, the step she takes towards me, lost completely in the scene, is what tells me that this is our perfect fit right here.

This is our Lila. My Lila.

NICK

What?

LILA

There is nowhere on this earth I could go
that would make me stop loving you.

Wil has actual tears in her eyes. They slip over the edge of her lashes.

LILA

You think I care that you're mad?
At least that's something.

NICK

What's that supposed to mean?

LILA

You gave up on us, Nick.
You quit on me. Why?

NICK

'Cause you're leaving! You're leaving me.
What else am I supposed to do?

I can't tell what pulls tighter at my heart—saying those words to her or wondering while I say them if Wil's feeling like she's looking through time. Seventeen was so long ago, but the wounds it cut are raw as they ever were.

LILA

Tell me you love me. Say it to me.
Right now.

NICK

Don't.

LILA

Nick. Please. Please.

"That's a cut," says Greg, beaming. And piece by piece, the room comes to life again. Everyone was under the spell. "Let's do . . ." He turns to Nancy, poking his script, and she gives us the next scene.

And the next. Then three more.

Wil is there for two hours on-camera with me, up for any-thing—improvising teenage flirtations, a monologue about losing a first love, even a slow dance. What has the room in tears is the final goodbye scene. The tragic end of an unlikely love that wound up being as big and bright as the moon. There's applause when we're through.

Greg gives me a *look* and I know Wil's got the part.

"I'll walk you out," I say to her. Wil has the script clutched to her chest and I follow behind her as she navigates the tiny studio, headed for the door.

Outside, she turns under the dappled shade of a tree coming up through the concrete and shakes her head at me, grinning. "What the fuck?"

"*What the fuck.*" I echo her words but slower, almost reverently.

"Oh my god . . ." Wil sighs. She puts a hand to her forehead. "I'm *shaking*. I'm sweaty. I'm . . . Dax, thank you."

Worst mistake you can make is looking into Wilhelmina Chase's eyes when they've just found the afternoon sun. Because the color you'll find there hasn't been invented or dreamed up yet—it's that good.

"I didn't do anything. That was all you."

Wil laughs. She's giddy and silly and *happy*. "I hope I get it."

"If you don't, I'll eat that script."

Again, she laughs. "You're so incredibly weird."

"I know."

For a second, we just stand there, looking at each other. Wil's lips part like she might say something, then she looks away from me, off across the street. "I'm gonna get going."

"Right," I say. "Yeah. Sure."

We share a smile and she ducks away, heading up the pavement towards her car.

"Hey," I call after her.

Wil stops and turns. "Huh?"

"I really hope you get it."

"Me too."

And I don't say it because it's the nice thing to say, I say it because it's true and because, if she does, there's nothing on earth that can stop us from getting anything we want in this industry. This is what we've both been waiting for.

Now

WILHELMINA

I cry the entire drive home.

Not because the story is sad, but because I think I just had the best audition of my life. It was easy. It was natural. I didn't have to worry about the next line. I was present. After seven years, seven frustrating years of feeling completely erased from this industry, I felt welcomed home.

And doing it with Dax made it so much better. So much more real.

The next few nights I fall asleep praying to no one in particular that my phone will ring. But days come and go and there's no call.

On Monday morning, my community service starts. One hundred hours. It'll take me about a month, eight hours a day. And within six seconds of stabbing my first cigarette butt, I decide that, yep, I hate this. The only upside is that it's a nice distraction from staring at my phone, waiting for the call.

I keep to myself most of the day. Head down, poking trash like it's got Katrina's face printed on it, and dumping it into a bag. Somebody drives by honking and blasting the *Marnie* theme song at one point, and I fight back the urge to laugh as they pass. I used to be really fucking famous. Now, I'm wearing a reflective vest on the side of the 101. If that's not perspective, I don't know what is.

Twenty minutes go by and that same car comes around again and pulls to the side of the road. I get a tight, nervous feeling. Maybe it's some deranged fan here to murder me or maybe paparazzi hoping to sell the saddest picture ever.

But then, Daxon Avery climbs out.

The buzz among my fellow community servicers is immediate. The trash-stabbing stops. Everybody stares. I keep forgetting that Dax didn't slip into obscurity. All his star has done in our time apart is rise.

"Can I help you?" our foreman asks.

"I'd like to help out," says Dax pleasantly. He pulls the sunglasses from his eyes and tucks them neatly into the collar of his T-shirt. "If that's alright with you."

The foreman goes giddy as *fuck*. Clearly, he's a fan. "That would be—let me just—hang on right there, I'll go get . . ."

"I think he's in love," I say, as the foreman all but sprints for the supply box in the van.

"I'll let him down easy," says Dax.

"What're you doing?" I shove my stabby-stick pointedly into the patchy grass.

"Wilhelmina, I am a hardened criminal looking to serve my community. You of all people should understand this." He grins. I try to ignore the hammering that's started in my chest.

Our foreman returns with a spare orange vest and a stick and hands them over to Dax. "I saw you in *Son of a Gun*," he says, completely fangirling. "I saw it twice. You're so funny. Could I get a picture?"

Dax spends five minutes with him. Posing for a selfie. Talking about what it was like to make the movie. Someone calls the foreman over and I watch as he disappointedly peels himself away from his conversation with Daxon.

"Nice dude." Dax pulls on his orange vest. It tugs up the sleeve of his T-shirt. Biceps. He has *biceps*. Not jacked, overdone ones, but gently defined, kissed-by-the-California-sun ones. And I don't know who's more taken with them: me, or the foreman who's sneaking looks back over his shoulder.

"You're not supposed to be here," I say. Cars whiz by. The wind ripples Dax's white T-shirt.

"Well, neither are you, but hey, here we are." He leans on his stick, stuck into the ground. "I actually came because I have something to tell you. It couldn't wait, and it wasn't a phone-call kinda thing."

"What?" My heart trips over its feet, running wild inside me.

Dax takes his time with it. He licks his lip. Looks around thoughtfully. Waves to the foreman. I want to smack him. At my expression, he breaks and grins. "You got the part."

I scream. I full-out scream like a jungle ape and jump and throw myself at him for a hug. Dax hugs me back. The wind whips our hair. He spins us around and I'm laughing and sobbing. "Are you serious?" I cry.

"One month. You ready, Chase?" Daxon asks.

"Holy shit. Holy shit. Holy shit!"

"Okay, no slacking on the job. Let's go. Spit spot," he says, trying not to laugh as he hands me my stick.

Tears on my face, I burst out laughing. "Get out of here!" I point towards his car, but if he tries to leave, I'll full-body tackle him to keep him here. It's normal for a second. Like we're kids, like we're seventeen, like we're alone. Just as it was.

"What're you doing after this? Wanna get something to eat? Celebrate?"

I'm about to say yes. But then I remember my resolve. What if it's not just dinner? What if it starts out that way but then his hand brushes mine in the car, and suddenly he's close and smells so good I can't stand it and I hurl myself at him because we're freaking magnets and it's basically inevitable. I shake my head. "I can't," I lie.

Daxon nods slowly. "No worries. That's totally fine. Another time, maybe," he says, and we walk together, poking garbage and shoving it into a trash bag—so far from where we've been but closing in on a new normal. Except that I want to jump on him right here, cars whizzing by, and feel his biceps underneath my fingertips and kiss him until my lips go numb and hear that rasped, whispered way he used to say my name as I plunged my hands into his hair.

Stop, I tell myself. *Cool it.*

Instead, it's the fact that he's here, next to me, all afternoon that I decide to tuck away in my memories. The sweat on his brow. A smudge of dirt on his cheek. The way he helps load the van at the end of the day. Our sweaty hug goodbye. I replay it over and over.

We're about to start something life-changing. Career-altering. All the things I left years ago—the media attention, interviews, photoshoots, premieres—it's all coming back. Whether I'm ready for it, or not. It's coming. And what it'll do for me, how many doors it will open, I'm not one hundred percent sure. But holy shit, I'm ready to find out.

In less than a month, we'll be in South Carolina on location. I'll be in pearls. He'll be perfect in suspenders. And if I happen to survive, it'll be a fucking miracle.

Now

DAXON

∞

From the moment the wheels lift at LAX to the rumbling thud of them touching down in South Carolina, my stomach, my heart, my lungs and all of my intestines are knotted tight. Opportunity isn't just knocking here—it's kicking the door down.

A car waits for me outside baggage claim, driven by an older man in a suit and tie. This is the thing you never really get used to about making movies: how much the studio will shell out to keep you comfortable (if it's in your contract, and my agent showed her stuff).

Some productions put you up in a hotel. But property out here is cheap, so the driver pulls up in front of a tract house at the far end of a suburban neighborhood. My home for the next few months.

Call it habit, but I pull my phone from my jeans pocket and bring up ye olde family group chat. Really, the chat is just a place to document the fact that me, my twin sister, Rainie, and our dads all play this ongoing game called We Never See Each Other Because We're Constantly Traveling For Work, and between the four of us, I have no idea who's winning. I text the group.

> Made it to South Carolina

Dad texts a thumbs-up emoji. Pop does the same. Rainie won't text me back for hours or days because that's just how she is.

My dads are always quick to text back the bare minimum. Because if it's not a fixer-upper with good bones, they won't make time for it. *Won't* is the wrong word—maybe I mean *can't*. Literally can't. Their filming schedules are so tight, you'd need an industrial wedge to pry them open. Which isn't their fault; it's probably a good thing, actually. But a busy schedule and involved, attentive parents are two incompatible things.

I climb out of the car and step out into a humid night, thunder crackling distantly. And then six seconds later, it starts to pour with rain. I mean *pour*. My T-shirt, my jeans, they're both stuck to my skin as my driver and I pull my suitcases from the trunk. The last case, I realize about a quarter of a second too late, has its zipper half-open, and when the driver lifts it from the trunk, the lid splits completely from the base.

Legos. That's what hits the sodden pavement. They scatter in a thousand different directions, barely illuminated under the orange glow of the streetlamp. I had to pack the Falcon. Had to. But the reason for that is nowhere I can find it as I stoop in the rain and feel around the sodden ground for a thousand tiny plastic bricks.

"Hey!"

I look up and squint against the darkness at a figure running down the adjacent driveway. Wil's immediately soaked, short hair sticking to her face and neck, but she doesn't stop, doesn't make a fuss.

"Hi." I raise my voice above the downpour.

"The fuck are you doing?" Wil says.

"Regretting my life choices," I tell her.

"Will that be all, sir?" asks the driver. He raises his eyebrows the smallest amount and I know he's waiting for a tip. I dig in my jeans pocket for my wallet and fish out a twenty.

"You still do the Lego thing?" Wil squats down and begins raking pieces towards her in the dark, collecting them in her fist.

"Old habits."

"What's this supposed to be?"

"It *was* about three-quarters of the Millennium Falcon."

"Oh, Daxon," Wil says solemnly. "So nerdy. So, so nerdy."

"No, I mean, it's—it's a hobby. Lots of people . . ." I mumble, my voice getting lost in the rain. Then a laugh comes ripping out of my gut. "It's extremely nerdy. Thank you, by the way." I nod to her fistful of gray and black Lego pieces. "Also, hi." I stop and really look at her. Right away I wish I hadn't, because the tornado of fluttering that starts up in my stomach is life-ending at best.

"Hi," she says, then adds, "neighbor."

We dump the pieces we've collected into the suitcase and I zip it tight. Wil grabs the other, smaller case.

"What brings you to South Carolina, Wilhelmina?"

Wil snorts. "I heard it rains Legos and dweebs named Daxon Avery here and I thought *I gotta see that.*"

I glare at her. "Cruel woman."

"Come on, come over to my place. Dry off your spaceship." Wil signals for me to follow her across the driveway.

"It's a sailing vessel, technically, but that's not . . . important," I trail off.

"Oh my god, Daxon," she says, turning the knob on the front door, "please shut up." She laughs.

Now

WILHELMINA

The entryway to my incredibly empty temporary home is . . . incredibly empty. And dark. Like, who designed this place?

Dax leaves his bags by the door. I lead the charge into the living area, which morphs into the kitchen and dining space like a traditional apartment. Except super nice because this is being paid for by bigshot Hollywood money, so on the one hand you've got low, crappy lighting, but on the other hand, nonsense furniture that's expensive.

Here's another thing I forgot about that comes with being famous—people will throw a lot of money at you in ways you wouldn't expect. In the type of limo they send you to ride to your premiere in. The swag bags you're given at events. Free, fancy food at exclusive restaurants.

"Welcome to my haunted . . . Restoration Hardware?" I say, gesturing grandly and confusedly around before perching on the arm of the couch. "Bathroom's over there if you wanna change or anything." I point out a closed white door down a dark hall.

What I don't want to admit to myself is that Dax looks fine wet.

Like, *fine*. And I don't want him to change his clothes, I just want to look at him a while longer, his T-shirt clinging to his torso.

Dax pulls his shirt out and away from his stomach, which is *toned*. What the actual fuck is happening? He flaps the material, trying to get it to dry, and I almost have to reach up and physically rip my eyeballs away from staring at him with my hands, like I'm Bugs Bunny.

I shouldn't be ogling him like this. I know that. Deep in some forgotten cavern in my chest, I completely know that. He's my co-worker for fuck's sake. I need to focus. This isn't some balmy, beachy vacation, this is work. A job. My first in, like, a millennium.

But *oh*, I know and he knows that we are so much more than two people on the same payroll.

"I'll be okay," Dax says, taking in the place. He nods towards the wall behind me. "You've got a fireplace? That's cool. Wanna light it?"

"We could," I say. "But I don't know how."

"To . . . start a fire?" Dax asks me, quirking his brow. "You break into houses for fun—isn't arson next on your list of hobbies?"

"Alright, Tom Hanks in *Cast Away*, whatever. Let's see you do it."

"Oh god, that's a great movie," says Dax, tipping his head back in comedic reverence.

Then, like he's been here a thousand times, Dax heads into the kitchen and starts opening drawers. He's in there six milliseconds before he emerges tossing one of those fireplace lighters up into the air then catching it again, as though to prove a point.

"Grab two of those," he says to me, pointing to a basket of logs wrapped in orange and black paper.

I do what he says and bring them to the fireplace. "Now what?"

Dax reaches up and takes one from me, his forearm brushing my hand. My stomach somersaults at the feel of it, and I watch him move fluidly, loading the log into place. "Hand me the other one."

I hand it over. The rain is loud and clattering against the chimney outside and the echo fills up the quiet room like another living thing sitting between us. Dax clicks the lighter to life and presses its flame to the log. I watch the fire catch, kissing its way along the paper with a crackle.

After a moment, the room is glowing. Dax sits back on the floor, arms behind him, legs long, and pulls off his shoes. I drop down to the floor beside him. When I glance at him, and he looks over at me, it's like not one second has passed since the summer we were seventeen. There's quiet except for the rain and our breath. I look around for something to say.

"This is weird—"

"This is nice—"

"Jinx!" we shout at the same time.

Fuck, I missed this. We both erupt in ugly laughter and Daxon leans all the way back until he's lying flat on the floor, his body shaking. I lean against a nearby chair, grinning giddily into the fabric as I watch him. He's exhausted-laughing. The infectious, ridiculous kind that takes you over and doesn't let go until you're wheezing for air.

Plus, he's wearing his glasses. The dorky grandpa aviators that he makes look sexy. I'm in so much trouble.

"Oh my god—" he starts, but I cut him off.

"No, you have to buy me a Coke. That's the rule."

Dax's perfect face falls as he realizes what he's in for. I am a totalitarian jinxer. He gestures grandly as though to ask *where the hell am I supposed to buy you a Coke at midnight in a South Carolina suburb in the pouring rain?*

"That's not my problem," I say.

He scoffs, incredulous. Then he's up and heading into the kitchen. I'm up, too, like a freaking jack-in-the-box, springing to my feet and literally skipping after him, wet hair sticking to my neck. Dax dips and pulls open the fridge, rooting around the bouquet of chocolate-covered fruit, and random, trendy organic whatever, until he zeros in on a little red can.

"Free Coke. Sweet." I snatch it from the fridge before he can grab it. But that's not to say he doesn't try, swinging around for it as I twirl away, trying a bunch of ridiculous moves like holding it above my head or dancing just out of reach with it held behind my back.

What I didn't bet on was how fast he is now. This is has-a-personal-trainer, up-with-the-sun, jogs-for-fun Daxon. My Daxon struggled to climb the tree in our backyard. His favorite sport was *Mario Kart*.

He darts one arm out and catches me. Locks me in and pulls me close. The laugh falls off my face slow, but all at once, like egg yolk slipping down a windshield.

Our faces are almost touching, the Coke can slippery in my fingers where I clutch it behind my back. Dax digs around with his free hand inside his jeans pocket and fishes out a black wallet. He flips it open one-handed. Coaxes a dollar bill out with his thumb.

I raise my eyebrow at him and try not to count the dusting of freckles across the bridge of his nose. Fourteen. *Damn it.*

"I didn't say how much it costs," I point out. "You're short."

Daxon rolls his eyes at me and maneuvers another dollar bill out. He's able to collect the bills in his fingers, close the wallet and stuff it back into his pocket without dropping it, which is weirdly the sexiest thing I think I've ever seen.

"Oh, dang, I should've mentioned. We don't take cash," I say, and instantly bite back a laugh. Dax looks ready to drop-kick me to another galaxy, but he can't hold that expression long and the laughter takes him, starting in the eyes and melting its way warm and flowing across his cheeks. Down to his lips.

Those fucking lips.

Probably because I've been staring at them, I don't notice the way he's looking at me. He's closer. Not just his face but his entire body. Our shoulders touch. Our stomachs brush. His eyes say *what's it gonna cost?*

Don't. Don't do it. Stay focused. But I can't help myself. I can't physically stop it from happening.

For the first time in seven dry, terrible, lonely years, I crash into him like a wave devouring the shore.

Then

WILHELMINA

∽

It only takes a handful of weeks after Dad introduces her to me for Katrina to start moving her things into our house. Into my mother's side of the bedroom. Into her end of the closet. Until, by the end of July, she's a permanent fixture. I, however, am gone as often as I can be.

The night I kissed Daxon Avery, I decided something: He was always supposed to be mine, and I would always be his. And that's all that mattered.

So, the next night, I climbed the trellis outside his bedroom window and knocked on the glass. Dax appeared there, after a minute, in his *Star Wars* pajama bottoms. I beckoned for him to come out, hoisting myself up onto our old spot on the roof. He climbed over the sill and sat beside me. It was warm out. No wind. No clouds.

I touched his face. Held it in my hands and looked into his eyes. "You're the only person who makes me feel found instead of lost," I told him. Which, by the way, is the truest thing I know.

Lost Wil is loud and performative. She's the one who signs autographs, who poses for selfies with her fans. She's Marnie.

But Found Wil exists only right here. Where it's quiet. Delicate. Soft. Heartbeats and stars.

He kissed me long and slow. "I'll always be that for you. I promise."

My throat tightened; my heart soared. I kissed him, and it was a long time before we came up for air.

Since then, the summer has been ours.

I follow Dax into ice-cream shops and out again with towering cones, dodging paparazzi. Up every last step in a movie theater until we hit the back row and spend zero percent of our time actually watching the screen. He drives, I ride shotgun, and we tear across the scorching asphalt of Los Angeles with the windows down, laughing, our hair wild.

Tonight, we park at the Griffith Observatory, kill the engine and climb onto the hood. I tuck my head into his shoulder. The soft, sun-worn, time-faded plaid of his shirt tickles my cheek.

"How many do you know?" asks Dax. His finger tracing shapes in the air against the stars.

"Who cares?" I mumble into his arm, kissing a meandering, shapeless trail against his shirt.

He laughs. "Pop knows stars. Did I tell you that he was an Eagle Scout?"

"No, you didn't tell me," I murmur. I'm drunk off of this. Off the normalcy. The dependability. Not much in my life has ever stayed this long, this consistently. My fingers clutch at his elbow, pulling myself as close to him as I can get, our ankles crossing, my flip-flops forgotten. Dax's dads are nice guys. Welcoming and kind. The few times I've been over and seen them there, they asked how I was, how my family was. They're talented designers. They've earned every ounce of their fame. Only thing is, and I doubt they planned it this way, but they have about six minutes a day to be dads.

I hate the look on Dax's face when they're supposed to show up for him but can't because they're filming or demolishing something for HGTV. Maybe if I hold him long enough, I can absorb all the shitty things in this world so he doesn't have to see them or feel them or let them bite him. The way he does for me.

"Some are easy to pick out," says Dax, still going on about the stars. "Like Orion's Belt. It's those three stacked ones. See 'em? In a line like that?" He glances down at me. I meet his eyes and my fingers dig into his arm, something big lodged in my throat. Dax's eyebrows pull into a worried line. "You okay?"

"Yeah," I say quickly. I add a big, phony smile to throw him off the scent but Daxon was a bloodhound in another life, I'm convinced. He pivots his body towards me.

"What's wrong?"

I shut my eyes. Breathe out slow to calm my heart. Mom collected chickens. *Everything* had to be chickens with her. Cookie jars and matching plate sets, a rolling pin, an apron. All chickens, all the time. Our kitchen was a shrine to her ugly, perfect chickens. Now, they've been bubble-wrapped, and put in a box.

Dax's words echo in my ears. *What's wrong?* Every other thing in my life is what's wrong. *Marnie*'s series finale episode premieres this Friday, and once it's aired and over, then what?

What about us? Nothing that has ever taken a breath or seen the sun or existed ever, at all, has been more right. I can't lose us.

"No, it's okay," I say, and open my eyes. "I'm . . . okay, it's like—I was just, uh, I . . . am in love with you." The words come out of me like trash from a can somebody's kicked over. A bizarre mismatch of almost-sentences in a hundred different colors of awkward until finally, the truth. I hold my breath.

Daxon's eyes slip from mine. My heart sinks. Shit. I'm freaking him out. It's too much, too soon. But then he looks at me, hungry and touched, sincerity blossoming out of every inch of him. "Wil," he breathes, reaching for me. "I've always . . ."

But he stops himself. There's turbulence in his dark eyes, but I barely have time to read it before they're up and away, focused on a cluster of stars.

"You've always . . . ?" I try to feed him the rest of the thought like it's a line in a script and he's late with his cue. Dax nibbles his bottom lip.

"I got into Yale for drama."

A steel fist wraps its crushing fingers around my heart and squeezes.

He didn't say it back.

Why didn't he say it back?

I blink at him, numb and frozen, breathing hard in and out through my nose. I didn't know we were applying to colleges. "Y-Yale? You got into . . . you're—Yale? Like, Connecticut Yale?"

"Connecticut. Yale." He nods. "They have this drama program that's *really* good."

When I try to breathe in, nothing happens. Reality has crept in and lays itself down between us. "That's . . . across the country," I say.

"Right," says Dax, nodding. "Connecticut."

I'm tensing, bracing for the sky to crack and crumble down on us. The fact that it doesn't makes it worse somehow. I sit up on the hood of the car and pull my knees into my chest. Dax's hand brushes the small of my back then falls away and we're quiet for a long time. Too long, probably.

He didn't say it back.

"I was just kidding," I say after eighty-four years of literal crickets. I steal a half-glance at him. "Before. When I said that I . . ." But I can't say it again.

Dax sits up now, too. I hear him drawing his legs in under him, pretzel-style. "You were?"

"Yep." I say it confidently, easily, and stare out towards the valley below us. Tiny taillights, bumper to bumper, on a distant freeway.

"Bullshit," Daxon says. His voice is rough with something that isn't usually there and goosebumps rise on my arms.

I shoot my words at him like venom. "Did you mean Yale? Because yeah. I agree. *Bullshit*."

"Wil." He runs a hand down his face, tired.

"Yale, Dax? *Yale?* Seriously?"

"Yeah, Yale. Seriously. I want to act. I want to *learn* how to act."

"And the show we've been acting on for, what, *five* years was some group hallucination?"

"*Marnie* wasn't acting. It wasn't craft. Not really, anyway. It's . . . not enough."

All throughout my body, magma starts erupting. It creeps into my cheeks, into the tips of my ears, down my legs, behind my knees, into my fingers and toes. My mouth goes tight as I try to keep in words I know I'll never be able to take back.

But . . . fuck. *I'm* Marnie. And I'm not enough for him.

"I hate you for not saying it back," I say. The heat behind my eyes is heavy and pressing, determined to push through. I blink it back and move to climb off the hood. Dax's hand reaches out, fast but gentle, and tugs on the arm of my hoodie. When I look at him, I want to die.

His eyes are full of tears. "Jesus, Wil," he breathes, "do you know how goddamn in love with you I am? Have been for . . . since we *met*. Every day, every second." He glances back up at the stars, and as a couple tears slip from his eye, Dax's eyebrows get taut, his jaw sets, his lips frown. "But the semester starts in two weeks. I'm leaving in two weeks." His eyes shift to mine then drop away.

When I close my eyes and imagine Daxon, I see colors that no one else can. But this awful truth is colorless. My shoulders droop. Electric panic and anger ricochet through my body, slicing and sharp, as I take stock of what I now know:

Daxon Avery is in love with me.

Daxon Avery is walking out of my life in two weeks.

Now

DAXON

In so many ways, Wilhelmina Chase is a tidal wave.

Ferocious and headstrong, always guns blazing. She's a current that grabs you firmly from the middle of your soul and drags you along with her, surging across cities and years and wildest dreams and moments like this one.

But also, she's dew on a quiet morning, whispering across the grass, covering everything. Mist on your shirtsleeve. Aching and quiet and soft. Though this woman in front of me now is the rip tide I don't want to fight, I can see the glistening stillness, the vulnerability, just under the surface.

She leans into me and I'm ready to let her carry me away.

My back flattens against the cool metal of the refrigerator as Wil's hands move up my chest and against my neck and up further into my hair. I hold her to me like she's my high ground.

Her lips, her hands, her body pressed against mine, and breathing is the literal last thing on my mind. *It's happening. Okay. Be cool, Daxon. Oh my god. No big deal, just the thing you've been missing like a limb is* actually *happening.* Wil's hands slip up under my shirt and I feel the coolness of her fingers splay against my stomach, running their way across my skin.

"Abs," she mutters incredulously between feverish kisses. "You have fucking *abs*? Who the hell are you?"

Against her lips, I grin. My hands drift in a wayward mess across her torso, her chest, towards her jaw, her ears. They dip through her hair and I can remember being seventeen with Wil in the back seat of my car on a warm summer night and really touching her hair for the first time and thinking how there was nothing softer in the world.

Now it's cool and damp against my fingertips. I run my thumbs across her cheekbones.

"I gotta be honest," I breathe out, dragging my lips towards her neck and chuckling softly, "I have no idea what my name is, currently." Then I stoop and collect her in my arms, pulling her off her feet and up so that her legs wrap and lock around my hips. I cross the kitchen and sit her on the counter. My heartbeat is the loudest thing I've ever heard. It thunders in my ears like the storm outside has moved in. "Wil," I rasp. It comes out like a question, because it is. My eyes trace their way across her face, which is flushing pink all the way up from her neck.

Seven years. It's been seven Wil-less years. With only glitchy memories for comfort when I close my eyes at night. But god, it's been worth the wait. Hell, I'd wait seventy years for her. Seven hundred. They'll bury me one day, but if she called my name, I'd crawl to her from the grave.

Except, I'm the one who walked away. Who drowned us. Who lowered us down into the earth. I don't know if I can forgive myself for that, and I'm pretty sure she hasn't. Not really.

There's a microsecond where I see a flash of YES in her expression. Then it's gone. Wil's face falls, her eyes bugging. She sits up and hastily unlocks her legs from around me.

"Oh my god," Wil says. Her voice is hoarse and she clears her throat. "Holy shit."

My hands, which are at her hips, freeze. "Are you okay?"

"I just—I . . . *No*. I'm not. I shouldn't have . . ." She shakes her head and rakes her fingers through her short hair, tucking it back behind her ears. Her palms come together, fingers beneath her chin, and I know that look. She means business. "Look, Dax, I don't know what I was thinking. I'm—and *you're*"—she appraises me wordlessly, but I catch a glimmer of something in her eye—"and *we*—but I can't. Okay? I can't. If I'm gonna do this movie, I need to focus. I can't be distracted thinking about how it feels to touch your abs. Which I'm not thinking about, by the way," she adds before catching her breath and inhaling deeply.

"It's okay," I say. "I get it." But inside me, I'm a lava rock recently drenched in ice-cold water, steaming. I can see where she's coming from. It's not a casual thing, returning to something this monumental after seven years away. The stakes could literally not be higher.

"You do? Okay, good," says Wil. "Because now that I'm thinking about it, I think we need a . . . pact."

My brow twitches upwards. "A pact?"

"Between you and me. A pact. While we're working together, we shouldn't . . ." She gazes around the room, searching for the right way to phrase it, I'm guessing. "We shouldn't hook up. Okay? Friends?" She extends her hand to me like a mayoral candidate running for re-election. I shake it gently, my lip curving upwards, despite the disappointment squealing through my body like a piglet on the loose.

"Aye aye," I tell her soberly. "Friends. But if it pleases the court—"

"You're not on trial. Or a pirate. Daxon, you are so weird."

I search the air above her head for what feels like the right salutation and come up empty, shrugging. "I pledge allegiance to the pact." My hand slaps to my chest, above my heart.

"*Stop.*" Wil rolls her smiling eyes.

"Your majesty, if I may," I say, grinning. "I can one hundred percent respect the terms of the pact, but let the record show . . . *you* kissed *me.*"

She scoffs. "Did not!"

"Absolutely did too," I counter.

"Excuse me, why are you talking? You never bought me my Coke."

I can't help the wide grin that slides its way across my lips. Wil is trying so hard not to match my smile. I see it in her eyes, blazing and beautiful and bright. But she fixes her lips in a tight line and cocks her head at me, waiting for my answer. Meanwhile, my brain is replaying the last five minutes on a dizzying loop. The cool touch of Wil's hand against my stomach, the way her fingers curled and her fingernails dug in a little.

Chances of recovering from this are negative five thousand.

"Pretty sure I did," I say slowly, quietly, shrugging.

Wil's eyes widen a moment, her mouth popping open incredulously, but she chokes on any comebacks and instead swallows hard, shaking her head at me.

All she can say is, "I think the rain's stopped." Her eyes are on the kitchen window beyond me.

The kitchen is quiet, except for my desperate heart still pounding away in my ears. My hand flexes at my side as a strange, nagging guilt suddenly passes over me. "I didn't plan on . . ."

"No," Wil says quickly. "I know."

"Because I'm sorry if things are weird now."

"No. They're . . . not weird. Everything is super normal. Completely normal."

I take a step back as she lowers herself from the counter, and hold a hand out for her that she takes, steadying herself, and then drops right away. The coolness of her touch crackles like a lightning strike against my fingers.

"You sure?" I ask.

"I'm sure. It's all good, Avery. Don't sweat it."

But the air is thick with a strange new awkwardness we've never known together. Minutes ago, we were clutching each other like life support, like those breathless weeks after our first kiss, when summer and each other were all we had.

It's the worst idea ever to start something. Not that I've been feeling nothing for her all these years—I think it's safe to say my flame for her has been set to simmer, and I don't think it could ever truly go out. But at the start of a project like this one, with so much to offer both of us career-wise, it's the best move to leave things in the past.

"I think I'm gonna, uh, get goin'," I say.

"Oh my god," Wil snorts. "Please be more Midwestern."

"What?" I say, mock-offended.

"Ya ready to rock and roll?" says Wil. She really hits those O's, making them round with a Minnesota lilt. I laugh.

"Shut up, Chase."

"Bite me, Avery."

Our eyes meet. Wil's teeth claim her lip. Blushing so hard I can feel the heat in my face, I clap my hands and rub them together like somebody's Midwestern dad. "Night, Wil."

Slowly, I head out of the kitchen towards the front door. I can feel Wil somewhere close behind, and when I turn, she's leaning against the doorframe of the tiny foyer, the firelight behind her glowing like a portal to somewhere entirely made of magic.

"Night, neighborino," she says.

And it's a Ned Flanders reference, I know that, but Christ, if it isn't the sexiest thing I've ever heard in my life.

Now

WILHELMINA

⌒∾⌒

Our first day starts with a dance lesson.

Which isn't something completely new to us. *Marnie* had a signature dance we were forced to learn together. Not to mention there were musical numbers for Marnie herself all the time, so when I wasn't doing press or appearances at the mall, I was usually in a vocal rehearsal or a dance studio. Dax, on the other hand, completely lucked out because it was rare that his character got called on to do any of the singing or dancing.

And, honestly, that was for the best, because Daxon is uncoordinated as fuck.

We have a scene coming up in a little over two weeks where Lila and Nick waltz at a function her family is throwing. He's good enough to fool the guests into believing he's a real gentleman, and Lila is hopeful that maybe, finally, he'll be accepted by her classist parents.

So when I show up to the local studio and find him already there, wearing slim-fitting joggers and a T-shirt, looking like a total pro, I'm shocked. He's chatting animatedly with the dance teacher, an older woman who has clearly fallen in love with him in the minutes they've been talking.

Join the freaking club.

Except, when I come in, he stops. Looks. Smiles. His hand

lifts in a greeting and I'm hit in the face by what happened the night before. How that same hand curled so confidently around the back of my thigh, fingers digging in like he was holding on for dear life. How the other splayed large and sure against my back.

I run my hand across my forehead like an eraser across a whiteboard. If this pact is going to stick, I can't think about things like his lips or the heat off his chest. The sound that slipped from his throat when my hands dipped beneath his shirt.

Or his abs.

His *abs*.

No. I've gotta keep it lowkey and professional. This is my *job*, my *life* on the line. From now on, it's focus, perform, and earn back the place I once had in Hollywood.

I wave back to Dax and set my things down. Friends. We are friends. Completely normal friends.

Who do not fantasize about each other at all.

"Alright, we can get started," says our instructor. "Let's have you both over here on the floor and we'll do some warm-up stretches."

Dax's eyes hit mine and I instantly want to laugh. He always had that power. No matter where we were, but especially in a situation that was traditionally unfunny, one look from him would send me keeling over with delirious giggles.

It was like we used to speak a language together that I couldn't speak with other people, at least never the way I knew it with Daxon. A glance. A shrug. Flaring his nostrils from across the room. A sideways grimace. I was always done for. I've missed it so much.

And now, laughter starts deep in my gut and spills out before I can contain it.

"Are you alright, Wil?" the instructor asks me, her eyebrows low and concerned. I bite down hard on my lip and nod.

"All good. Sorry."

For ten minutes, we stretch. When I dare to look Daxon's way, he crosses his eyes at me or sticks his tongue out. I return the favor. God, it's nice. The vibes between us are right where they were when we were kids and all we had was each other in a room full of adults and with an ocean liner of responsibilities no child should know. This is light and sweet and fun in a way the vibes could never be with anyone else.

"Alright, let's get up and I'll walk you through the steps. It's simple. We call it a box step. Daxon, you'll be leading."

"I accept the nomination," says Dax with a salute.

From where I'm standing beside him, I gently jab my elbow into his side. "Shhh." But the grin on my face is impossible to get rid of.

Our instructor clears her throat softly and Dax and I straighten. Shit. That's right. We're working. I take in a breath and let it out. It's time to focus.

"We'll start left foot forward, and step to the side with the right," says the instructor, walking through the steps at half-speed. "Bring the left foot together with the right. And shift your weight here to the left leg, because now the right is going to step backward, and the left will step out to the side. Then right comes in together with the left. So, you can really see how we've made a box here, yeah?"

"Yes," I say.

"Uh." Dax lets out a laugh. "Sorry. No. Could you do it again?"

"Of course. Once more. A box, just like this."

She moves through the steps again and again until we can mimic her without totally fucking it up, and then the instructor comes behind me and, with one arm on my shoulder, the other at my back, pushes me around to face Dax.

"Now we'll try together. These hands go up and hold." She lifts my elbow into the air and Dax reaches up for my hand. Before she can place our other hands, his lands warm and wide against my waist.

The goosebumps are instantaneous. Everything inside my body rises, but it's not nausea, it's this floating feeling, like glowing lanterns swelling towards the stars.

Our eyes meet. His are so sweetly brown. Melting milk chocolate. They're safe, they're home, they're exactly where I want to look until my eyeballs turn to dust. Daxon's Adam's apple bobs as I watch his gaze dip to my mouth and back up again.

"Not at the waist, Daxon, but up here at the top of her back, please." The instructor takes Dax's hand and pulls it off my waist to land between my shoulder blades, and I wrestle with a sudden urge to let out a feral, dissenting shriek that would shatter the mirrors along all four walls in here.

But I don't. Because we're *friends*. Normal, ordinary, neutral friends. Except, where his hand used to be, my skin is sizzling.

"Wil, you'll place your hand just below the top of the shoulder, like this," she says, and moves my spare hand to the place on Daxon's arm where muscle definition blossoms just enough for me to feel it beneath my fingertips. "Are you alright?" she asks me, suddenly concerned. "You're flushed. Do you need a break?"

"No." I say it too fast. Too loud.

Dax pulls a weirded-out face at me. "You good, Chase?"

"Totally," I lie. "I'm fine. Let's keep going."

For half an hour, we box-step around the room, clunky at first. So clunky and baby-deer-ish that we have to stop and laugh at each other several times until the stern sound of a throat clearing brings us back to ourselves.

"And again, please. One, two . . ."

"Come on, Bambi, keep it together," I say.

Dax fixes me with an animated doe-eyed look, blinking rapidly for effect, and I almost lose it again. But I can't. I have to find some kind of balance between the wailing, flaming way I need him and want him and must have him, and the reality of this situation, which is that, if I don't nail this performance, there won't be another chance.

That's the thing about chances—they're numbered just so.

My first chance was bright as the North Star until it was extinguished. And the boy steering me around the room in big, bobbing circles chose another path and didn't look back. Now he's brought me this second chance. Held it out like a fine glass sculpture of something perfect that could shatter at any moment.

I can't let it.

Then something weird happens. Daxon leading me around the dance studio doesn't feel messy and awkward; it becomes fluid and clean. We box-step quicker now, turning and moving together, and it's not anything I'm doing. Actually, I'm pretty sure I'm holding him back. This is all him.

And it is so needlessly hot.

By the time the instructor dismisses us, I'm glad. I don't think I could stand another second in there, sweat at my hairline, my hand clutching Dax's, our heartbeats so close together that I could feel the magnet pull starting.

"You're weirdly good at that," I tell him as we fill cups at the water fountain.

Daxon pulls a face at me, full of mock incredulity. "I'm not *weirdly* good at it, I'm extremely good at it."

"Okay, let's not blow the roof off the place," I say with an eye roll.

"I'm kinda thinkin' *Dancing with the Stars* for my next project. How 'bout you?"

"I would pay money."

He grins and downs the rest of his water, wiping excess from his bottom lip with the back of his hand. I bite down on my own lip. *Stop. Fantasizing.*

"It's not bad," he says.

"What?"

"This. Real dancing."

"No?" I say. Dax looks around the empty studio, our instructor having left us at the end of the lesson. There's some local ballet class here in a few minutes, but I'm not in a hurry to leave, even if we're shooting all night tonight.

"You ever think it was weird that we never had a prom?" asks Dax.

I nod. "I guess." There are so many childhood things we never got. Because the moment we stepped on that set, we were treated like tiny adults with enormous responsibilities and never-ending pressure towards perfection. There wasn't time to be children.

"We deserved that."

"A prom?"

"Yeah," says Dax. "Rental tuxes, those flower wrist things, you in some great dress."

"Corsage," I say.

"Bless you?" says Daxon.

I push his shoulder. "The wrist thing. With the flowers. It's called a corsage."

"I'd have gotten you one," he says, really reflecting on it.

"Oh, so we're prom dates in this imaginary scenario?"

He grins, eyes swooping across my face and then back to the studio. Dax puts a fist to his hip. He nods around the room like he's decorating it in his mind. "You think I'm gonna let Garrison Boyle beat me to asking you? No. No way."

My mouth drops open, aghast and playing along. "Garry B? You would deny me a chance to be escorted around a smelly gymnasium with such a stud?"

Garrison was not a stud. He was an asshole. An entitled actor kid who played a featured extra on *Marnie* all six seasons.

"I would lie down in traffic to avoid it," says Dax seriously. He sweeps a hand across the air in front of our faces. "Ah, yeah, I can really see it. Streamers, of course. Balloons. Disco ball."

"Terrible DJ," I add.

"Wilhelmina, this is *my* vision," Dax sighs, playing exasperated, "and in my vision, the DJ is once-in-a-lifetime awesome. Nothing but hits. Straight bangers all night."

"Even the slow songs?"

He nods, stoic. "Especially the slow songs."

"And we'd waltz underneath the disco ball, is that right?" I ask, grinning.

I can see it, too. A dark room full of satin and silk and flowers and hairspray. Bright, anxious smiles, the flash of a photographer's camera lighting up the darkened bleachers in the background. Not the kind of camera flash I'm used to running from, but the kind that's warm and full of promise that the picture coming from it will be sweet and treasured.

Not agonized over.

Not mocked in a tabloid.

Not pasted permanently in the back of anyone's mind, taunting.

"No," he says with a scoffing laugh. "No, no. No waltzing. But we'd dance."

"To what?"

Daxon's body pivots towards me. We're both leaning against one of the ballet barres attached to the long, mirrored wall. The sleeve of his T-shirt tickles my arm as he moves to look down into my face.

"Huh. Well." He exhales a measured, thoughtful breath. "We're going back, what? Seven-ish years? So, that's . . . Ed Sheeran? 'Perfect'?"

The second he says it, I can tell he regrets it. It's all in the way his eyebrows fall and his lips part and the quick, recovering smile he slaps on his face. "Actually, I take it back," Dax says, and the uncomfortable moment of reality has scurried away to its dark corner. "It's 'The Middle.' Zedd. That is the song right there."

"With Maren Morris?"

"Yes, indeed." Daxon extends his hand to me, palm up.

"Baby, why don't you just meet me in the middle?" he says, deadpan. "Can I have this dance?"

My knees give and I slump over laughing. "One . . . hundred . . . percent no," I splutter, heaving for air.

"Aw, come on, Chase. I'm light on my feet," says Dax.

When I straighten up, his smile is gentle and familiar and warm like the sand on a sun-drenched beach. His eyes are so many things—amused, smart, silly, but also truthful and hoping. I flop my hand into his.

"*One* dance," I say, and Dax leads me out into the middle of the room. Which is such a blatant mistake for me to make given last night, and the pact, and the fact that we are co-workers, friends, nothing more. But as his soft hand tugs me along, I go without complaint.

I go like a bee to a blossom, starving.

Here, without an instructor to move them into proper position, Daxon's hands come to rest low on my waist near my hips. I reach up and lock my arms around his neck and we sway a little, side to side, around in a circle.

It's so sublimely ridiculous. I know that. But there is a niceness to it that I've never known, that I—*we*—deserved to know as kids getting tossed around the sea of young Hollywood. Daxon's eyes are on mine and we leave it like that, spinning delicately across the floor to music only we can hear.

I tighten my grip on him. He does the same to me. Our gazes shift to something wanting and heated, and Dax leans down to press his forehead against mine.

"I'm sorry I never asked you to prom."

I shut my eyes hard. "Daxon . . ." It's barely a sound. I'm

surprised it can be heard at all over the way my heart is fucking running for its life like a girl in a horror movie headed up the stairs.

"Yeah?"

There's a nuclear wave of anxiety that starts somersaulting around my stomach. Because it would be so nice to let myself give in. To kick the pact under the nearest shelf and forget about it. But I can't. I lift my head away and take back my arms. "I gotta get back," I lie. "Prepare for tonight."

Dax straightens up, nodding and blinking around the room like the streamers and balloons have been ripped from the walls of his imagination. "Yeah. That's . . . yeah. Good plan."

The door to the studio opens. A flood of little ballerinas spills in, tutus and satin slippers bringing both of us back to the present moment. To where we are. To *who* we are. Celebrities in a tiny town.

"Oh my," says a young instructor in dance attire from the doorway. "I'm sorry, I didn't realize y'all were in here. They said the private session was finished."

"Hey, no, don't worry about it," says Dax with a lazy wave. "I was just heading out."

He throws me a half-smile that's friendly and pure Daxon and so pretty I want to keep it in a jar in my room. But I know that smile. There's weight underneath it.

Maybe even disappointment.

⌇

TO THE STARS - OFFICIAL SCRIPT

EXT. THE PIER - DUSK

A glittering boardwalk. Game booths and
prizes. Cotton candy. A balloon loose and
drifting towards the stars. We can smell
the warm summer air. It's 1939 and
NICK—seventeen, handsome, with a wise-
beyond-his-years charisma—rearranges the
pins at a ring-toss game.

                    NICK

        Let's see you do that again.
            I'll bet you can't.

His mark is an overgrown frat-boy type,
1930s edition. Built, wealthy and
unimpressed.

                FRAT BOY
        (slapping change on the counter)

            You're on.

NICK hands FRAT BOY the first of three
rings. FRAT BOY cocks an arm back, ready
to throw. We're tight enough on his face
that we suddenly see his eyes drift from
the game and we pan left to see . . .

LILA, seventeen, beautiful, and disgusted
as she takes in the boardwalk. She's
dressed in a way that drips wealth,
clutching a handbag close to her as she
passes between the booths with another
well-dressed girl, AMY, sixteen, blonde,
flushed and grinning ear-to-ear.

                    FRAT BOY
        (lowering the ring and staring after AMY)

                    Holy hell.

We catch NICK's eyes as they hit LILA's
regal frame. His entire face, smudged with
a little dirt against his cheek, softens.
FRAT BOY turns away from the booth in
pursuit of the girls. NICK's eyes flick
down to the forgotten change on the
counter. He considers giving it back.
A beat. He pockets it.

                        FRAT BOY
            (stepping into sync with the girls)

        You two look hungry. Dinner's on me.

FRAT BOY pulls a wad of cash from his
pocket and begins to count it out. AMY
laughs. He winks at her.

                        FRAT BOY

                Anywhere you wanna go.

LILA comes to a stop in the middle of the
busy boardwalk. We're tight on her face,
sizing this kid up. We know from a twitch
at her mouth that she's decided he's an
asshole, and she's about to have some fun.

                         LILA
                  (faux-sincerely)

        Aren't you charming. Dinner? On you?
            Anywhere we wanna go?

FRAT BOY

That's right.

LILA
(almost to herself)

Where do we wanna go? Hmm . . .

AMY

I'm starving. Anywhere is f—

LILA
(cutting across her, protective and final)

Somewhere you won't be.

AMY
(aghast)

Lila.

LILA

We're leaving.

LILA loops her arm through AMY's bent
elbow and tugs her roughly away.

FRAT BOY

Hold on a second! You can't just run off.

LILA

Watch us.

FRAT BOY hurries forward and skids to a
stop in front of them.

FRAT BOY

I believe this young lady said she was
starving. We can't have that.

                    LILA

            She'll live.

                    AMY
        (staring moonily at FRAT BOY)

            I am starving.

                    LILA
    (off AMY's lovestruck, googly eyes)

            You'll live.

LILA gives AMY's arm a significant tug,
beginning to walk away. She's always been
AMY's guidepost, her trailblazer, her
anchor to reality. It's a role she hates
but does well, and would never entrust to
anyone else. As if anyone else could fill
LILA's shoes.

FRAT BOY
(taking hold of AMY's other arm
to stop her)

We'll try everything they got. You and me, up
and down the boardwalk all night. You like
crab legs? They got crab legs. Hot dogs, too.

LILA
(sharp, suddenly poisonous)

Take your hand off her.

AMY

Li, it's fine.

FRAT BOY

Cotton candy? Saltwater taffy?
How 'bout a ride on the Ferris wheel?

LILA

We're not interested. Your hand.
Take it off her.

AMY yanks free of LILA's grip to clutch
FRAT BOY'S arm.

                    AMY

          I'm interested.

If her sister would allow it, AMY would be
a spontaneous, free-willed person, strik-
ing every opportunity like lightning. LILA
is Lila. Smart and exceptional and always
right. But AMY is Amy. Full of stardust,
chasing happily ever after in a blindfold.

                  FRAT BOY

     You see? She's interested.

LILA stands alone now, staring in disbelief
after FRAT BOY and AMY as they make their
way towards the Ferris wheel. There's no way
she's leaving this asshole alone with her
baby sister. FRAT BOY and AMY climb into one
of the swinging loveseats and lower the
safety bar down, AMY giggling. LILA charges
forward towards a gruff TICKET-TAKER.

TICKET-TAKER

That's three tickets for a ride, ma'am.

LILA

I don't have any tickets. Listen, my sister—

TICKET-TAKER

Three tickets, or you don't ride.

NICK

Three tickets.

NICK extends the tickets out towards the
TICKET-TAKER, appearing like magic at
LILA's side.

NICK

You can keep an eye on your sister there.
On me.

                          LILA
                        (warily)

                    No, thank you.

The Ferris wheel has begun to spin, AMY
and FRAT BOY rising into the night air.
AMY's laughter trickles down as FRAT BOY's
arm slips around her shoulders.

                          LILA
                      (muttering)

     And once again, it's all up to me. God,
       what an impressively terrible choice.

The TICKET-TAKER slips the tickets into a
pouch at his waist.

                     TICKET-TAKER

                    Go ahead, son.

It's not a bad idea. Two pairs of eyes are
far better than one. She folds her arms

across her chest and stares bitterly up at
AMY like all the hard work she's put in
with that girl, pushing her towards a
shimmering reputation, never letting one
curl on her head fall out of place, is all
about to come to nothing. The truth is
that AMY has a spirit free as a summer
storm, and LILA's is sitting quietly in a
fragile, corked bottle.

                    LILA

     As a matter of fact, I will ride.
                  With you.

She appraises NICK. Doesn't let herself
linger on his good looks or threadbare
clothes.

                    NICK

     You sure about that? You're looking
        at me like I'm something squashed
              on your windshield.

LILA

Yes. I'm sure. I'm plenty sure.

NICK

You don't know me. I could be anyone.

LILA
(bitingly)

Could you be a dear and help me
watch my stupid sister?

NICK
(squinting up the wheel at AMY
and FRAT BOY)

It'd be my pleasure. Only thing is, we
don't know each other. And I'm nothing if
not a stickler for manners, so that's not
gonna cut it. I'm Nick. Nicholas Greene.
And you are?

LILA rolls her eyes then straightens her posture, giving him her best well-bred debutante's introduction handshake.

LILA

Eliza Patterson. Pleasure.

NICK
(recognition sparks)

Eliza *Patterson*.

LILA

That's what I said.

NICK

Patterson. Like PATTERSON STEEL, Patterson?

LILA
(uninterested)

Uh-huh.

TICKET-TAKER

Come on, girl. In or out?

NICK

She'll ride. With me. Sounds like she
wants to. Damsel in distress asks for your
help, you help. Ain't that right?

LILA

I am not a damsel in distress. And I don't
want to ride with you, it's just that—

NICK

You look like you do.

LILA

Then you need to get your eyes checked,
because I don't.

Couples on the Ferris wheel jeer down at
them, catcalling LILA to shut up and get
on already. She squints up at them, highly
offended.

NICK

I've got exceptional vision.

Oh shit. He's funny. And the short-sleeved
shirt beneath his suspenders is a little
too tight in the arms, favoring what is
clearly a physical laborer's physique. It
sends her stomach plummeting to her feet.

LILA steps towards the Ferris wheel car
and sits down on the farther seat.

LILA

Okay.

                    NICK

                    Really?

                    LILA

    I said okay. Would you sit down, please?

    NICK can't believe his luck. He does a
    terrible job hiding his victorious smile
    as he quickly lowers himself into the seat
    beside her, pulls the safety bar down
    around them, and catches her eyes as they
    lift off into the air.

"Cut!"

Greg's voice slices through the night, magnified tenfold by a megaphone. He's sitting just behind the cameras where crewmembers whisper into walkie-talkies and hair and makeup stand ready.

It's two in the morning. The humidity is clinging to us, and in this wig, my head is one giant bead of sweat. But inside my chest, my heart is bouncing on a tiny trampoline, my stomach right up there with it. Because it's *happening*. I'm *back*.

I'm a working actor again.

"Back to one!" Greg says. The car lowers back down to the ground. Dax and I step off. We're re-powdered and fussed over. Our costumes are smoothed and tugged into place. I go back to my first mark and Daxon goes back to his and I catch his eye.

"Hi," I mouth, fuzzy with lack of sleep, but high on the feeling of being back on a set. Of being *wanted*. Dax shows me his tongue. I wrinkle my nose at him.

I'm glad it can be normal tonight. Or as close to normal as Dax and I get.

What isn't normal is the re-run of last night skipping glee-fully through my brain. Kissing Daxon Avery is one of those limited-edition things that should cost, like, twenty-five thousand dollars and come with a Rolex.

Across from me on his mark, he worries a loose strand of his brown hair away from his dark eyes. Something in the lower part of my stomach stirs.

I love the color of Dax's hair. It's an ordinary brown when you first look at it. But when you run your fingers through it while he lays his head in your lap, you can see pieces that are lighter. Like a toasted almond. Like tea before the milk. Little bits where the glimmering Los Angeles sun has pressed light to this strand and that one.

He gives up fixing the unruly piece with a laugh, and the hair and makeup team descends to help.

For one impulsive second, I want to rip our proverbial "no hook-ups" pact apart like a mountain lion to tissue paper. I want to charge across this set and grab him by the costume collar. Send everyone home. Shut down the whole fucking thing. And give into the volcanic way I want him.

But I've never been good at wanting something and also letting myself have it. So many years ago, I wanted *Marnie* so badly, but never felt worthy of it when I got it. Even when she was my primary identity, when I thought I was on top of the world, I still felt like I was holding on to that purple wig for dear life.

So, here's how it's going to be, I decide. Because if I don't decide, my brain is going to continue to feel like a washing machine set eternally to spin.

It's one thing at a time. First, this movie. Performing CPR on my suffocating career, my public image. And not only that but falling back in love with acting. Performing. Stepping carefully into the skin of someone else and lifting them off the page.

Maybe somewhere else, another time, another life, Dax and I could be something. Not something fleeting, but something permanent.

He left, remember? An old, nagging voice whispers to me from the back of my mind. *He left you. And that was when you were actually friends—best friends—so in love you could snap. You don't think he'd do it again now? Now that you're nothing?*

Stop, I tell myself firmly, my fingers forming a tight fist at my side. He left because it was the right thing for him. He wanted something and he let himself have it.

Seven years have shone a light on that reality for me, brighter with each passing year.

Does that mean I've completely accepted it?

No. It's still biting at me. It's just that its teeth aren't as sharp as they once were.

Aside from pacts, and kissing or not kissing, and torturing myself by meeting his eye for a second time and receiving a genuinely happy smile from him in return, here's what I know for sure: Daxon Avery is the best friend I've ever had in my life. Breakup or no breakup. And bringing me in for this project after I spent eons being shooed out like a freaking rodent means a lot. Especially after shouting that I hated him for leaving so many years ago, and worse—believing it.

We do twelve more takes, and at four in the morning, we wrap. Dax and I are golf-carted back to our trailers, which sit opposite each other. Like they used to do. At the top step of mine, I turn.

Dax does the same thing from his.

I don't know what exactly I want to say to him, but this is the first moment we've been truly alone since last night and something needs to be said. My stomach lurches as I try to at least cough up some snarky little comment.

"Hey," he says, beating me to the punch for once in his life, "wanna come over? Run lines?"

Now

DAXON

W il knocks on the door of my rental at eight that morning, and even though I'm running on fumes, itching for a real night's sleep, I have to stop myself from sprinting to answer.

Relax, Daxon. Deep breath in. Deep breath out. Be cool.

The first night of filming is always weird and funky, and no real amount of rehearsal is going to get you where you need to be on that first take. The costumes are starchy, the lighting keeps getting adjusted, the lines, the accent, the characterization—all of it is bumpy, at best.

Except that, last night? It wasn't. Nothing was off, nothing took too long or didn't hit right. I should've known, honestly. Nothing Wil touches is ever less than the best you've ever seen.

Her short, copper hair is wet from a shower and pushed behind her ears, her tired eyes hidden behind sunglasses. And in her hands are two coffees, with a script and a tabloid magazine tucked beneath her arm. "Rise and shine, my little Thirty Hottest Under Thirty superstar."

I roll my eyes and take the coffee from her, shutting the door behind her once she's in.

"Yikes."

This is the sort of thing that makes my stomach shrivel up. Eyes on me like this.

Since puberty kicked down my door and I grew like six inches overnight at seventeen, my body's changed and kept on changing. Which, as a fat kid with a warped body image, was a lot to process.

There are so many people on this planet who are fat and gorgeous exactly as they are. Handsome and capable. Worthy and strong. With love they deserve. They don't need to change. I know they aren't less-than.

But as a pre-teen star of a huge kids' show, I never felt like one of those people. I always felt wrong or shameful. We actually did an episode of Marnie about Dougie being bullied for his weight, which was eight different shades of awful.

Dad and Pop frequently suggested that I work with their personal training team. Not out of judgment, I don't think, but from a place of caring. Maybe a little pity. And I hated the gym. There's a unique kind of embarrassment when you walk into a gym as a fat person, that kept me away for a long time, even when my body went from bigger to straight size.

But I figured out as I grew that exercising doesn't have to be miserable and humiliating. That if it feels right and my body's happy, that's enough. And I like feeling stronger. I can run further than ten feet. Lift weight I never imagined.

Which, in Hollywood photoshoot land, translates to a fairly embarrassing spread of me in the tabloid Wil had under her arm, where I'm pulling a white T-shirt up over my oiled stomach, faking like I'm getting undressed and smoldering at the lens.

"You're number five!" she says, flipping the page to a picture of my face. "How do you feel knowing four people out-hot-ted you?"

"I'd like to thank Dad for his cheekbones, Pop for his confidence, and the mystery woman who donated her eggs to my cause for, uh . . ." I drift off, trying to be funny, but on two hours of sleep, failing spectacularly.

"For your debilitating nerdiness," says Wil.

"Yeah, that feels right."

We laugh and she pulls the sunglasses to the top of her head. "Freaky—this place is exactly like mine." I watch her walk into the living room and stop at the dining table where the Millennium Falcon sits, partially assembled. Even the way she turns her head three-quarters back to me is dry with sarcasm. "Minus the *Star Wars* Lego. Oh, Daxon." Wil shakes her head solemnly.

"Look, it's Lego or competitive bowling. You pick your poison, Wilhelmina."

She turns for the couch with the kind of smile you try to bite back but can't, and sets her coffee down on the nearby table. I watch her wiggle out of her flip-flops, sit with a bounce, and pull her feet up and under her crossed legs. I sit beside her. My arm stretches out along the back of the couch. Not close enough to hold her, but close enough that if she wanted me to, I would.

In about four milliseconds, I would.

I almost pull it back because the temptation is so real.

This pact between us . . . I hate it, but it's the right thing to do. I can respect it. I know how important this chance is for Wil and I'm not going to do anything to threaten that.

Wil, who's been turning pages in her script for our upcoming scene, glances up at me. I catch her eye, and we smile and look back down to the thick packets in our hands.

Heat.

Heat all the way from my hairline to my little toe.

Electric heat.

Dangerous heat.

"Page thirty-two?" Wil asks.

I nod and bite my thumbnail for something to do that isn't *walk my imagination back through our kiss in the kitchen*. You haven't lived until Wil Chase grabs you at random and kisses the soul out of your body. Ten million out of ten, would recommend.

TO THE STARS - OFFICIAL SCRIPT

EXT. THE PIER - NIGHT

NICK helps to lift the lap bar as the
Ferris wheel comes to a stop and they
climb out. AMY and FRAT BOY wander the
game booths, laughing, genuinely seeming
to have a great time together. LILA scowls
after them.

LILA

Alright, she's had her fun.

(lifting her cupped hand to the side of
her mouth to call out for AMY)

Time to g—

NICK
(cutting her off)

You know what you need?

LILA

A restraining order?

NICK grins at her and shakes his head.

NICK

Cotton candy.

LILA

No, thank you. I'm just fine.

                              NICK

              I don't think you understand what
                        you're missing.

                              LILA

                  And what am I missing?

                              NICK
                  (in disbelief, accusingly)

              You've never had it before.

                              LILA

                              So?

                              NICK

          So, you have no idea what you're missing.

        His endless enthusiasm is unfortunately
        incredibly contagious, and as LILA looks
        ahead to where AMY and FRAT BOY have turned

a corner to another row of booths, she
decides to let herself try something new.

                    LILA

          Show me, then.

NICK offers her his arm with a victorious,
beaming smile.

                    NICK

          It'd be my pleasure.

We see NICK steer LILA to a nearby booth
selling cotton candy and offer a stick of
pink fluff to her. LILA plucks off a tuft and
tries it. She's horrified.

LILA

You can't eat this!

(she laughs)

It's pure sugar.

Spotting AMY, NICK places a hand on LILA's
back and steers her behind a nearby game
booth, trying to covertly overhear AMY and
FRAT BOY's conversation.

NICK

Okay, now, very important: keep your voice
low and keep yourself out of sight. This
is the perfect place to spy on those two.

LILA

I'm not spying, I'm just being concerned.
There's a difference. And I can't hear
anything they're saying from here.

NICK

Not a problem. I can help. I read lips.

(adlib nonsense)

My "adlib nonsense" impression of Lila's sister, Amy, is so high-pitched that my voice cracks and Wil chokes on her coffee as she goes to take a sip.

"JESUS!" she cries between heaving laughter. "Prepare me next time!"

I lean my head back and let the laughter take over, my script slipping down my stomach and sliding to the floor. "Oh god, we're fucked," I say.

"No," says Wil, her own laughter ebbing now. "We'll be okay. That was cute. That was, like, prime Dax."

"*That* was cute?" I ask her, grinning but furrowing my brow with doubt.

Wil swallows, her eyes falling to her lap then sweeping back up to hit me with a *look*. I can tell she's tired. That she's been awake all night, high as a fucking kite on the one thing she loves most in this world. I would know—I'm right there with her.

And maybe part of her is relieved to be here with me. At least, part of *me* is relieved to be here with *her*.

Okay, all of me.

"What?" I ask her.

Wil studies me. "I just gotta know," she says, an eyebrow lifting. My stomach tenses, waiting for what she'll say. "Do you think you should've made the Top Three?"

I chuckle and reach for her. "Okay, that's it, now you're gonna get it." Wil shrieks as I pull her over to where I'm sitting and we laugh, our smiles doofy ones, happy ones.

She slips unapologetically onto my lap, a leg on either side of my hips.

Our eyes meet.

She bites her lip.

"Can I just tell you . . ." she starts. "And I'm delirious and sleep-deprived and not thinking, really, but I am. Because I can't stop *thinking* about this. About you. How much I fucking missed you."

Her fingers reach out and brush my hair back with a reverence, an earnestness that I'm genuinely concerned might make my heart explode out of my chest.

Goosebumps flush down my body.

"Dax?" Wil breathes, and it's like she's asking if we can rip up that pact and grind its smoldering pages into the cement with our heels. "Did you miss me too?"

I pull her as close to me as I can get her, hands taking her face in their grasp.

"You have no idea," I say. But there's no air in my lungs so it comes out strangled.

And then I'm seventeen, nervous and fumbling. But at the same time, I'm twenty-four, grown and sure.

And her script is sliding off the couch, forgotten, my hands are tangled in the coolness of her damp hair, she's pulling away my T-shirt before ripping off her own and if you asked me about the pact we made last night, I would look you dead in the fucking eyes and, with all the seriousness in the world, tell you I've never heard of it.

TO THE STARS — OFFICIAL SCRIPT

EXT. THE PIER - NIGHT

In NICK's mind, this is starting to count
as a first date. In LILA's, it's her first
taste of rebellion, and it's delicious.
This boy is unsuitable in every way. But
after holding up his end of the bargain
and helping to spy on AMY and FRAT BOY
from the Ferris wheel, his smile eases the
tension in her soul. She's willing to give
him this chance.

NICK

What's it to you if your sister's running
around with a guy like that?

LILA

Amy has a responsibility.
And I'm older, I'm supposed to make
sure she sticks to it.

It's a line her mother has been repeating
to the two of them verbatim since infancy.
All well-bred southern girls are destined
for proper marriages to wealthy, well-bred
southern men. You don't pop the bubble of
a life spent attending society dinners and
afternoon teas; you don't let yourself
even hold the needle.

                    NICK

           Which means . . . ?

Upstairs, Wil lies with her head in my lap on my bed,
wearing only my Han Solo T-shirt, which fits her more like a
dress. I will one thousand percent be high-fiving myself about
this later. But for now, I lean against the pillows, idly curling
sections of her red hair around my finger. Afternoon sun spills
in through the windows and we read through tonight's scene.

                    LILA

The choices she makes now determine her
   entire future. She doesn't have time to
ride Ferris wheels and share popcorn with
         someone so . . .

NICK

So . . . what?

LILA

Someone who would find themselves far more
comfortable in a zoo, I'll bet.

NICK

Yep, that's it. I was trying to put my
finger on it, and you're right. A gorilla.
That's what he reminds me of.

(a beat)

So, you're husband-hunting. That it?

Wil lowers her script. "What's that sound?"

I listen and realize it's my phone, which is lying forgotten on the carpet almost completely under the bed. Wil sits up and I lean down, fishing with my hand until I pull it up and press it to my ear. It's one of our second assistant directors, Kim.

"Are you able to get to set a half hour before your call time tonight?"

"Sure, yeah. What's up?" I say.

"Greg wants to have a quick cast meeting before we shoot."

Wil watches my face as I speak, and I trace a pattern on her knee where she sits, now in front of me—a lopsided, lazy heart. She grins at me. I grin back. "Sounds good." Our eyes are locked on each other.

"Great. I'll give Wil a call."

"Oh, she's right here, I can pass the message along."

As soon as I say it, I have to stop myself from cringing. Wil and I are friends. We have so much history. It's expected that we spend time together away from set, right? We're the leads. We have to build up the chemistry. But how much of that we should let people in on is one thing, and whether or not this is anything at all is another.

"Oh . . ." says Kim, and it's a loaded "oh." Like, *oh.* "Great."

"Great," I parrot, and then pull a face at myself. "We'll be there."

"Good. See you both soon." She hangs up.

"Oh my god," says Wil. She swats my thigh.

"I panicked."

"I noticed."

I pull both of my hands through my hair in exasperation, my stomach churning now with embarrassment and anxiety. All of the things you're not supposed to do after you sleep with your best friend and co-star for the first time in seven years, I've just done. I slapped a label on us. Hell, I flipped on a flaming neon sign above our heads with arrows pointing at us that reads: THEY JUST HAD SEX.

"I didn't know what to say. What should I have said?" I ask her, my eyes wide. Wil was always the smooth one. She always had a plan, a maneuver, the perfect cover.

"I don't know," says Wil. "Not that I'm pantsless in your bed!"

"I didn't say that!"

"It was heavily implied," she says.

"Okay, so . . . they know. Maybe." I lick my lip and stare at the mattress. A moment passes and then I can't help myself. Our pact is on the floor, bleeding out. I have to ask. "By the way, what does this mean?"

"My pantslessness?"

"Among other things," I say, and my lips rise at the corners.

Wil's eyes draw a long, slow circle across the ceiling as she thinks of an answer. Finally, they land back on me and her jokester's smile settles into a soft frown. She's not a tidal wave. Not now, anyway. She's quiet and softer, the mirrored surface of a glassy lake.

"I don't know," she whispers.

"Me either," I say.

"Maybe," Wil starts, "it shouldn't have happened. I mean, we had a pact. I told myself I was gonna take this seriously and focus and . . ."

It's a little like taking a knife to the balls but I nod, cool and calm and hoping desperately that the shattering feeling in my chest isn't translating to my face. "Right." I swallow and there's something heavy in my throat.

"Dax," says Wil, and her voice is weirdly measured, like she's about to tell me that I'm adopted or something. "I'm sorry, I can't do this with you right now." She slips off the side of the bed and onto her feet, looking for her jeans and pulling them on. "This opportunity is everything to me. It has to be. I have to . . ."

"Focus," I finish for her. "I know. But I just . . . you and me . . ."

"I know." She buttons and zips, looking at me, and I wish she *was* tidal-wave Wil. That she would come rushing over me, sweep me somewhere far away where we could be whatever we wanted, and I would tumble through the water, completely okay with there being no air, with not being able to see the surface. Everything would be her, would be Wil. In my lungs. In my bones.

"So . . . we're . . . ? Where do we . . . ?" I say, and watch her turn and change back into her own T-shirt.

Wil tosses me Han and I catch him one-handed. Already, he smells like her. Sweet, understated citrus and something underneath, indistinguishable, that makes me feel homesick.

"Friends. We're friends. Okay?"

She's right. I know she's right. That's the smart thing. I try to set my expression in a steely, no-big-deal look. "Friends," I repeat. "Yeah. Okay." I can't help spewing another question, anything to prolong this moment. Wil in my bedroom. "This still, uh"—I work the fabric of the shirt between my fingers—"meant something, right? I mean, it's okay if it didn't for you, but for me . . ."

I need it to have meant something. Because to me, it's everything.

"Yeah," Wil agrees with a smile. "It did. It does."

"It was better than nothing, right?"

Wil's gaze hits the floor and her smile only grows. When she looks back up at me, it's with an eyebrow that's subtly arched and her tongue caught between her front teeth, delighted and embarrassed, maybe, but her eyes are sparkling. "Best nothing I ever had."

I make a point of sitting across the room from Wil at our production meeting. I even go so far as to angle my chair slightly away from where she sits across from me in the circle.

That's right, folks, nothing to see here.

Very casual.

But what I can't stop myself from doing is shifting my eyes to hers across the busy space. They slice through conversations between the crew and cast around us, tear through gossip over takeout containers balanced on laps, and scripts in hands, poised to note any changes. And when they meet, all the things inside of me—organs, blood, guts, you name it—turn into warm blankets straight from the dryer.

"Alright, lemme have your attention here real quick and we'll get on with shooting."

Our director comes to the center of the circle and we give him a brief, appreciative round of applause. Wil's eyes hit me from where she sits. I like that feeling. Her watching, me *knowing* she's looking, while a film reel of this afternoon plays over and over in my head.

We're complicated. We have history. There's the whole public perception piece to think about, the press. Our jobs.

But those hazel eyes looking into me, through me to every memory we've shared, every time I've thought about her over the last seven years? God tier.

"I wanted to let you all know that we've had a casting change. I know it's last-minute. But you know this business; scheduling can be catastrophic at best. The role of Lila's mother, Mrs. Patterson—and I can't believe I get to say this, you're all in for such a fucking treat—will now be played by the legendary . . ."

I watch him extend an arm towards the doorway, watch as a woman appears, slender, tall, fake-tanned, blonde, with a face so familiar it kicks me right in the stomach . . . especially when my eyes leap to Wil and catch her blanched reaction.

In an instant, she's seventeen, watching her world begin to shatter all over again.

"Katrina Tyson-Taylor!"

Then

DAXON

For the last two weeks, we've gotten really good at pretending I'm not leaving, that summer won't ever end.

Tonight is it, though. Where we have to end it.

Tomorrow, I'm leaving for Yale.

I didn't tell Wil that it was me, that I was the one who set things in motion to end *Marnie*. I should've. The second that acceptance email came in and I knew I wouldn't be renewing my contract with Magicworks, that's when I should've told her. I know that. But when I look at her face, when I think about what she's up against, combined with the fact that I'm about to pop our perfect bubble of summer and loving each other out loud, I can't.

I pick Wil up around four, and we go to the beach. The weird thing about LA beaches is that during the day they're like the surface of the sun, and then right around late afternoon/early evening, somebody turns the temperature way down and you need a sweatshirt, maybe a blanket. Wil is wearing my sweatshirt not fifteen minutes after we get settled on the sand.

I'm sitting with my legs wide and she's sitting in front of me, leaning back against my stomach. The breeze coming off the water sends the smell of strawberries from her hair up into my face, just to make this that much worse.

"First break is in November. I'll come back then," I say.

"I don't wanna talk about it."

"Winter break is longer. I'll be back then, too."

"Dax . . ." Wil sits up and pivots around towards me. Her eyes hit mine and I know what she's going to say.

"I know," I tell her. "But maybe we can . . ."

"Maybe."

I lick my lip. Suddenly, every organ in my body weighs a ton. "Because I don't wanna not be . . . us."

"Daxon," Wil breathes. She reaches out for me and pulls me close to her, arms wrapping around my neck, and everything goes still—even the roar from the waves diminishes. "That's all I wanna be. Us. Always. You're the only thing I have left."

"Me, too." My arms fold around her and we sit like that for a long time, breathing each other in, trying to memorize how the other feels in our arms.

We're out all night, under the stars, walking the shoreline in bare feet, pointing out the winking lights of ocean liners, wondering where they're headed. Pretending nothing is going to change, but being so fucking aware of it that the passing seconds hardly feel real at all.

At six the next morning, we wake up in my car, sunrise drenching the windshield. I squint against the color if it. "We should go," I whisper.

Wil looks at me from the passenger seat, lowered flat the same as mine. She reaches for my hand and holds it tight and fast to her chest, tucking her chin around it. "Don't go to Yale."

I blink at her. "What?"

"Just . . . stay. With me. Maybe we can call Harris and Bill and the Magicworks team and save *Marnie*. Maybe it doesn't have to be over."

Slowly, I adjust the seat so it's fully upright and take my hand back from her gently. I would follow her into space without a helmet, into an inferno without a drop of water. And for a second, I'm about to tell her *okay*, I'll stay.

But I can't obliterate a dream before I've even given it a chance to fly or fail. My jaw is locked tight as I stare out across the sand towards the waves. I *want* to go to Yale. To learn how to do this right, to make a meaningful career out of acting.

"The movers are coming at eight to get my stuff. I gotta get back."

Now

WILHELMINA

∽

"No fucking way."

I've paced a squished, white trail into the carpet of my trailer, walking back and forth for the last half hour. Camera-ready, but stalling. Dax sits on my trailer couch. He has on that sober, worried face he makes when I'm spiraling, and he knows better than to get in the way.

"I know," he offers.

"She doesn't even fit the part."

"I know."

"And why the hell would Greg bring her onto this project *knowing* my history with her? It's gotta be some PR bullshit thing, right?"

"Katrina's got a really big team. I'm sure they pushed for this. Greg can only do so much."

"What do I do? Do I quit?"

When I whip around, I catch Dax's expression. And it's the briefest, wildest sadness. It's a look that makes my numb feet stop mid-step.

"No," he says.

It's not the word, it's the *way* he says it that kicks my heart into gear. Firm and sure. *Strong*. I don't have to arm-wrestle the decision or tiptoe around it—Dax just made it for me: I stay.

My feet bring me slowly to the couch. I lower myself down next to him, our thighs touching. My costume dress is soft against the rougher material of his costume's pants. "I can't do this. How am I gonna do this?" The words spill out of my mouth in a whisper and disappear into the air between us.

Daxon's hand brushes the side of my knee. "Listen to me, okay?" Our eyes connect. I nod. "This whole thing is a test. And Katrina? She's that friggin' essay question at the end where you think *there's no way I have it in me to answer this*, but if you're gonna pass? You have to."

My eyebrows tug together into a knitted line. "The hell are you talking about?"

"Think Miss Kathy."

I give an involuntary shudder at the name. Our on-set teacher all the years we worked on *Marnie* was this strange, awful woman named Kathy who exclusively wore denim dresses paired with eccentrically embroidered vests. She hated us. Mostly me. And every time we were called over the PA system to report to school, Dax and I would look at each other and pretend to vomit.

"I try not to," I say, grimacing.

Dax grins. "No, I mean, those tests she gave us. The really hard ones? Remember?"

"I will go to my grave being haunted by those tests. They were college level! We were eighth graders."

"Exactly," says Dax, "but we had to pass."

"What we had to do was torture ourselves via flash cards to cram for her annoying tests, on top of learning pages of dialogue for the next day's scenes."

"On top of trying to scrape the bottom of the barrel for any semblance of childhood," Daxon adds.

"Don't know her," I say. We laugh.

"You can do this," says Dax, more sure than I've ever heard him in his life, so sincere. "Because you have to. For your career, for this movie, for . . ."

"For what?"

I want to hear him say it. The fire inside my gut needs to hear him say the word *us*.

Which is completely useless, because there's no us. We are not a thing. We are two humans who know everything about each other and grew up together in the same shitty Lost Boys vortex under a spotlight aimed right at our faces.

We're two vines. Tangled at the root. Growing towards the sun without realizing that, hey, guess what? Our version of the sun is each other.

My eyes search his face.

He leans in quickly. Gently, softer than he would typically, to press a kiss like butterfly wings to my painted lips. And there's my answer.

"But will there be Jell-O?" I murmur when we've pulled apart.

Dax takes my chin in his forefinger and thumb and grins. Nobody pranked like Daxon Avery back then. He'd swipe things off set, and the next day, we'd find them floating in the middle of a Jell-O mold. Or, my favorite, the time we filled Miss Kathy's school bag with cubes of red Jell-O as our "senior prank" and watched gleefully as she left for the day, leaving drops of red, melting gelatin in her wake.

"There will always be Jell-O," he promises.

There's a firm knock at my trailer door and Dax's eyes ask me if it's okay to answer. I nod. He gets up and pushes the door slowly open. It's one of our production assistants.

"They, uh, need you guys on set."

Daxon glances back to me and I nod. "We'll be five minutes," he says. "Can we get hair and makeup?"

"They're saying they need you right now."

"We need five minutes."

Adult Daxon has a confidence that my childhood Dax didn't. But it's more than confidence, it's this mixture of maturity, patience, and unflappable kindness that he offers to everyone automatically. Craft services. Our crew members. Assistants. Producers. Anyone. Everyone. It makes me want to grab him and pull him in and never let go.

"I'll send over hair and makeup," says the production assistant. We watch him wander off, probably to massage his temples, wondering how he ended up here, babysitting emotionally damaged former child stars.

Dax shuts the door and leans against the kitchenette countertop across from my trailer's sofa. "Do you need more time?"

"Why do we need hair and makeup?" I ask.

The left side of his mouth lifts into a smile that's friendly. "You, uh . . ." he gestures at my face.

"What?" I get up and turn around to face the mirror hanging above the couch. Mascara has tracked its way down my cheeks on both sides. "When was I crying?" I ask, bewildered.

"When we came in," says Dax.

"No, I wasn't." The absolute last fucking thing Katrina

deserves from me are tears. She's not getting anything from me—ever. My heart picks up the pace. I turn to Dax. I need him to know I'm strong. That she won't break me. "I wasn't."

"Okay," he says. And we both know it's bullshit, but he lets me have this and that means more than anything.

∞

TO THE STARS - OFFICIAL SCRIPT

EXT. THE PIER - NIGHT

                    NICK

So, you're husband-hunting. That it?

                    LILA

Shhh. I can't hear them.

                    NICK

I didn't think the Pattersons ever
    actually came out all this way,
        but this makes sense.

LILA

What?

NICK

Myrtle is good as anywhere to find somebody
from money. Plenty of oil tycoons with
summer places out this way. Then you've
got the fishing families—at least, the ones
bringing in the big bucks.

LILA

We're here on vacation.
That's all you need to know.

NICK

'Course you are. So's every one of 'em.

(gesturing to the crowds walking
along the pier)

Difference is, they're dressed for it.
You, on the other hand . . .

LILA

Excuse me?

NICK

I missed the invitation to the Royal Ball.

LILA

You're dressed like you deliver newspapers
and I haven't pointed that out.

NICK

You literally just did.

(gesturing to his clothes)

And this is grocery delivery boy,
at least.

LILA

Be quiet, please. And be useful,
for god's sake. Can you see them?

NICK

Listen, I don't know you.

LILA

What a shocking revelation.

NICK

I don't. I don't know you. But what I know
is that you can't push people into anything they don't wanna be pushed into.

LILA

And what does that mean?

NICK

Your sister over there? She's gonna wind
up doing what it is she wants to do. You
can't stop her. Not really.

LILA

Is that so?

NICK

Yes, ma'am, it is.

LILA

And how are you so sure?

NICK

I know people. Know how they work.

There's a beat. LILA takes in the boardwalk, the night air rippling through her
pinned-up hair. NICK takes in LILA.

LILA

So, you deliver groceries, that it?

NICK

Matter of fact, no. I don't.

LILA

Milkman?

NICK

Nope.

LILA

Enlighten me, won't you?

NICK

I work with cars.

LILA

Cars?

                         NICK

                         Cars.

                         LILA

                    You're a chauffeur?

                         NICK

                       Mechanic.

                         LILA

                  And you like cars?

NICK clocks AMY and FRAT BOY a few booths
away, where FRAT BOY is leaning in to
whisper something in AMY's ear.

                         NICK

          Look at that, he's making a move.

                    LILA

                    What?

LILA looks around and gasps.

                    LILA

        She couldn't make this any harder
                for me, I swear.

NICK pulls a quarter from his pocket and
flips it, catching it deftly with one hand.

                    NICK

                Watch this.

                    LILA

        What are you going to do?

                         NICK

            Have a little faith.

                         LILA

            Absolutely not.

    NICK raises his hand and flings the
    quarter. LILA cries out. It sails forward
    to clang off the side of the game booth
    where FRAT BOY and AMY stand close
    together. They jump apart, startled.

                         NICK

            You're welcome.

                         ∞

Katrina isn't filming tonight, but she lingers on set, waiting,
watching from behind Greg like this is her movie.

    Every time Greg calls cut, this clawing feeling scratches its
way up my body from my stomach, wrapping strong, spindly
fingers around my throat because it's absolutely only a matter
of time before she tries to talk to me.

    Or worse: What if she doesn't talk to me at all?

I don't *want* her to talk to me. I'd rather eat an opossum. But somehow the notion that she wouldn't, given the chance, makes me want to puke. There's this enormous iceberg bobbing in the water between us, it feels like. Made of memories of years ago.

Of *weeks* ago, with the arrest, the breaking and entering.

Around one in the morning, we break for a meal. I stop at crafty to load up on tacos and licorice, and as I'm debating whether or not I need more guacamole, a hand touches my shoulder.

"I have my bib-thing, don't worry, the costume's safe." I turn around, assuming it's costuming.

Except it isn't.

"Hi there," says Katrina. The smile on her thin lips is calm and confident, but not friendly. I can feel my organs shriveling.

"Katrina," I say, my heartbeat deafening in my ears.

"Isn't it funny," she says, "they always say if at first you don't succeed, try, try again. And you're living proof of that. Nice to see you booked something after such a *long* time."

There aren't a lot of people who intimately knew me in the early days after *Marnie* where I couldn't book a job. Dad and Katrina watched me fall apart, every day another chunk of me falling to the ground when the phone refused to ring.

It's funny how I wanted to shed Marnie like a second skin and step away someone new, someone that was wholly me, but she didn't budge. I was walking around without an identity, Marnie's shadow glued to my heels like I was Peter Pan.

I was screaming at the top of my lungs for someone to notice me and care.

When my agent suggested I take a break from auditioning, I started going out. All the time. For hours and hours, club after club, bar after bar. I was eighteen. Nobody cared. Thankfully, that was when I met Margot. She was the reigning queen of the LA scene back then, a place where it was hard to find someone trustworthy. In that way, Margot was rare.

But Katrina?

I look into her pale, venomous eyes. "Thank you." The words come out of me mechanically. Icily. I'm vaguely aware that my plate has started to shake slightly in my hand.

"You know, I'm really looking forward to this. You and I have our first big scene on Wednesday, bright and early."

"Can't wait." My tone is as even as I can make it.

"It's amazing what strings you can pull in this industry if you're at my level. Anything you want, you can get." Something in her eyes flashes and I have my confirmation.

Hahahahaha, shit. Mystery solved.

She sought this role out. I wouldn't be surprised at all to find out she manipulated her way in. Forced whichever actress was originally playing Lila's mother out on her wayworthier ass.

"Neat," I say, and the sound is dry as cracker dust. I glance at my quaking plate. "I'm gonna go."

"See you tomorrow," says Katrina. And weirdly, or maybe not so weirdly, given that it's *her*, she makes that sound like a threat.

When I've turned my back to her and started to walk away, the panic starts bubbling in my stomach. *What if I can't do this?*

Now

DAXON

⟳

I guess I should probably have seen it coming, like Godzilla rising up out of the sea, but when Katrina steps on set, Wil starts to crumble.

I catch Wil panic-eating licorice at crafty during lunch as the crew finalizes the lighting for her scene with Katrina. Wil wears a blue cotton robe over her costume, her wig tied back and away by a black net to keep its 1940s style preserved.

"How many feet do you think you could get if you put all the pieces end-to-end?" I point at the enormous plastic jar of Red Vines.

Wil covers her lips with her hand, her mouth full of candy. "I heard that if you do that, you end up with a giant dork. Wait, how tall are you again?"

The worry in my gut for her softens at the familiar melody of her sarcasm, and I roll my eyes, playing along.

"Show me your tongue," I tell her.

"Why?" Wil glares suspiciously at me.

"Show me."

She sticks it out halfway, and it's exactly what I thought it would be: bright red. "Nope, that's not gonna fly."

"What?" Now she looks worried. "What're you talking about?"

"You guys start shooting in, what? Half an hour? Your tongue's red. Like red-red."

"Shit," says Wil. She pulls out her phone from a pocket in her robe, turns the camera to selfie-mode and points it at herself, examining her tongue. "Fucking Red Vines," she says.

"I'm a Twizzlers man, myself."

"Daxon."

"What?"

"Shut up, please." But she smiles at me and I'm all fluttery, light and soft all over.

There's no pact anymore. I'm pretty sure we sent it running with its tail between its legs. In its place is something that doesn't seem to have boundaries or a name. Which is strange, sure, but *thrilling*.

"Come with me," says Wil.

In her trailer, she brushes her teeth and tongue four times until the licorice red is a pale, forgotten pink stain. I sit on the couch and watch her. Not in the creepy *I'm watching you* way. Just watching, mentally pinching myself that we're here. After seven lonely years. We're here. Together. I mean, not *together*, I guess. But, regardless, we're here. The wildest part is I still have no idea where that actually is.

"How are you feeling?" I ask her.

Wil turns from the sink. She shuts off the water and leans her hip against the counter, arms folding across her chest. I watch her eyes as they travel the wall space above my head. "Close to death. Thanks."

"Okay, so better than I thought," I say. A smile whispers its way across her lips and I grin back at her. "Talk to me."

"I'm not trying to be dramatic, but . . ." Wil starts.

"Um, bullshit."

She glares. "I think if I got too close to her, she'd full-on stab me."

"Can we blame her?"

"*Daxon.*"

I laugh. "Look, regardless of who broke into whose house, this is work. She doesn't have the luxury of stabbing you mid-scene. Her PR team is good but they're not *our client murdered someone and everything's fine* good."

"I know you're right," says Wil, letting out a sigh drenched in pure anxiety, "but I can see her trying."

A production assistant taps on the door. "Wil, five minutes!" Wil grimaces at the carpet.

"You know what you need?" I ask her.

"A bulletproof vest? Maybe a crucifix?"

"A night out. Let's get a group together and go out tonight."

Wil slinks towards the door, shaking her head. "I can't go out with a severed head."

"*Or,*" I say, "completely intact, having just demolished another day kicking ass on this movie. We'll get a beer. There'll be mediocre music. And only the cool people."

"So you wouldn't be coming?"

"Watch it, or I'll feed you to Katrina."

Wil flashes her tongue at me. She puts her hand on the doorknob, then looks back. "What time?"

∞

Katrina has this completely bizarre ability to suck all the air out of the room when she comes into it. I've heard people say that all the greats do this. Real stars feel bigger, feel larger than life, when you're lucky enough to get close to them.

Bob is one of these celebrities, but Katrina? Katrina stops at every mirror and stares herself down. Katrina doesn't greet the caterers at crafty, let alone make eye contact with them when she places a lunch order. She snaps her fingers to get the attention of our production assistants. That's not greatness. That's some classist bullshit assholery.

But Katrina is an industry vet, who's made a career of starring in sitcom after sitcom, so she gets this weird free pass in Hollywood to be a jerk but still wind up on top.

"Let's go! Are we going? Greg, are we ready?" Katrina's voice is loud and direct and slices through the set like a buzzsaw.

Wil stands just off her mark, having her lipstick touched up. Her hazel eyes roll around to me and I smile at her, trying to put her at ease. Hoping that maybe the secret language there's always been between us will reach her and stop the hammering I know her heart is doing.

"Let's get quiet on set!" calls our second assistant director. Wil takes her mark, pulling a little on the edge of her costume blouse.

Here it is: one of the big scenes. The first of two blowout fights between Lila and her mother. Katrina fusses with the back of her wig, shooing away the hair and makeup crew who had flocked to her to help.

"Action," says Greg from his director's chair.

TO THE STARS - OFFICIAL SCRIPT

INT. PATTERSON HOME FOYER - EVENING

VICTORIA PATTERSON, 50, is elegant and
well-mannered with a vague air of royalty.
Everything about her, from her hairstyle
to her shoes, looks expensive. Angry, she
comes downstairs to find LILA just getting
home from a day spent with NICK.

                    VICTORIA

    I have been sick with worry over you.
             Where have you been?

                    LILA
                  (flustered)

Mama. You scared me. I didn't see you there.

                    VICTORIA

We have guests turning up here any minute
now and you look like you've been hit by a
         cyclone. Explain yourself.

LILA

Not now, Mama, I have to change.

Already the tension between Wil and Katrina is so thick it's gelatinous. But what's great is that it works perfectly for this scene. Since meeting on the Ferris wheel, learning to trust him and spending a day together on the beach, Lila's been sneaking out to be with Nick, trying to keep him hidden from her mother. This is the turning point where her secret comes out.

VICTORIA

Eliza, tell me where you've been.

LILA

Out at the beach.

VICTORIA

With who?

LILA

Just some girls.

LILA edges towards the staircase, hoping
to escape before the truth about who she's
been with gets out. VICTORIA puts a finger
up to stop her.

                    VICTORIA

               Which girls?

                      LILA

          Alice and Mary-Kathryn.
          You don't know them.

                    VICTORIA

        What is that? Right there on your neck.
                 That mark.

                      LILA

     I was being careless, I was out too long
       in the sun. I'm sure it's just a burn.
          I'll head up and get changed.
             Who's coming tonight?

                         VICTORIA

              Stop. Come here. Let me look.

                           LILA

              Mama, I need to get ready.

At a look from VICTORIA, LILA grudgingly
steps closer to her mother and moves the
hair off her neck to expose what is clearly
a hickey.

                         VICTORIA

                           Who?

                           LILA

                       Who, what?

                         VICTORIA

              What is his name, Eliza? The boy.

LILA

Mama, I told you, it's a sunburn,
that's all.

VICTORIA

Tell me this minute. I know it wasn't a
gentleman. No respectable man touches a
young lady like that, let alone at all,
without thinking about marriage, and I
know that can't be, because we haven't
set eyes on this boy.

LILA

Nicholas Greene. Nick, Mama.
His name is Nick.

VICTORIA

Greene? I don't know any Greenes.
Who are his people?
What does his father do?

LILA

Mama, I'm a mess, I've got to get changed.
The wind was wild on the boardwalk and I—

VICTORIA
(cutting her off)

Answer me, young lady.

LILA

His father works cutting steel. Nick works
part-time fixing cars, part-time on the
boardwalk during the summers.

VICTORIA

Steel?

LILA

Yes, ma'am. Mr. Greene works for
Daddy's company.

VICTORIA takes this in and it's a bitter
swallow. This is her worst-case scenario.
A blue-collar distraction, a stain on
their image.

                    VICTORIA

            No. I forbid it.

                      LILA

    Mama, listen to me. Please. I could have
    him over. You and Daddy could meet him.
        He's smart. He's a hard worker.

                    VICTORIA

    I will not have my oldest daughter getting
        foolish with a mechanic with no family
            name, no money. I forbid it.

This is LILA's worst-case scenario. Given
her choice, she'd keep NICK to herself,
but there's no turning back now that the
secret's been spilled. LILA backs away
slowly towards the front door, looking at

her mother, her lifelong model for how not
to step outside the lines, like she's
never seen her before.

LILA

You can't do that.

VICTORIA

Lila, I am not playing here. Do you hear
me? I need you upstairs and fixed-up right
now. And I don't want to hear another word
about you bothering with this boy.

LILA

Mama. Please.

VICTORIA

I said not another word!

                                    LILA

                    You can't keep me from him.

                                  VICTORIA

            Upstairs and that's it, Eliza. That's final
                and we'll hear no more about it.

                                    LILA
                                 (crying)

                                I love him.

                                  VICTORIA
                        (harshly, dismissively)

                    You don't know what love is.

                                 (a beat)

                You don't know what it'll cost you.

    "Cut!"
    The sound of Greg's voice makes me jump. Not because
it's insanely loud, which it is, but because for the last few

minutes, I've been somewhere else entirely. I've been rooted in the Pattersons' foyer, watching generational privilege and trauma whip out its fangs. Watching Wil earn the accolades I know are coming her way.

The subtleties in her face, as Katrina's character spits terrible things at her, grab me by the shirt collar and shake me around enough to feel my bones rattle.

Tiny, blink-and-you-miss-it things she does with her eyes, minute twitches at the lips, the way you can almost see the breath rushing from her as her face pinkens with anger.

This is real for her.

I think about how we play pretend for a paycheck, but for Wil, this is as real as it gets. A fake mother she can't stand, twice over.

"Reset! Let's go back to one." Greg motions to the cameras, then gets up from his chair and takes to the set, bringing Wil and Katrina in for a huddle. When they break, I catch Wil's eye. She's trying to pin back a victory smile, trying to stay focused and in the moment. But she's proud of herself for something and I know she's just been praised.

Katrina, however, goes back to her mark at the top of the stairs, and her lips form a bitter line as she waits for the scene to be called to action.

She's gotten feedback, and it wasn't an ass-kissing for once.

∽

The local crew likes a place in town called Betsy's, this shoebox bar where the beer is cheap, so that's where we go.

It's Wil, a couple production assistants, two or three extras, and some of the main cast, like Vanessa, who plays Lila's younger sister, Amy, and Sean, the Frat Boy.

Wil and I order a round for the group. We sit together at the bar, trying to toss peanuts into each other's mouths. I miss every single one, but she makes them all, which completely tracks. And god. It's so normal. Like nothing broke us, like we didn't wait seven years for this.

"Sorry, could I have a picture?"

A woman dressed in white with a bachelorette sash across her torso approaches timidly and gazes at Wil like she's the moon.

I know the feeling.

"Sure," says Wil, flashing me a wide-eyed look as the bride-to-be gets close and lifts her phone in front of them for a selfie. Wil's left hand, which was resting under the bar against my thigh, retracts and my skin goes cold without her touch.

It's possible that maybe it's not real at all, this thing we're doing. But I would reach up, fearless, and pull down every star in the sky if I could make it real, if it could be as it was. I'd carve out my heart with a toothpick if I was sure she wouldn't run.

Maybe I'm *not* sure, though. Would she run away if I tried to make us something permanent? She's changed in subtle ways over the years, like leaves once green starting to burn. I can't predict her every move anymore.

"Here, let me," I say and reach out for it.

"Oh my god, Dougie!" the bride-to-be squeals. "I forgot you got hot! I mean, shit. That was rude. Sorry, I'm drunk."

We all laugh. "Would you be in it, too?" she asks, and I nod, tell her sure, then pose myself on her other side and lean in with a smile. The flash goes off and the bride breaks away from us, giggly and excited, talking animatedly with her hands the way Wil does when something lights her up. "I wanna buy you guys a shot." She flags down the bartender.

"Hell no," argues Wil. "You're getting married. It's on us."

Tequila in tiny glasses and a plate of lime wedges slide towards us across the counter. Wil counts us down. We bump our glasses against the bar with each count, then toss them back.

"Hey!" says the bride, grinning ear-to-ear like she's just had the best idea anyone's ever thought of. "You guys remember the *dance*?"

"Well," I say, "I think it's physically impossible for us to forget. I still have scars. Emotional scars."

"Oh god," groans Wil. "The Baldovia Boogie?"

This is a *Marnie, Maybe* classic from season three, the heyday of our show. To defeat a rival from her kingdom of Baldovia in a talent competition, Marnie, who can't let anyone know she moonlights as a world-famous popstar, invents a dance to perform with her best friend, Dougie, that is so sublimely cringey, but wins her the competition, because of course it does. And now, the world will never let us forget it.

I have never walked through an airport without someone asking to see it.

Last Thursday, I was pumping gas and did a half-assed, one-handed Boogie for two excited teens. It's my Ghost of Christmas Past. But with Wil finally by my side, the last thing I am is afraid.

"Could we do it for TikTok? You guys, come here!" She waves over her friends, and Wil and I exchange a look. "Baldovia Boogie!"

Wil's eyes get big and she shakes her head at me. I, on the other hand, flash her a grin and nod my head.

"Daxon. Nuh-uh," she whines.

"Sunshine, sea stars, shine as bright as we are . . ." I start to sing the completely bananas lyrics in a high, terrible rendition of her teenage singing voice, and Wil glares at me. I hold my hand out for her and turn to the bride. "Ready?"

"I have it!" a woman from the bridal party cries, holding up her phone. It's been attached to an auxiliary cord feeding into the bar's speaker system. Bar regulars turn to watch. She presses play, the way-too-familiar beat starts, and Wil groans as she reluctantly flops her hand into mine and I pull us out into the middle of the room.

Wil hides her eyes with her free hand, flushed red as a stop sign, dragging her feet through the motions. But I can see her lips just under her hand and they're wide with a grin, so I make a grab for that hand, too, and spin with her in time to the music.

She's laughing at herself, at the goofy face I know I must be making. At life, I guess, timing, this right now, after so much time apart. I watch Wil find her way to the right steps.

There's a lot of embarrassing arm-ography involved in the Baldovia Boogie. Clapping over our heads and flapping chicken wings, then some stomping for ultimate obnoxious-ness. The choreographer who cooked this up for us almost a decade ago is probably stirring his cauldron of poison apples and cackling evilly somewhere.

But it's us. Wil and I. *Us*. And tonight is a memory I'm locking away inside my soul—beneath a tag that reads: *Property of Wilhelmina Chase*.

Now

WILHELMINA

Going from having everything—a thriving acting career—to every door being slammed in my face was a little like what I think getting whacked in the head with a shovel is like—sudden and painful as a motherfucker.

So, having this bridal party take turns leaning in for selfies with me, pushing drinks into my hands, tearing up as they tell me about remembered *Marnie* birthday parties their parents threw them, is a little like if that shovel held out its hand, shook mine and said *you know what? I was an asshole and I'm sorry.*

"Do you feel like Elvis?" Daxon asks me.

We wait out in the comforting darkness of the late night for our driver. His fingers brush the side of my hand just as the night wind kicks up. It's a warm and soft breeze, whispering through our hair, fluttering the cotton of his T-shirt.

I ball up my hand into a fist and knock it into his side playfully. "Shut the fuck up, Avery."

"This just in, Marnie and Dougie spotted fighting to the death in downtown wherever-we-are," quips Dax, grabbing for my arm and twisting me around so that I fold into him, stomach to stomach.

"You're drunk."

"No, I'm just floating," he says, grinning up and away from me to look at the stars.

I lean my head into his chest and shut my eyes. "You're drunk," I say again, fondly, but this time it's muffled. His arms wrap me up. The street is quiet. After a minute or two, I lift my head and meet his eyes. "I'm sorry for the stuff I said. How I acted when you left. It was shitty and immature."

Dax's blissfully happy-drunk face shifts, fading into the pain of a memory. "I'm sorry, too. For everything. All of it."

"You needed to leave. Yale was the best possible thing for you at that time in our lives. You did the right thing. *I* needed to grow up. And I don't know if I actually did, but . . ." I laugh, but it's empty-sounding. Tired.

"You did. Trust me."

These words leave his lips in a whisper. It occurs to me that I really thought his heart was brittle glass, and that I enjoyed dropping it. Now, though, I want to sit down and glue every single tiny shard back together until it's strong again, and then I want to pass him the glue bottle and say, *Me next.*

⁓

In the car, in the dark of the cool leather and tinted windows, we kiss each other like there was never any time spent apart. And also like we lost each other for a hundred years. A thousand years. A cool millennium. It's sweet, slow, found. Desperate, ravenous, searching. Away from the cameras, from excited eyes and grabbing hands. Away from the world as it was and as we know it.

The skin on his arms and hands is so soft, so warm, and he pulls me to him. Holds me tight and close against him.

Breathing is the last thing I'm thinking about, but every tiny breath in between kisses, my brain is filled with the smell of him. That good Daxon smell. Fresh laundry. Safety. Home.

Feverishly, I kiss my way down from his lips towards his jaw and along his neck, where I catch a sound escaping his throat good enough to make me forget we aren't alone.

"Here we are, Miss Chase, Mister Avery," says our driver, avoiding eye contact with us in the rearview mirror. I pull myself off Dax, blood rushing to my face as I smooth my hair and drag my thumb beneath my bottom lip to wipe away what I'm completely sure is smeared lipstick. The pair of us smile in the dark at each other like complete dorks. Dax brushes some of my hair behind my ear tenderly.

Then I reach out for a fistful of his shirt and pull him towards me, my other hand on the car door. "Come upstairs?" I breathe.

"If we make it that far."

Now

DAXON

〜

I missed so much while I was pretending not to miss Wil.

When I was at Yale, all I wanted to do was put my head down and *learn*. I wanted to absorb everything like a kitchen sponge and then wring myself out on stage, on set. I did it, too. Starred in a few off-Broadway productions, booked a Judd Apatow feature in a supporting role, then a couple more supporting things, Greg's limited series, and here we are: my first lead.

I wanted those roles to feed me, and they did, sure, but just enough to keep me alive. Not to nurture my soul the way my childhood years on *Marnie* did. That time was momentary in the hugeness of time and space, but it was ours, Wil's and mine.

I remember going around back then thinking that there must be more, it must get better. In reality, there *was* more. It did get better. Bigger sets, bigger stakes. Better directors and costumes, and dialogue so purely delicious it was like filling my mouth with maple syrup. But there was something missing, too.

The last girlfriend I tried to make anything real with pulled me aside before the red-carpet premiere of our film, *Son of a Gun*, pushed her finger in my chest—not accusingly, but firmly, with intention—and told me, *"She's really lucky."*

I remember asking, *"Who?"* but I knew.

"The girl you're in love with. Whoever it is you can't let go of."
I tried to deny it. There was no way something I'd felt at seventeen could stand untested, refusing to diminish as year after year tried to knock it down. But I knew we were done.

And now here's that missing piece: Wil.

I get up obnoxiously early and try to fit in time to run. I asked Wil if she wanted to come with me, but she squinted at me wordlessly for, like, forty-five seconds, so I took that as a no and headed out solo.

There's a TV in the kitchen at Wil's place, and after my run, I grab the remote and turn it on.

I scroll through a couple channels until, sure enough, there are my dads. Pop: handsome, Mexican, always so proud, with so much confidence, so much heart. Dad: half my DNA, tall and white and charismatic, talking a mile a minute about the exposed wooden beams in a living room they're gutting.

Pick a renovation-related subject and they know everything. How to build a home. How to gut tile. Why fountains are almost always a mistake. This show is their entire world, their third child—their *favorite* child, I should say.

I don't know why, exactly, but I pull out my phone and I call them. It rings and rings and rings, and finally, I get voicemail. Hanging up, I try again. Right to voicemail this time. A text comes in from Pop:

> Filming right now. Talk soon. Love you!

Having famous parents is a mixed bag, I know. Anything I want, it's available to me. It's privilege and connections and recognition without opening my mouth. But so much is missing—things like knowing my dads as people, rather than parents.

We've never had the time.

Suddenly, my fingers are sifting through my recent contacts and tapping on my sister Rainie's name. It rings three, long, faraway-sounding rings.

"What?" she grunts. "It's, like, two in the morning here. You better be dying."

I work my hand through my hair. "I tried to call Dad and Pop."

"Did you also try asking the Vatican for a ride on the Pope Mobile?"

"Believe it or not, that's next on the list."

I can hear the annoyed scrunch of Rainie's eyebrows from her tone alone. "Why'd you call them?"

"I . . . have no idea."

Rainie takes in a slow, highly unimpressed breath and sighs it into the receiver. "Where are you? Aren't you on set somewhere? It's late."

I sigh back, the sound staccato and as exhausted as I feel. "I'm in"—I stop for a second, prepare myself for her response—"Wil's kitchen. Or maybe it's the dining room? This place is all one big room."

"Did you just say *Wil's kitchen?* Is that, like, some weird euphemism?"

"No. God. It's—you know what, forget it."

"What's wrong?" The entire tone of her voice shifts from unamused to actual mild concern.

My teeth work my bottom lip. "I hate to say it, but I think I need advice."

"And your first call was Dad and Pop?"

"It's about a girl."

"And your first call was Dad and Pop?" she asks again, drier this time.

"You're right."

I don't tell her that I was thinking about them, and the enormous, Grand Canyon–sized hole between us. How talking to them, getting any time with them at all, feels like yelling back and forth across a huge crater in the earth and only catching every other word. And even then, demolitions and crown molding still lure their interest and enthusiasm away.

"Dad and Pop don't know shit about girls. I would know, I lived it. If you need girl advice, you call me first." My sister, a proud and out lesbian, is a magnet for gorgeous women— models, mostly. She may actually be the Queen Lesbian. And she's right, I should've tried her first. "So, spill."

My hand reaches to scratch slowly at the back of my neck while I work through the scattered, thousand-piece puzzle that is me and Wil. It's like we've found all the edge pieces, we've got a border going, but the middle? Chaos.

"I hooked up with Wil."

This is probably a conversation I should be having with a guy friend. Like Blake, an actor I met working on *Son of a Gun*. Blake is extremely chill. He likes hot yoga and spends his free time at his family's ranch riding horses. Blake's the kind of dude who doesn't say much but, when he does, it's wise. Unlike Rainie, who generally prefers to roast me.

Rainie's voice has enough sarcasm to fill the Chrysler Building. *"What? No way. How? When? Where?"* She stops and snorts out a laugh. "I mean, that was a given. Go on."

"Really? It was a given?"

"Daxon," Rainie scolds, "you've been pining for this girl for most of your life. Now you're making a movie with her where you're cast as star-crossed lovers? I mean, come on. There will be banging. That's a given."

The hand at the back of my neck travels up through my hair towards my face, where I let it drag itself down to rest over my eyebrows, my finger and thumb pulling them in tight and letting go. "Okay, yeah. I get it. You're right."

"Of course I'm right. I'm always right. You had sex and then what?"

"I don't know. It was . . ." I trail away. It was the same, sparkling. But it was different, better. The way the smell of her skin hadn't changed, even after all this time, the way we broke together like crystal shattering and held on to each other for dear life. It was everything.

"I don't know what we are," I explain.

There's a silent beat on Rainie's end. My face tightens while I wait for her verdict.

"Hm," is all she says.

"What, 'hm'? What does 'hm' mean?" Beneath my ribs, my heart is contracting.

"Do you read the stuff about Wil?"

"Stuff?"

"Yeah, the tabloids, social media shit. Have you read any of it?"

The number of times I've googled her over the years is embarrassingly high. Frankly, if my account hasn't been flagged for fervent stalking, I'd be shocked. I'm kidding. But I've looked her up. Scrolled her barren Instagram. Wil's never been big on social media, and her account is about six pictures from a handful of years ago, mostly of delicious food eaten or a trip to the Bahamas with Margot and other glamorous friends. A selfie of her newly cut hair with a classic Wil half-smile, all at once confident and daring, bold, perfect. Not needing me.

Gossip sites like Wil because she's a name people remember, and she's usually out late, ducking in and out of nightclubs across the city, climbing into expensive cars, flipping off the paparazzi.

"I've seen some of it."

"I love Wil, you know I love Wil. If I could trade you for Wil, I'd do it." Rainie gives a chuckle that's all air. "Wil is someone who's got a front row seat at the shit parade. Do you know what I mean? She's going through it. She's *been* going through it for years."

I nod, even though no one is there to see me do it. In the pit of my gut, something hot and sparking has started up because, of course I know. If anyone knows, it's me. But, then again, I was gone for so long from her life. There's probably a lot I don't know. My voice is defensive. "I know. I know that."

"Okay, then you know that when you're living in fight-or-flight like she probably is, you do stuff you maybe wouldn't do normally. Like bang your dorky friend."

"It wasn't that simple. We . . . we were gonna have a pact not to . . . hook up. Have sex. I don't know, it was sort of nebulous. And really fucking easy to break."

"A . . . pact? Like, what are you, a coven of witches? Was there a blood ritual, too?"

I sigh. "No. No blood ritual. That's on Tuesday."

"So you had a pact and you broke it?"

"Yeah. And then she re-established it, and then we broke it again. And . . . one more time. And a couple of times after that."

"Okay, gross. I'm hanging up now."

I run my fingertips along the cool countertop, scratching at the grout. "I just don't know what to do."

"Dax, I don't know. Okay? I'm not there. I don't have all the answers or anything. I just know from what I see online and read that she's clearly in a bad place. Maybe she's not thinking things through."

"So it was a mistake. That's what you're saying." That pit inside me is hotter now.

"Don't flip out," Rainie says, calm.

"I'm not flipping out," I shoot back. My heart is racing.

The last thing I really want to be is one of Wil's impulses that sound fun in the moment, like partying all night or stealing an engagement ring, but wind up with her barfing on Sunset Boulevard or getting herself thrown in jail.

"Look, I know you. You'd do anything for her. Be anything. Go anywhere. Climb something really tall and jump."

My mouth opens to tell her that she's wrong, but I shut it. Because she's right and we both know it.

"Dax, breathe. I understand that you like to know where you're going and what time you'll be there and how many minutes it's gonna take to get there, okay? But I don't think that's Wil. And if you're gonna jump into something with her, pack a parachute, okay?"

"You look like you've been up all night."

It's a woman's voice, a familiar one. Katrina Tyson-Taylor.

We've got a night shoot, and after staying up late into the early morning with Wil before getting up to run, I got a total of maybe two minutes of sleep. Worth it, though.

"Thanks," I say. I'm not unkind; she hasn't done anything to me directly. But I hear the walls going up in my voice. The gate coming down. Some loyalties you just don't shake.

"Here," she says, handing over a coffee in a to-go cup. "From crafty."

I eye it for probably too long. Then I reach out and take it. "Thanks." Me hungover has a stunning vocabulary.

"I didn't poison it," she says happily. I take a sip. It's bitter and hot, but it soothes the ache in my head. "That much," Katrina adds, winking.

For someone with Emmy awards for their sitcom performances, I never found her super funny. She's got good timing, but she's bland. Forced. If Wil's dad's funny flows smooth and easy downstream, carried by the current, Katrina's is that one river rock standing straight up, water knocking against it, creating a splash without moving anything forward.

I force out a grunting laugh. How fast can I sneak away to craft services for a hangover-curing breakfast burrito? But before I can escape her, Katrina tips her head and makes a fond clicking sound with her tongue. "I remember you so well from all those years back," she says. "You've really grown up."

I splutter and nod, coughing. "Happens," I say.

"I mean, congratulations on this," says Katrina. She gestures around, her blue eyes impressed. "Big win. Everything's going to change for you now. You watch."

Awkwardly, because I think that's my default setting, I toast her with the coffee, a little sloshing out of the lid and dribbling down the cup to land on my shoe. "Shit. I mean, thank you. Yeah, I'm really grateful this came along."

"Have you celebrated?" she asks.

"What do you mean?"

"Well, have you gone out? Had a proper meal? Glass of wine?"

"I—" I don't know how to answer this one. The past few weeks with Wil come to mind, though.

"Let me take you out tonight," Katrina says suddenly. "My agent is in town visiting. You know him? Max Perry. WME."

Do I know him? Name me one person in this industry who doesn't freaking know him. Max is a star-maker. He's ruthless, notorious, effective. He gives Jaws a run for his money.

"I've heard of him," I tell her.

"I'll introduce you!" She nods excitedly. "He'll love you."

What would Wil say? My heart sinks as I imagine the betrayal on her face. But then it's rising, breaking through the atmosphere because this is Max fucking Perry. My career is flashing before my eyes, getting bigger, better, stronger, completely real by the millisecond. How many doors would open? Hell, screw doors. Windows. Chimneys. Gigantic, spontaneous holes in the wall.

There wouldn't be a house anymore, just wide-open sky.

Directors whose films make me feel lightning-struck would call me directly with offers. Scripts would arrive at my doorstep and I'd open them up and sink into the possibility of being handed a golden statue in front of my peers.

Christ. It doesn't get more real than that.

"He would?" I say. "I don't want to get in the way or any-thing." Except that I *really* do.

"No, no, no, no, no," Katrina says. "He loves this kind of thing. It's casual. Don't stress about it. I'll send a car for you around eight tonight and we'll toast and celebrate you with Max."

Last chance, say no.

I almost do. My mouth opens, I'm ready to let it fire, take the high road, the road that whatever I have going on with Wil is balanced precariously on, but I hear myself—or maybe it's my ego—say, "Okay, thanks," instead.

"Great! I'll tell Max you're coming."

Then Katrina heads off towards costuming and I'm stand-ing there, minutes from Nick and Lila's teen-years breakup scene, trying to remember how to function. Because if Wil finds out, she'll kill me. Or worse: leave.

Then

WILHELMINA

"Don't go to Yale."

"What?"

"Just . . . stay. With me."

"The movers are coming at eight to get my stuff. I gotta get back."

Sitting in Daxon's car, cool beach air fogging the dawn-lit windows, I don't know what to say to that. So I don't say anything. Dax drives, I watch the world blur by.

My fingers pick at the shredded ends of my shorts. Pulling the threads out of the fabric altogether. I don't stop until I have a tiny fistful, and that's when I realize I can't fight the pressure in my throat, behind my eyes, for much longer.

Daxon is leaving. It's happening right now, in front of my eyes, as the minutes tick by. And I don't know if he's really all that sorry.

And I don't know if I can breathe without him.

He pulls up in front of my house and I sit there, frozen, staring at my legs.

"I'll call you when my plane lands," he tells me. He won't look my way.

I bite down on my tongue until I can't stand the pain any longer and finally turn to him.

"Stay."

"Wil . . ." Daxon shuts his eyes.

"Stay."

"I can't."

I try to swallow down the thick, painful lump in my throat but it's impenetrable. "You can," I say. "You can. I need you."

"This is important to me," he says. "I really want to do this."

The tears continue, silent and constant. And I don't do anything to stop them. Even my nose has started running, and I don't care. My fingers yank back the lock on the car door and I push it open, slamming it behind me.

"Wil!" Dax is up and out in seconds, jogging up the drive. "Wait. I need you to understand."

But I don't want to fucking *understand*. I want to rewind the years and go back to twelve, back to that first audition room, back to the sweetness of his round, friendly face. I want to do it all over again, over and over, on an endless loop.

I whip around and stop. "Well, I *don't* understand," I say.

"This is my dream. I want to be a real, professional, trained actor. I wanna win an Oscar! Yale can get me there." His face is earnest. His eyes are fragile. That's what guts me.

"What I don't understand is how you're so okay with leaving me behind." My entire face is stiff, my nostrils flaring, my lips in a tight line. I could breathe fire if I tried.

"I don't want to," Dax says. Actually, he kind of shouts it. And I see in his eyes that he's broken. His chest rises and falls as we stand there, six feet apart, shattering. "I love you, Wil. I don't want to leave you. But if I want to grow at all, I have to."

It's the *I love you* that injects lethal venom directly into my heart. My eyes narrow. I've never heard my own blood pounding in my ears as loudly as it is now. "No you fucking don't," I yell at him. "If you leave, no you don't."

Dax stares down at his shoes. "I gotta go," he says when he looks up at me. "I love you."

"I hate you for leaving."

My voice carries across the quiet, dewy lawns of my neighbors. It fractures the early-morning songs of doves nesting nearby. Wings take to the sky. My shoulders heave. Daxon looks anywhere but at me, pausing to take in the house we spent so many evenings wasting time in—nights we could have become something a lot sooner.

"Bye, Wil," he says, and he goes.

I march myself to the front door. Daxon's car roars to life and begins to pull away from the curb. The regret is instant. I turn around. His car is just starting to slip out of sight.

I run.

I run full-out, all screaming adrenaline, like if I stop, I'll die.

Like a dog, I chase his car up to the stop sign, crying out, "Wait! I'm sorry! Come back!" But Dax doesn't wait, and he doesn't come back. He signals his right turn, and goes.

"Daxon!" My voice breaks and I stop running, slump over and pant.

No.

It never occurred to me that he would *go.*

And the last thing he heard me say, before he got in that car and drove out of my life, was that I hated him.

My feet carry me back to my door. But it opens before I can turn the knob, and Katrina stands there in a robe with coffee in her hand.

"You look like shit," she observes. "Want some coffee?"

What I want is to knock the mug out of her hand. But instead, I push past her. "I can get it myself," I grunt and walk to the kitchen. There's one chicken mug left, but someone's pushed it all the way to the back of the cabinet and I have to stand on my tiptoes, fishing for it.

"I thought one of those was missing," Katrina says. She settles at the bar, slipping onto one of the stools. "They're ugly as sin. Your daddy's so lucky to have someone with taste moving in. Leave it out when you're done and I'll pack it up."

I don't answer her. Mostly because I'm afraid that if I open my mouth I'll throw up on the kitchen rug.

"So, kiddo, what's next?" she asks, flipping through a newspaper.

Kiddo. It's one thing to go right ahead and slip into the open parking space my mom left when she died, but it's another to expect me to be happy about it. Or, like, want to engage with it at all.

I add milk to my coffee and stay standing, six feet from her, my back pressed against the counter. It's not far enough, in my opinion. "What do you mean?"

"Magicworks must have something planned for you now that you're done with your little show. They take care of their stars, don't they?"

She knows that isn't true. Fuck her for saying it.

"I'm going to bed," I say and walk out.

∽

The sound of fingernails drumming against my bedroom door wakes me, an entire day later.

"Hey, girly," says Katrina. She snaps her gum, poking her pointed face in through a crack in the door Jack Nicholson–style. "Mani-pedis. Let's go."

I'm face-down in bed, but I won't get up for her. The inch I raise my head off the pillow is all she's going to get. "No, thanks," I say.

The door opens all the way, slamming loudly into the doorstop. Katrina swears, then gives a high, hooting laugh, apologizing to nobody. She's got car keys in her hand and they jangle annoyingly against her hip. "Let's go, let's go. I made us an appointment. We can get your eyebrows waxed while we're there."

Slowly, I unravel myself from the sheets and turn over, coming to sit in the middle of the mattress. I blink at her. "What time is it?"

"Twelve thirty," she says. "I don't know how the hell you sleep like you do. I've got an internal alarm clock that goes off every morning at six."

"I don't want to go anywhere. You go. Have fun."

"Oh no, you're going. Your dad wants us to spend a little quality time together. Come on. Up, up, up."

To shut her up, I go. I get hair ripped off my face while Katrina literally never stops talking. I climb into a spa chair and pick a spot on the opposite wall to stare at, drifting away into my own head.

I chased him up the fucking street.

Like a Labrador. And he didn't turn around.

Dax called last night from the Connecticut airport to tell

me he landed, but I couldn't find it in me to answer. He ended his voicemail with *I love you,* and I can't delete it. I'm gutted by it; I'm *thrilled* by it.

And I have to keep reminding myself that he's gone. He left. That this might be the last time I'll ever hear him say it.

"Where's your little friend? Jason? Jackson?" Katrina chews her gum at me from the neighboring spa chair. My eyes sink to the bubbling tub of water where my feet soak. It's hot water, I know it is, but I don't feel it. It's like I can't feel anything.

"Gone," I grunt.

"Boo," says Katrina. "He was cute."

"He's an asshole," I say, but I don't mean it.

Without spending any time thinking it through, I stand up suddenly and step out of the gurgling water. The kind older woman just sitting down to do my pedicure asks if I'm okay, but I can't answer her. I can't open my mouth, or a hard racking sob will come falling out, and I'm not ready for it yet.

I leave wet bare footprints across the floor of the salon, Katrina calling my name as I run outside and keep running. On the corner, I pull my phone from my shorts pocket and buy a plane ticket to Connecticut in about four and a half minutes. Middle seat. Leaves tomorrow.

It's not going to be over like this. I won't let it.

Now

WILHELMINA

Out of hair and makeup, standing across the hall from me with two coffees in his hands, is Daxon. He's got the beginnings of a smile on his lips. The small kind. The intimate kind—the one where only he and I know something.

There are so many somethings only he and I know.

Butterfly wings swoop low in my stomach. "Thanks," I say, taking the cup he extends to me.

We fall into step, heading towards set. And then it hits me, like reality likes to do, that I need to be careful here.

It's been *seven years*. And this whole time I thought he was the one with the scissors behind his back, so fine with severing the tie between us for cold brick and columns and ivy, and whatever else they had at Yale that I didn't.

But he was right to leave. Plays, musicals, short films, action movies—he's done all of that because he made the choice to walk away from what was comfortable.

"This call time," he says, rolling his eyes.

"*Ugh*." I add an overdone laugh and Dax laughs along with me, but there's an underlying tension between us, a strange kind of awkwardness that wasn't there earlier. I raise the coffee to my lips and drink, my throat tight. "Thanks for this, by the way. Perfect. Exactly what I needed."

I want to pull him into the nearest closet and forget for a

while that anything bad has ever happened anywhere. But I don't have time. There's a script in my trailer with new lines I need to learn. We have blocking to rehearse. I can't sit around idling with Dax; I have to prioritize my own success. Especially with Katrina crouched just out of sight, ready to pounce on me the second my guard is down.

"You okay, Chase?"

"What are we doing?" I ask him. My eyes dart down the hall, checking for listening ears. Nobody's there.

"Drinking liquid sugar and trying to stay conscious?" says Dax.

"No," I say. "You and me."

His eyes darken a little and they drop mine. "I don't know. What are we doing? 'Cause Wil, I . . . it's been so long, but I never . . . it never . . . I still—" But he cuts himself off with a sigh. "Do you know what I mean? If you wanted to . . . I don't know—be something? I want that, too."

I'm not looking at him, because I can't. Because if I do, I think maybe I'll burst into flames and melt into a bubbling puddle. My lungs suck in a deep, steadying breath, and in an exhausted panic, I push what we could be further from me.

"You know what you mean to me. You're my best friend," I say, instead of what I want to be saying. Which is that even after the sun has swallowed the earth, and the stars start blacking out, and the universe begins to shatter, I will love him. That is my only constant.

"Don't do that," Daxon breathes. His eyes are big and soft and sad, so sad. They're full of sudden tears. "Let's be more than that. This is real to me, it means something. Everything."

"Dax—" My bottom lip begins to tremble. It's too early to rip myself apart from the inside out like this. The look on his face is enough to bind myself to him forever.

But, god, I'm so terrified to lose this chance that I can't let myself have him.

"I can't," I breathe. Which is a lie, because I could. So easily, I could. Like spreading butter across hot bread, I could. "Everything I've ever wanted . . . a comeback, my chance to perform again, those have to come first this time."

"Okay," says Dax, "then put them first. I'll happily be second. But I don't want to be nothing."

I shake my head at him. "It wouldn't be that easy."

Two crew members carry a ladder past us and we both straighten up and nod a greeting their way. When they've gone, Dax turns to me again. "It *would* be easy."

"I have to go learn my lines," I say. "I'll see you."

"Wil."

But I don't turn around.

∞

TO THE STARS - OFFICIAL SCRIPT

INT. LILA'S BEDROOM - EVENING

It's goodbye. The thing that's been
tapping on their shoulders since that first
night on the pier. Inevitable and cruel,

of course, but also slow. Taking its time
about things. Ripping through them inch by
inch. She can't stay. He can't go. And
there's nowhere for them to find equal
footing here.

                    NICK

 So, you're going to school. So what? We
 can do long-distance. I'll write you. You
  can come back on breaks, or I'll visit
 you. I'll save up for it. It'll be just
             like it is now.

                    LILA
                  (angry)

 Stop it. Stop it. No, it won't. It won't.
 I'll be thousands of miles away and you'll
   be here with an entire life to live
              without me.

                    NICK

  I don't want a life without you.

LILA

Forget me, okay?

NICK

How the hell am I going to forget you?
Huh? Tell me just how.

LILA
(crying)

I don't know just how.

NICK

Can't forget what's carved on your
goddamn soul, Lila. You think you'll be
easy to get rid of? You won't be.
You'll take me eight hundred years just to
stop thinking about, let alone forget.
I will love you forever.

Now

DAXON

∽

"Max, meet Daxon Avery. This kid's gonna be huge."

Max Perry is a head shorter than me and built like a tank. He was absolutely one of those high school football players that got jacked at seventeen and still carries that confidence. But there's something poetic about his size; Max looks like someone who would crash through any wall for his clients. He feels safe. A sure thing.

"Daxon, tell me about yourself. What've you done?" Max asks after we've all clinked glasses of scotch.

I choke down the first sip of scotch. If this stuff wasn't brewed by Count Dracula in a mossy basement cauldron, then *fuck*. But Max downs his in one go and I feel weirdly compelled—*ha, get it?*—to finish mine quickly, too.

I tell him about *Son of a Gun*. Then my role in Greg's limited series, *Kill Switch*, an action-adventure based on a bestselling graphic novel.

"Very good," says Max. His eyes slide to Katrina and he tips her a wink. "You're getting out there. And this kinda thing is right where you wanna be next," he says. "Romantic lead."

The truth is that I have no idea what I want next. *To the Stars* is probably going to determine the course of the rest of my career. And it's a solid script, sure. But do I want to do romance for the foreseeable future?

"What if I want to win an Oscar? That's a bucket list thing for me."

Max signals our server for another round of drinks and I suck down the rest of my glass, trying not to puke on the table as it goes down like lava.

"Then I'd say *join the fucking club*, kid." He grins. "I'm kidding. Look, you wanna win something? I have the best scripts in the industry hitting my desk every day. Take this." He hands me his card and I reach across the table to take it. "And call me when this wraps. We'll set something up, have you come in, see what's what."

"Uh, wow, okay," I splutter, grinning. The scotch is slipping down the curves and ridges of my brain like they're waterslides. "I will. I absolutely will. Thank you so much."

"I knew you'd be a fit," says Katrina. Her eyes trace my face over the rim of her glass.

For two hours, we talk Hollywood. Directors, producers, people we love and admire, people who are probably over-rated, and people who are coming up that excite us. Katrina apparently knows everything about anyone who's ever had a SAG-AFTRA card, and gossips sloppily with Max about co-stars who know someone who knows someone, while downing martinis like water.

I am zonked halfway through my second scotch. I watch their lips move to keep myself from slumping forward onto my empty steak plate. Finally, Max is beat, and after he makes a show out of treating us to dinner, he offers to grab us a car, leaving Katrina and me alone at the table.

"What did I tell you?" she asks me, slipping out of her chair and settling down into Max's, the one next to mine.

"He's the whole package. Anything you want, he'll get you."

My head starts nodding and I can't stop it. I'm like a wind-up toy trying to stay conscious. "Yep," I say heartily, still nodding, "yep, he's the real deal." Not that my agent isn't. But Max is playing on an entirely different level.

She leans towards me with her elbow on the table, a cloud of booze radiating from her skin and off her teeth as she smiles. "Anything you want, Daxon," she repeats. "Anything."

"Yeah," I say uneasily. My eyes dart around us as my feet try to remember how to move. I feel like human Jell-O, equal parts wobbling and immobile. The restaurant is dimly lit, with dark floors and walls. It's exactly the kind of place you bring someone so that you can get close and fly under the radar. "Why don't we, uh, let's . . . Max. With the car. Let's . . ." I scoot my chair back and stand up, the room spinning.

"Whoa, Daxon, let me help you." Katrina locks her arm around mine, steering me towards the hostess stand and the exit. I blink hard, trying to get my bearings, trying not to trip over my feet in front of Max Perry. "First rule of this biz is never let them catch you wasted," she whispers in my ear.

"Oh, I'm not," I argue, as she pulls me out into the night, but I am.

The lights out here, warm and white, contrast so starkly with the ones inside that it's like the sun has come up suddenly. Max is out there laughing with the valet, but Katrina keeps us back.

In my peripheral, a car pulls up and I twist towards it, ready to get in and get home.

"Daxon," Katrina says, her fingers tight on my arm. I turn to her.

"Yeah?"

"Stick with me, and I'll help you get where you want to go."

"Uh," I grunt, "that's—"

And then she starts laughing, overly loud. "You are *so funny*! I'm such a sucker for a funny guy."

"What the fuck?"

It's Wil's voice, sharp and clear. She and the actress playing Lila's sister Amy are dressed for a night out, walking to the door from the car that just pulled up. The look on Wil's face is blind rage and the color in her cheeks changes like a traffic light, first drained of blood, then murderous scarlet.

"Wil," I say quickly. My eyes are unfocused, especially in this light. My head swims. My stomach reels. "It's not—"

But the look on her face cuts me off. Her hazel eyes narrow, her painted lips form a thin line.

Chumming up with Katrina is unforgiveable.

Wil charges past us into the restaurant.

"Oh, shoot. She looks mad," Katrina says in a faux-sorry voice. "I'll sort it out."

"No—" I start, but a booming voice cuts me off.

"Daxon! Over here!" Max waves me forward from the car window. "I just thought of a role you'd be perfect for. Get in, I'll give ya the pitch and we'll get the ball rolling."

I genuinely don't know what to do.

In my boozy fog, I make a choice. Is it a good choice? Nope. But I try to rationalize it and come up with the fact that, anything Katrina says, I can defuse and explain to Wil later. This is one of those jump-now-or-miss-it moments. So I'm gonna jump.

I go to the car.

Now

WILHELMINA

$\backsim$

"Lemme see if I can get you a water while we wait," says Vanessa, my on-screen sister. She flags a passing server and they walk off together to the bar. "Stay here, I'll be right back."

I can't blame her for suggesting it. Blood is pumping rhythmically in my ears like the doom-laden drums that play before King Kong emerges from the forest, or something.

God, that sounds like a thing Dax would say.

Dax.

And Katrina.

My eyes are wide and searching the restaurant for a place to step away. Get some air. Possibly vomit. It's dark in here, lounge-y. The live tinkling of piano keys plays against clinking silverware and conversation.

"How many?" asks the hostess.

I look at her, but my eyes can't focus on her face. "I— you know what, I just need . . ." and my feet start backing up. I keep going until I full-on bump into an older man in a suit jacket. "Oh god, so sorry. I'm so sorry. Are you okay?" But I don't wait for him to answer. I keep going, down a hall lined with pictures of Hollywood icons—Sinatra, Marilyn, Elvis—until the sign for the restroom appears and I push in.

It's empty. I breathe alone in the dim lighting. Let my shoulder sag against the tile wall beside the sink and tip my head, shutting my eyes.

Daxon Avery and Katrina Tyson-Taylor. Out to dinner. Like two old friends.

Which can't be fucking possible because he *knows*, intimately and without any doubt, the extent that that woman has upended my family. I saw Max Perry there; I get it. But also, I don't.

My fingers press against my brow as a headache spreads mercilessly. I can't be here. With people staring. I turn for the door, ready to tell Vanessa that I need to head home, when it opens.

My eyes drop immediately. "Excuse me," I murmur and go to step around this person. But they shut the door behind them and stand in front of it, blocking me. When I look up, my heart plummets what feels like fifty stories.

Katrina.

"Stuffing your pockets with free tissue?" she says.

There's no fake nicety. We're not on set, not at work. She's free here to say and do whatever she wants.

"Let me out," I say, my voice low and curt. My eyes are focused on her right shoulder, unable to lift to meet her eye.

"There's a little bottle of hot sauce on every table, bet you could swipe a few without anyone seeing. Maybe sneak the saltshakers, too."

My breath is ragged and slow, quivering as I finally raise my head and look into her face. Well, not *her* face. The face she upgraded to a couple years back. My eyes narrow.

"I have nothing to say to you."

Which is a complete lie. I want to throw names at her. I want to go off. Her birthday was a few days ago, and I swallow back the urge to ask how she rang in seventy-five.

"I'm sure you don't," Katrina says. "Not without your lawyer present, anyway. How you got off with just community service, I'll never know. Must have hired a real shark. Well, not you—your daddy."

"Shut up," I snap. "Move. I'm leaving."

She doesn't. Katrina looks over me at her reflection in the mirror, taming a few flyaways. "Not yet. I went to lunch with an old friend the other day. Harris Bastian? You know Harris. God, he put in years on that little show you did. I'm so glad to see him moving up in the world."

Just the sound of Harris's name sends a prickling shiver down my spine. And though my stomach has balled itself into a lump of coal, I don't let my face reflect how I'm feeling. "I said *move*."

"Speaking of moving up," Katrina continues, like I didn't say anything. She unpins a sparkling barrette from her hair, smooths the piece it was clipped to then refastens it. "I was shocked to see you'd booked something like this. After how many years hiding away? You must've pulled some strings somewhere. Daxon, though, *what a fit*. The perfect romantic lead. He's really going somewhere. I'm so glad he didn't renew his Magicworks contract all those years ago. He would've been sucked in for who knows how many more seasons of shitty kids' TV. No, it's a good thing he ended that show when he got the chance. I heard he graduated from Yale with honors, is that right?"

Wait . . . what?

Didn't renew his contract.

All the blood that was boiling in my ears begins to freeze. My hands had turned to fists at my side, and now they're shaking, fingernails shoved into the skin of my hand so hard they could draw blood.

It's a good thing he ended that show when he got the chance. It's not true. That's not what happened. Dax would've told me. He would've told me before we got canceled, I know he would've told me.

"I told you to *move.*" My teeth are gritted.

"You didn't know," says Katrina, delighted. "Ouch." And she steps aside to let me pass.

"I know everything," I tell her confidently. Which is totally a lie. But it sounds so good and true coming out of my mouth, low, with finality. "And I never forget."

I pull open the bathroom door and slip out, call a cab and get myself home.

∽

TO THE STARS - OFFICIAL SCRIPT

EXT. THE BOARDWALK - AFTERNOON

It's September now. The pier is quiet, the
Ferris wheel still. No music, no laughter,
just a moody sky above NICK and LILA as
they stand looking over the water, saying

goodbye before LILA is set to leave for
school.

                    NICK

        This isn't the end for us,
            Eliza Patterson.

                    LILA
                 (cold, numb)

        Don't lie to me, Nick.
        It doesn't suit you.

NICK stares across the water like he can
imagine the battle beginning to rage on
distant shores. His life here is over.
Summer with Lila, in this town.

                    NICK

        When I get back, I'll find you.

                    LILA

        When you get back?

                    NICK

War's coming. I intend to fight.

                    LILA
                 (horrified)

   No. Nick, you can't.

                    NICK

   It's the right thing.

                    LILA

        No!

                    NICK

      Lila . . .

LILA turns her back on him, angry tears slipping down her cheeks. We see her breaking,
see her walk the thin edge of despair, watch

her as she teeters, towards a hard new
reality: this could be life or death.

But she takes a breath and wipes the water
from her face. Below them, the sea rages.
Above them, thunder cracks and lightning
splits the sky. Her mind is made up: if she
lets him go now, maybe she can forget him.

                    LILA

        So, go. Leave. Go on. Go to war,
          get blown up for all I care!

                    NICK
                (stunned, hurt)

                Stop it.

LILA pushes NICK in the chest. She's weak,
he isn't hurt from it, but it's her words
that nearly knock him down.

                    LILA

        Go! I hate you for making me
          love you like this.

NICK

Listen to me: You go to school, and you
excel, you hear me? You graduate with
honors. Take over your daddy's company one
day. I wanna read about it in the papers.
I wanna see your name and your picture and
know you ended up alright.

LILA

Stop it.

NICK

You do everything in this world
that you want to do.

LILA

I mean it, stop. Stop it right now.
Just go!

NICK
(turning to leave)

And when I think about you, Lila,
it's gonna be with a heart full of love
and no regrets.

I have almost nothing left in me to give, but . . . there's something about this scene that sparks a flame. We've lived this moment, me and Dax. Not at the brink of the Second World War, maybe, but at the breaking point of our world, of each other. The wet on Lila's face is real. The pallor Nick wears, the desperation in his eyes, that's real, too.

And the anger Lila feels as Nick leaves her before she can leave him, leaves her for something that could take him from her, from the earth, forever, well, that's not hard to summon.

We wrap the scene. A production assistant brings me a water. The lights switch off. The on-set chatter comes alive, and Daxon tries for the eleven millionth time to get my attention, to talk to me, but I walk away. I walk to the golf cart waiting to drive me to my trailer.

Once there, I stand still and alone in the quiet.

From the moment Dax answered my one call from jail, I handed him my pounding, bloody heart on a silver platter. I didn't mean to, it just happened. Because he's Dax. My Dax.

And yet, again, I'm standing here wondering what deficiency I must have, what kind of wrong I am, to be so easy to leave behind.

I'm remembering those months when Katrina took over my home. Boxed up my mother's things. Pushed in, pushed me out. And now she's done it again. And Dax let her.

I pull my jacket tighter around me and leave the trailer. Dusk is settling and it's hot, but there's a wind that sifts its fingers through my hair, finally free of my long, neat Lila wig.

"Wil!"

My stomach drops fast and heavy, like an elevator someone's just cut the cables on. It's Daxon. I don't answer him. I walk half the length of base camp, as fast as my short legs can carry me. He follows me the whole way. I breathe into my nose and out my mouth, an old trick my mom taught me when I'd get hot-headed as a kid.

Maybe I can tell the director that I need some time away.

My eyelids scrunch closed and I breathe in, counting to four, and breathe out again, counting to six. I can't stay here and look at Dax every day and say words so much like the ones I used to say seven summers ago.

"Wil, hang on."

But at this, the air comes ripping out of my mouth in a snarling sound. "Get away from me, Daxon."

"I want to explain," he says from six feet away. His shadow is long in the dying sun. The edges of it brush my shoes and I fight the urge to back up.

My jaw is clenched. "No."

"I know you saw me with Katrina. *Nothing* happened, okay? It wasn't like that. It was a business dinner with her agent."

I roll my eyes. "That is the last thing I'm thinking about right now," I say. My voice is frigid. "How many *fucking* years, Daxon? How many years have you been my best friend? A part of my family? You know everything about me, you know what getting *Marnie* meant to me. I can't believe you chose not to renew your contract and didn't tell me about it first."

Dax is visibly taken aback. "How did you know—?"

"I didn't." The words come out of my mouth slowly, with a weight to them. "I had to hear it from Katrina. *You* should've told me."

"Wilhelmina." He says my full name in a pained whisper and I literally feel my heart shatter like a mirror ball, reflecting back moments of our lives as they once were in the scattered pieces around our feet. Dax's eyes are big and soft, terrified. He swallows and his throat bobs. "I—it's complicated."

"It's not fucking complicated, Daxon. You took something from me. You left me drowning. And then you hid behind Yale and never thought for a minute that maybe I deserved the truth about why."

"Look, I'm sorry. I'm sorry you found out like that. But I'm not sorry that I went to school. It was the right choice. And this thing with Katrina is nothing, I swear. It was business," he argues. "It wasn't personal."

My skin is prickling with anger. "This business is always personal."

"Wil, come on. It's me. And I fucked up when I was seventeen. I didn't handle it right. I'm sorry for that, I am. When I heard they were canceling the show, I had no idea it was because of me. We were on for so long, Wil. Things end. It was time." He looks around the lot, eyes scanning for listening ears. "Let's go sit and talk this out."

Dax steps forward, his arm reaching out to me like he expects me to take his hand. I recoil.

So much of my body is made of pure anger now that I don't know where that stops and the good parts, the rational, understanding parts, begin.

"No," I say.

"Wil."

"Fuck you," I tell him. "I'm leaving."

"You're . . . leaving? For how long?"

I nod and shut my eyes a moment. "I can't do this right now."

When I open them again, I can tell his jaw is tight, the muscle there jumping as his gaze slips away from me and he takes in a deep breath.

"No," he says, and the sound of it is firm. It's a tone I've never heard before.

"No?"

"We're gonna talk this out. Right now. We've come too far."

"No, *we're* not going to do anything anymore," I spit, and start to turn.

"Would you hang on a second? Please?" Dax's words cut across the space between us and hit me hard in the chest, and I stop. "Everything we've been through, all those years, I deserve two minutes of your time."

"You just had 'em," I say, voice cold and static like it belongs to someone else.

Maybe I'm taking the easy way out. Except, where Dax is concerned, where *Katrina* is concerned, nothing is easy.

I turn around and I walk off the lot and call a car. I'll take a red-eye home.

My hand digs in my pocket for my phone and I pull up Margot's contact, needing a familiar voice to drown out the distant sound of Daxon calling my name.

Then

WILHELMINA

$\sim$

Autumn hits Connecticut in all the ways it doesn't in Los Angeles. It's *cold*.

I'm wearing a short-sleeved dress, a summer dress, and even here in the cab it's freezing. I hear myself tell the driver to take me to Yale. The word is bitter and ugly in my mouth.

The campus is enormous and busy. Cutting across it, trying to find the drama department, is like trying to merge across the freeway. My stomach is this turbulent because I'm nervous as fuck.

What am I going to say to him?

There's a little coffee place beside the drama-school building. I duck inside. I've got my dad's old ball cap on my head, and I pull it low, try not to meet anyone's eyes.

Before I'm anything, I'm Marnie. And I don't have time for that.

I order the biggest coffee they have and chance a glance around the shop. Students sit at small tables with their laptops and textbooks. Good, smart, normal people who chose college over cameras. I should want to be one of them. Why don't I want to be one of them?

At the back of the shop is a girl on a date with a brown-haired boy who's got his back to me. He's glancing at his phone way too often. She's watching him like he's the North Star.

I clock her hand reaching across the table to touch something on his face. She laughs. And that's when my heart plummets.

He straightens up and I'd know the bend of those shoulders, the rogue freckle on the back of his neck, the way his hair gets a little too long and curls around his ears, from another continent.

It's Daxon.

My feet are quick, unembarrassed, charging ahead. But my heart is screaming. My breath is quick and uneven. I'm four feet from their table when I feel my lips part and my angry, broken voice tumble out. "Dax?"

He whips his head around and I watch his face fall like someone's just poured ice down his back.

"Wil?" He stands up so fast his chair goes toppling backwards.

I didn't think I could get to a lower place emotionally. But I feel myself riding an elevator down to the basement level of my soul. I turn around and I book it. This was the literal worst idea I've ever had in my entire life.

I'm speed-walking across campus, head down, not even cold anymore but with no idea where I'm going. When I get to a crosswalk, I stop and punch the button. Behind me, feet come jogging up.

"Wil. Hey. What're you . . . ? When did you . . . ?"

I don't answer him. I jam my fist into the crossing signal button seven more times. *Come on.* Cars whiz by. I'm trapped.

"Wil. Come on."

"Don't." I turn my head and fix him with a deadly stare.

Dax shrugs out of his coat and holds it out to me. "Put this on."

I turn away from him. "Get away from me, Daxon."

The walk sign lights up in the coming darkness. I charge across the street, but I can feel him right at my heels.

"Wil, stop."

"I said *get away from me*."

His hand lands softly on my bare shoulder and I hate the way it's healing me, even in this brief second. I shrug away from him.

"Wil, come on." His fingers brush my arm, taking gentle hold. I yank it away.

"Who the hell was that?" I ask him. I can't keep it in anymore.

"Who?"

"*Who?*" I glare at him. He's not this thick. He was on a *date*. Four seconds after driving away and leaving me standing in the middle of the street.

"What are you doing here?" Daxon asks. His voice is soft, he's still a little out of breath from chasing me across campus.

"What's her name?" I say.

"Who?"

I roll my eyes. "Coffee girl."

"Hannah something. From one of my classes. We got partnered up on an assignment. That's all. Wil, what are you doing here?"

Like that sounds real. I roll my eyes and repeat his words back to him. "Hannah *something*. Sounds like you're really all-in on this one. Casual college Daxon, casually dating college girls with no last name as soon as we break up."

Dax's face falls. He blinks at me.

I've seen that look there before. Not from something I've

done or said, but from a late-night movie marathon with him. *Lord of the Rings*. It was towards the end, when I could barely keep my eyes open. This guy gets hit with an arrow in the chest but keeps fighting. And then he gets another arrow to the chest, and it's like, there's no way he's gonna make it. But he keeps fighting. He takes out a couple of enemy warriors, and then you hear the villain's bow creak, and the guy turns around and the last arrow takes him out.

Dax cried during that scene. Not a big boo-hoo cry. A soft, sweet kind of cry that he didn't want me to see. He brushed away a couple tears and pretended to cough. He's doing the same thing now.

I wonder if the words *break up* are his last arrow to the chest.

"We didn't break up," he says, voice wavering.

My lip starts shaking, I can't help it. "You didn't stop the car."

"I—couldn't."

"Bull. You didn't turn around." I cross my arms tight against the cold. The evening wind is bitter as it cuts through my hair. "I ran for you and you didn't stop."

"We didn't break up." Daxon says this so quietly, I barely hear it.

"You left," I say. "You left me. That's a breakup."

He swallows down what are clearly tears and pushes his coat at me again. "Put this on."

"Dax . . ." I shake my head. Like, come on, what does he expect from me? To be okay? To be normal? For everything to be just as it was?

"It's cold. Put it on. Please."

I stand there, breathing in and out, our gazes held steadily together. I take the coat from him and slip it over my frozen shoulders. The warmth, the familiar smell of him. It's enough to drug me. "Take me home," I say. "Wherever that is for you now."

Dax reaches his hand out to me and I fold my fingers into his.

∽

Dax's roommate is thankfully scarce, because when the door closes behind us, we reach for each other like it's been eons apart. Then we order a midnight pizza.

We strip the comforter and pull around the desk chair. Tie the sheets to the headboard and to the chair back and sit inside our makeshift fort, together and whole.

"I'm gonna stay here," I tell him at three in the morning.

"Of course you are," says Dax. He's braiding my hair, long down my back, from where I sit cross-legged in front of him.

"I'll be like the ghost haunting the dorm. They'll give me some kick-ass ghost name, too. Like *the Shadow of Suite 120*. The legend, the myth—"

"The trespassing vandal."

I turn around and wrinkle my nose at him. Daxon takes my face in one hand and kisses me.

"What are we going to do?" I ask.

Dax's fingers pick up again at the bottom of my braid, twisting around and around. Loose and messy, the way only a boy would do it. He lets go and it instantly begins to unravel.

He presses a kiss to my bare shoulder. Slowly, I turn around to face him. His eyes are soft, tired, emotional. Dax glances towards the window for a moment, and when his eyes come back to me, the look there is shattered.

"I don't want anyone else," he says.

"Me either."

"There's no one else. For me. Ever."

I climb into his lap. Wrapping my legs around his waist, I stretch my arms around his neck, and I lay my head down. "I have to go home," I murmur.

"You have to go home," Dax says.

"But not yet."

"Not yet. Please."

Now

DAXON

~∞~

I don't care who's watching. Whose heads turn as I call for her like the ground is crumbling beneath my feet.

This business is always personal circles my head over and over in her voice.

I stop, breathing hard, pulse jumping. If I could just talk to her, if I could get her to understand. I need her to understand.

I want her to know how sorry I am that I made her feel like she could hate me.

But what I know Wil needs is space. So, when she leaves, head down, and climbs into a waiting Uber, I don't stop her.

My teeth catch my bottom lip as it starts to shake.

Greg appears at my side, his hand pressing gently into my shoulder. "Dax," he says, "you good? It's okay. Come on, come inside." He steers me around to the larger, more permanent-looking trailer he's been based out of this entire shoot. Inside, it looks like a regular office. Blinds on the windows, leather chairs, a whole three-screen setup on the desk to review dailies and meet with studio execs. He sits on one side; I sit on the other.

"Talk to me," says Greg.

My hands tangle in my lap. "She left."

"Left?" His face falls.

"She's gone."

Greg drops my gaze and tips his head up towards the ceiling. He looks like Gandalf in *Fellowship* when he realizes they'll have to go into the Mines of Moria—like this is the last thing in the world he wanted to hear, and everything is about to go to hell.

"What happened?"

So, so much. A billion beautiful, irreplaceable things and one infinitely terrible thing.

At first, it was a summer plucked out of time, back doing what we love to do, together. Nights that stretched endlessly, tiny moments between scenes, glances when the camera wasn't looking. And god, just the feel of her so close, finally, after so long.

I don't know how much he knows about Wil and me, so I start at the beginning from that first *Marnie* audition when Wil brought the house down with enough pluck and personality to fill an ocean, and that it was then that I knew I was gone forever.

Greg nods and listens, stoic but worried, because it's a lot, our story, for someone whose job it is to keep us united towards one common goal.

And then I tell him about Katrina, and now, what a seven-year-old secret has ruined.

We talk logistics, how to proceed if we can't bring Wil back. Greg outlines contractual obligations and legal proceedings, and my stomach twists and tightens as I imagine that quitting this project would be the cherry on top of the shittiest thing that's happened to Wilhelmina Chase in a long line of shitty things she's been dealt.

"I'll do what I can," I say. "I'll talk to her. Can't make any promises, but I'll try."

Except that, before I do, I have one quick stop to make.

$$\infty$$

"Somebody really likes their Jell-O."

It's 11 p.m. and I'm the last person in this town's Piggly Wiggly supermarket, checking out with what looks like a literal metric ton of strawberry-flavored Jell-O mix. Little white box after little white box rides the conveyor belt towards Shirley, the checker. Honestly, if you told me she was the ghost haunting this place, I'd believe you, because this woman is probably eight hundred years old.

"Guilty," I say brightly, sticking my card into the reader. The fun thing about Jell-O is that when it melts, say in an extremely nice vintage car parked out in the sun on our base camp lot, it stains. Big time.

I may spend a few days with red hands, but hey, it'll be worth it.

All night, I'm up mixing red powder with water and filling the fridge in my rental to within an inch of its life, then waiting as it solidifies. In the morning, I feel just a smidge unhinged loading bags of the stuff into my driver's trunk. But what's a good revenge story without a little insanity?

We have a scene scheduled for today, Katrina and I. Her character gets to tell mine that he's trash and to stay away from her daughter, which feels extremely on the nose given what's gone down. And honestly, I don't intend to stick around long enough today to get that filmed. I'm planning on

coming down with a wicked case of the Find-Wil-Chases—
it's an epidemic.

It's 6 a.m. and I'm unloading tote bags of wriggling strawberry Jell-O from a Lincoln town car at base camp. Casually,
I walk them over to where Katrina's Aston Martin convertible
is parked, its top down making this all too easy.

The valet shakes his head at me, telling me no one's
allowed near the car. I shuffle around the bags in my hands—
surprisingly heavy, I have to say—and hand him a folded bill
that makes him change his mind.

Then I get to work. By the time I'm done, you can't see the
dashboard, you can't even see the steering wheel. Everything
in this priceless, precious car with its milky vintage leather
interior is now jiggling red cubes. It's already warm out. I give
this about an hour in the sun before it's melted.

And, sure enough, right about the time I'm telling our
producer that, unfortunately, I'm not feeling well and I can't
film today, a scream slices across the asphalt and fills my
twisted heart with the kind of joy that only comes with a
prank well done.

Today, revenge is sweet. Strawberry Jell-O sweet.

All that's left is to find Wil.

Now

WILHELMINA

∞

It's nearing midnight when I land at LAX, but still, cameras flash. Which is so supremely surreal. Like a memory feeding through an unfocused lens.

It's been a long time since cameras cared about me. And yeah, this movie is a big deal. I get it. Greg and Daxon and a bestseller-turned-blockbuster. But this is nothing like *Marnie*; they were everywhere. Anywhere I went, they followed.

Then, suddenly, almost overnight, they were gone.

Maybe I should be glad that I'm relevant again. But really, I'm thinking about how much I hate airports. How seven years ago, I was standing in the Connecticut airport with Dax. Holding on to each other for dear life as rushing currents pulled us in separate directions. He had school. I had a life across the country to sweep the broken pieces of into a dustpan and find a way to move on.

That was the first day I knew it was over between us.

We never said that it was, but I knew.

I keep my eyes on the pavement through the sea of paparazzi and curious travelers. How long until it gets out? That I've abandoned the set of this huge movie. That I had my one chance at a dream come true sitting pretty on a silver platter and I drop-kicked it into the ether.

On the way home, driving across Los Angeles, all I can see

are places teenage Dax and I used to haunt. Restaurants and shops. That one sloping street where he kissed me out in the road until a honking car brought us back to reality. We ran, screaming, laughing, for the safety of the sidewalk. Fingers tangled. Invincible.

And there, right up there is the observatory where we held each other on the hood of his car, looked up into the sky and only saw ourselves reflecting back at us—the brightest constellation.

I didn't know it then, but he had already extinguished the fire we both built stick by stick.

When my agent reached out about renewing my *Marnie* contract, I said yes without another thought.

Maybe I should've had another thought. Or several hundred. It was time to move on from that show. But I was clinging to Marnie like a cat on a shower curtain as the bath fills up, so unbelievably scared to let go and get wet.

I needed to jump for myself. Instead, I got pushed.

And now I know who did the pushing.

∞

I'm back in la!

Are you out?

Margot texts me back immediately:

Yes!!!!!!!!!! Impliquer on Melrose

> Get your ass over here!

By the time I walk into the swanky, dark restaurant, I can barely keep my eyelids from falling closed. But I missed Margot, and sitting in a private booth with her and Cassie and a few other girls I don't know well is a nice distraction. Even if I'm wearing yesterday's clothes and the skin around my eyes is swollen from crying into an airline napkin, it's still nice.

They pepper me with questions about the movie and the costumes, the hair and makeup. When one of the girls I don't know asks me about Dax, I say something vague and change the subject. Margot's eyes narrow slightly from across the table, but she doesn't ask. I love her for not asking.

We split two bottles of champagne between the six of us, and when I can't stay awake anymore, I call for a car.

"But you *just* got here!" Margot whines, standing with me on the curb while I wait. A few rogue paparazzi cameras flash in the darkness.

"I know," I tell her, pivoting away from their lenses. "I'm just so tired."

"Wil . . ." She gives me a look. "You're gonna tell me why you look like shit eventually, right?"

"You're so kind."

"I'm worried about you."

"I'm okay. Really. I swear. I just needed a little break, that's all." My car pulls up at the curb and I hug her quickly. "I'll text you. Get home safe, okay?"

"You're sure you don't wanna stay? We're going clubbing!"

"Goodnight," I call from the back seat. Margot rolls her eyes in a silly, dramatic way and waves me off.

But when I wake up, I'm still tired, like I haven't slept at all. I pour myself coffee. Still tired. Walk out into the backyard and sit on the side with my bare legs in the cold pool water. Still tired. It's only when I catch my reflection in the hall mirror that I realize what I'm wearing.

It's an old Magicworks company Christmas party T-shirt.

I must have pulled it on last night in the dark, half-asleep, half-drunk on champagne. My stomach twists. Not because I'm still mad, which I am, but because I know where I need to go to make peace with it.

∽

Benny still works Security at Studio 7B on the Magicworks lot.

His familiar face answers the buzzer.

"Wilhelmina Chase, no freaking way. That you?"

I laugh, genuinely. It's a weird sound, given that I'm half-dead. But it feels so good.

"It's me," I say with a pathetic flourish of my hands for effect. "I was nearby and thought I'd swing over here, see what they've got set up in 7B."

"You wanna take a look?" he asks. Thank god. I was imagining I might have to beg, or cry. Maybe wind back up in jail for trespassing.

Benny leads me down the familiar hall of machinery and wires. The old linoleum flooring is the same as it was seven years ago (and long before that). Faded spring-green and flecked with white. Beyond towering lights and ladders, just around a slight corner, is the stage.

It's currently set as a diner for some new show. For some new cast to gather in. To make something glittering and magical together under these lights for a live studio audience.

That's what *Marnie* was. *Magic*.

The authentic laughs from the studio audience after we delivered our lines. Sweet, tiny faces beaming and hoping for me to stop and say hi on my way out, or even just to wave from right there.

I walk out into the middle, to center stage. The ground is covered in tiny tape X's and T-markers, just as it was then.

Feels like a thousand hours went by of waiting for that tape to go down. For the lights to lock, for the camera to be ready and in position. Dax and I would make up the silliest shit to pass the time between scenes. Handshakes and secret languages. At some point, we tried learning Morse code so that we could blink things to each other from our marks even after the director called for quiet.

So many things were said here. Frail, silly, forgettable nothings. I mean, they were somethings to me back then. But in hindsight, all I can hear is what we never said.

"Can we turn the lights on?" I ask Benny over my shoulder. He nods, disappearing to flip the right switches.

This place was my home. Here, with the warmth of the lights on my face. The soft shadows of seats just beyond where I can see, empty and waiting. Where applause and laughter ghost through the air.

Studio 7B is the house that made me.

Literally, in the sense that it birthed my career. But really, I became *me* right here.

"Okay if I hang out for a few minutes?" I ask Benny. He nods and shifts away down the hall. I sit down on the stage and draw my knees into me, wrapping them up in my arms.

Dax walked away from this show, but I'm the one doing it now, walking away from everything I wished for. Relevance again, a career again. A chance, a real chance at being an actress again. At booking and succeeding and pushing past this soundstage on to bigger things.

I don't know what to do.

Behind me, distantly, a door opens with a squawk and shuts. Maybe that's my cue to get out. I wouldn't blame Benny if it was—a welcome is only warm for so long before it starts to go cold.

"Sorry, I'll get going," I call over my shoulder, not looking.

"Hey," says Daxon Avery. "You busy?"

Then

DAXON

~~∞~~

Bob's house always has Christmas lights. I've helped him string them up the last few years. He likes the old, vintage, colored ones, and he likes them on every outdoor surface possible.

This year, it's white lights along the frame of the house and tracing neat lines up and down the roof. The trees are wrapped in tiny golden lights with smooth, even lines. He's upgraded; these were definitely done by a professional. White light-up deer graze on the lawn, and I notice the grass I've always known to be a little yellow and dead in places is lush and green.

The chunk of driveway Wil accidentally chipped that summer she thought she could skateboard has been patched up without a trace. I feel my skin prickle, up my legs and down my arms. It's like someone else lives here.

But Wil's upstairs window light is on, and the warmth of it, the familiarity, is enough to settle my rattled bones.

She has no idea I'm coming tonight. I didn't even think I'd be home for winter break. And what I'll say when I get inside . . . I really don't know.

In the foyer, Katrina Tyson-Taylor is dressed like she's about to present the Oscar for best candy cane, decked in rubies and a red skirt that sweeps along the ground. She greets me with a martini in each hand. I nod and say hi and then slip away as fast as I can.

As I take the stairs two at a time, my heart sloshes excitedly in my chest like an over-filled water balloon. It's been weeks. Hell, it's been *months* without Wil. I realize as soon as my eyes hit her just how badly the distance—physical, sure, but emotional, too—has taken a toll.

She's been busy here with a crowd of new friends and I barely have seven minutes to myself between classes, performing in an off-Broadway production of *The Importance of Being Earnest*, and trying to stay alive. I get her voicemail when I try to call and my own mailbox is full of her voice, tired and annoyed that I'm not there to answer. We've both not replied to too many texts.

It's not what either of us wanted or expected that day we held each other at the Connecticut airport and promised we'd make things work.

As I knock gently against the doorframe, Wil turns from the seat at her vanity, her mouth falling open. "No fucking way." She scrambles to her feet, flying across the room into my arms. I lift her up, her legs locking around my hips. I even spin a little, giddy, laughing with relief.

I kiss her like I'm a phone with two-percent battery life and she's my charger; she kisses me like someone who's been fumbling terrified in the dark and finally finds the light switch.

"I missed you," I say against her lips.

"You have no idea," Wil whispers, her forehead pressed to mine. "Holy shit, I can't believe you're here. For how long?"

"Two days."

"Damn it." She frowns at me.

"Hey, just try and get rid of me for the next forty-eight hours."

There's a party downstairs. We hear the sound of silverware tapping purposefully on crystal, the din of voices and brassy Christmas music dampening as Bob's voice cuts in. There's laughter, because where there's Bob, there's automatically laughter.

"Come on," I say, and set her back down on her bedroom floor. Wil extends her hand, grabbing mine and pulling me from the room towards the stairs.

We descend slowly. The partygoers have all convened in the living room just beyond the staircase, and through the railing, we have a perfect view of Bob holding a glass of champagne and Katrina perched on the arm of a chair to his left. Behind him, the fireplace roars. Wil crouches on the top steps and I follow suit, like we're kids sneaking out of bed.

"You go through life, you don't know what you're gonna find. It's tough out there. It is. This house was dark for a long time."

A breath comes out of Wil, low and dangerous like a growl, remembering her mom. I watch as people's eyes drop to the carpet, fingers absently adjusting shirt buttons. I don't know what it is about death that makes people so fidgety. Better than the awkwardness of confronting your own sadness, maybe.

"This gal, this piece of stardust, picked me up off my ass and turned what I was thinking was the last chapter into a fresh beginning. I was lost and she found me." He raises his champagne glass to her and Katrina beams around the room, blushing. Wil's entire body stiffens next to me. I steal a glance at her and I'm pretty sure she isn't breathing.

"I'd get down on one knee, but who the hell knows if I'd

ever get back up again?" Bob chortles. He digs in his pocket with his free hand, pulling out a ring box.

"No," says Wil, desperately, under her breath. Her fingers grab my arm, tightening.

"Katrina Tyson-Taylor," says Bob, "how 'bout we add one more last name to your collection. Will you marry me?"

Katrina stands as Bob hands his champagne off to a friend, and we watch, Wil and I, as she wraps her arms around his neck and he dips her low and they kiss like the ending of some movie. I feel Wil's grip on my arm slacken, her hand fall away.

"You okay?" I whisper to her.

"Come on," she says. Wil charges down the stairs, and for a split second, I worry she's about to burst into the living room and make a scene. But she goes right past, towards the front door and then out over the threshold and into the cold. I follow her as fast as I can, carefully shutting the front door behind us and jogging to catch up with her. She's got her phone out and is texting furiously.

"What's going on?" I ask.

"Margot's coming to pick us up," she says, like I'm supposed to know who that is.

"And take us where?"

"Out. Barhopping. Dancing. I don't know. It doesn't matter. Just out. Away."

Barhopping? Last time I checked, we were barely eighteen. But the look on her face is determined, hurt, so I don't offer up this fact. I stand with her in silence and wait for a car to appear at the end of the driveway. It flashes its lights and Wil grabs my hand.

"Come on," she says, so I do.

"This is Margot," says Wil from the front seat.

"Hi," I say. "I'm Daxon."

"God, you're right. He's *cute*," says Margot to Wil like I'm not there at all. She revs the engine and reverses out of the driveway.

The radio blares and Margot plows through the narrow streets of the Hollywood Hills. I'm just starting to get a tingling feeling like death is tapping on the car window when she swings us up against the curb beside a valet stand and she and Wil pile out. All I can do is follow.

Margot knows the bouncer and he lights up when he sees her, practically throwing the velvet rope to the ground he's so excited to let her pass.

Wil loops her arm through Margot's and mine and we go in. To a nightclub. On Christmas Eve.

"How is this place even open today?" I ask Wil, yelling over the thumping of the music.

She shushes me "*Be cool.*" Which, okay, we both know I'm not. That never mattered to Wil before.

She orders shots and martinis and cans of Red Bull. No one checks our IDs. Instead, they giddily usher us into the back, where things get dark and swanky. Supple black leather booths, velvet ropes and curtains to keep the non-child megastars at bay.

When I order a Coke from a server wearing thigh-high leather boots, Wil cuts across me and makes it a Jack and Coke. She squeezes my arm. "You good?" I tell her I am. But what I really am is crazy uncomfortable.

I have zero interest in being one of those tabloid child stars tripping out of nightclubs at four in the morning. Crashing my Porsche on the way to jail. I can admit it, I'm a complete square. And that's fine with me. But the feeling that I might not fit into whatever world Wil is building here brings heat to the back of my neck and a slick to my palms.

Then there's Margot. Is this who Wil is friends with now? Watching Margot flirting with waitstaff, daring Wil to take shots, I start wishing for a time machine; let's skip ahead a couple years, outgrow this night.

Meanwhile, Wil has started ranting about her dad. "He's an asshole. He's always been an asshole."

"I don't think he's an asshole," I say, but Wil doesn't seem to hear.

"But this really makes it all stick out, you know what I mean? Like, saying how awful things were before Katrina? Sorry your kid wasn't enough to make you happy."

I touch Wil's arm. "Want some water?" There are three full glasses on the table, untouched by any of us, and I slide one over her way. But Wil shakes her head and tries to get whatever's left out of a pink slushy drink she finished fifteen minutes ago. "We should probably get back," I try again.

"I'm never going back."

I don't like the look in her eyes. This isn't the alcohol talking. It isn't even just the trauma of watching your father move on with his life well before you're ready for him to.

She says it like it's a fact, not a drunken whim. And that chills my bones.

A waitress appears with another cocktail, a tropical blue drink complete with pineapple wedge. Wil grabs for it eagerly and the fruit falls into her lap. I don't think she notices at all. "They can have the house, the Barbie dream wedding, all of it. I don't give a fuck," she says to no one in particular, and downs it.

Margot's up and dancing off towards the bathroom. As Wil starts to rise, too, I reach out and touch her arm.

"What are you saying?" I ask.

I swear the music is getting louder, the beat shaking the cups on the tables. "What?" asks Wil, frowning at me. "Why aren't you drinking? Have something. Do you wanna do a shot?"

I shake my head. "What do you mean you're not going back?"

Wil pretends like she didn't hear me.

She sticks her arms up into the air and yells out a loud *woooooo!* then sways, precious and happy but so drunk, so completely drunk with this booze Band-Aid.

"Let's get outta here," I tell her, and I stand up from the booth, extending my hand and hoping she takes it. Surprisingly, she does, and I guide her out and onto the sidewalk under a cold moon.

"I want to dance," Wil whines faintly. "Take me back inside. Let's dance."

"You said you're never going back. What do you mean?"

"Daxon." I frown softly, my eyebrows creasing low. "Don't worry about it. It's fine. Be cool."

I shake my head at her. "I'm not cool, Wil. And this?" I gesture towards the club behind us. "This is bullshit. Getting wasted at nightclubs with models? This isn't you."

"It *is* me," Wil says loudly. I see a few heads turn in the crowd waiting on the sidewalk to get in. Wil's eyes take them in and a softness touches her gaze, an embarrassment, a guilt, a fear. She grabs my hand and marches us down the sidewalk away from their eyes, a camera flash going off in the distance.

The thing is, it's not her. It's not. I've never known her to run away from her problems. But, at the same time, I've never seen her come up against something as big as Bob getting remarried. "Look," I say, "I'm sorry he proposed to her. It's messed up. It sucks. But it happened. You gotta accept that and move forward. You can't drink it away."

"*No*," says Wil, and her face is shadowy, her expression angry. I've overstepped. "It's not that easy. He didn't even wait to make sure I was in the fucking *room* before asking her, Daxon."

"I know. That was shitty."

"Why would he—I don't understand why he—" But she cuts herself off as a sob comes choking out of her mouth.

I take her hand in mine and squeeze. "He fell for her. That's all."

Wil hiccups faintly, and even in the dark I can tell she's flushed. "Why are you taking his side?" she cries. It's a harsh sound, almost a shout, and I can only blink at her, at this new person transforming in front of me.

"I'm on your side always," I say.

"Then *be* on my side, Dax. Let's go back in. I wanna drink, and I wanna dance. Celebrate never going back home."

"This isn't you."

"It is me!" Wil shouts. "This is what I want."

Everything we built together, years of trust and friendship, murmuring secrets in the dark and then keeping them locked away tight, feels like it's gone. My best friend, my girlfriend, is gone. "God, Wil, just—*grow up*," I hear myself say.

"Wil?" Margot comes tripping prettily towards us, assesses the tension, then takes Wil's arm gently. "You okay?" She looks at me like I'm a creepy stranger and my heart sinks.

"Get me out of here," Wil tells her, but she's looking at me, right into my eyes, and I know we're broken. "Anywhere but here."

Margot nods and slides her hand down Wil's arm until their fingers lock. It's like the fucking changing of the guard. An era has ended, and the next one just ate the first one alive.

"*Wil*," I plead. As much as I know we're done, I don't want it.

Wil doesn't say anything. She shakes her head at me and drops my gaze and lets Margot lead her to the valet. Paparazzi have appeared now, and their shouts slice the frozen air. Camera flashes illuminate the sidewalk, the passenger door of Margot's car as it pulls up curbside, and I watch Wil's face, devastated, as she buckles herself in and stares straight ahead.

A shiver flutters through my body. She's going to leave me here, stuck to this lonely sidewalk. I call out her name again as Margot pulls away from the curb. Wil turns at the sound, pressing her small hand to the glass, and the look on her face is enough to shatter me.

Alone, I'm swarmed and swallowed by photographers.

Now

DAXON

∽

"Daxon. The hell are you doing here?"

Bob Chase moves aside as I slip past him into the foyer of the home that's always felt like my entire childhood tucked neatly inside four walls.

Just the smell of it is familiar, comforting, like a hug from arms I didn't know I'd been missing.

"I'm looking for Wil. Is she here?"

"No, she's not. I was hoping she was with you." He studies me. "Aren't you guys supposed to be on set in one of the Carolinas?"

The breath that comes out of my mouth wavers like a laugh, but it's more of a tired sigh. "Yeah. Yeah, I am. We are."

Bob ushers me into the living room.

"Wil okay?" he asks me. His voice goes a little gruffer than I remember it and I realize it's the sound of a wall rising, a drawbridge retracting. Anything to defend the castle.

"She's mad," I say. "She's really mad. At me."

Bob's round, jovial face darkens. "Why?"

We're seated on opposite couches, a fire crackling in the hearth to my left despite the already warm California morning outside. Does he know what happened back then, why the show ended? They probably would have looped him in. Then again, maybe not. If he did, it was probably something he'd have shared with her, even when their relationship was fracturing.

I take a deep breath, in through my nose, out through my mouth. My knee jiggles, and I place my hand on top of it to keep it still; the other one starts going. The fire gives a roaring snap.

"Katrina's working on our project. The South Carolina one. It's been hard for Wil."

I hear Bob swallow. "I heard something about that."

"Right," I say. "Well, Katrina asked me to dinner with her agent."

"Max fucking Perry," says Bob, rolling his eyes. Then he puckers his lips and makes a kissing sound. "Ass-kisser. Bet he was all over you."

I can't help it, I laugh. Bob rolling his eyes is a dead ringer for Wil. There's humor in it without needing to say anything else; it's charisma and a loud opinion in one quiet second of time. I love this family, truly, completely. But my laughter doesn't ease the tension in my gut or in the room.

"Yeah, he was interested in meeting with me. But the thing is, Wil ran into us on our way out. I didn't tell her I was meeting with Max and Katrina. Which I realize now was not the way to play it at all."

"No," Bob agrees. "Probably not. She saw you with Katrina? Fuck."

"Fuck, indeed."

He chuckles softly at this. "So where does you being in California all of a sudden come into this?"

My stomach is like an eel, twisting, serpentine, inside me. I take in a shallow breath. Ending *Marnie* wasn't just taking away Wil's dream, but Bob's day job playing Marnie's father. "Do you know why *Marnie, Maybe* ended?"

"Hell should I know?" Bob grunts.

"It . . ." I breathe out slowly and rub a hand down my thigh and back up again, trying to wipe the sweat away. "It was me. I got into Yale for drama. And then contract renewals came up and I said no."

Bob sinks into the couch cushions, taking this in. He rubs at his nose with the back of his hand. "No fucking kidding," he muses.

"No," I say, "and the part that I'm still kicking myself over is that I didn't tell Wil."

"She wasn't ready to hear it," says Bob. "My girl's been Swiss cheese for a long time. Bunch of life-shit digging holes in her since she was a little thing. Her mom dying. All the things that went down with Katrina. I hate that I had a hand in that. But I don't think she needed to hear that truth back then, 'bout you and the show ending."

Swiss cheese. Such a Bob-ism. Air comes forcefully from my nose and mouth in a strangled laugh, but my eyes sting, my throat starts getting tight. "I've been beating myself up for not telling her. For years. I'd never lied to Wil before that. I guess I did it so she wouldn't hate me. Which is kinda selfish, because I should've done it, to protect her from one more hole in the cheese."

"Why's all this coming up now?" Bob asks.

"Katrina told her. When I was chatting with Max. Which is so fucked-up. I should've kept an eye on her. I could've prevented it."

"Whoa, hey, hang on. Go back a beat. When Katrina gets

an idea in her head, she's gonna see it through. You couldn't have kept her from telling Wil." His eyes soften. "Wil could never hate you, Daxon."

I swallow the rising lump in my throat and nod. "I really wanna believe that."

"Thanks for tellin' me about Katrina."

"Listen, Bob, I have to find Wil. She left set. No one knows where she is."

"Shit."

"Yeah. I know. She's so good in this movie, she's so natural. It's the perfect next step for her. I have to . . . make things right."

"You checked her place?"

I nod. I swung by before coming here, only to find her driveway empty.

"She can't be too far. Probably just cooling off somewhere she feels safe."

And it hits me in the face going ninety miles an hour.

Somewhere she feels safe.

∞

All the lights are on in Studio 7B.

And while the set decorations are unfamiliar, the room has the same cool smell of metal and polished wood, the lingering sweetness of hairspray and laundry starch.

The door shuts behind me with a creak and a crunch as it settles closed.

Wil is sitting center-stage, her knees up to her chest, arms wrapped around herself. For a second, she's twelve and being thrown from general obscurity into the Sarlacc pit that is instant, lonely, glittering child stardom.

In the next moment, she's seventeen. Fresh from losing everything she's loved and worked her ass off for—lost all semblance of normalcy for—afraid of what it means to climb out of that pit Boba Fett–style.

But ultimately, she's the Wil those past lives have grown into. Stronger than ever.

"Hey," I say. "You busy?"

Now

WILHELMINA

∽

My heart zips up into my throat at the sight of him, here. "Dax, what're you—why are you—how did you—?"

Everything I want to say, every question, apology and accusation goes into the blender inside my skull.

"I'm sure I'm the last person you want to see right now," he says, hanging back a respectful distance. "But I'd like to talk, if that's okay."

I'm literally stunned. Did he teleport? Fly his little Lego starship across the country to come after me? I want to throw up and cry and laugh simultaneously.

Goosebumps prickle along my arms.

I get up and brush off my jeans, avoiding his eyes. My hand works its way into my hair, pushing it off my face and pinning it hard behind my ear. "I don't—I don't really want to . . ."

"Yeah, I figured," says Dax gently. "So, I'll talk, okay?" He takes a deep breath. "The other night? I drank too much trying to keep up with Max Perry—who, by the way, must be, like, made of scotch at this point. Like, I'm pretty sure he ordered a barrel, and drank most of it himself."

Affection for Dax starts creeping. First up from my stomach where it flutters to life, then crawling up along my ribs towards my mouth. "He looks like a barrel, so that tracks."

Daxon laughs. "Oh, totally. Totally barrel-shaped."

My lip twitches up and then falls back into a measured frown just as quickly. I study Dax's hand where it hangs at his side. "Why didn't you tell me? Why did I have to hear it from Katrina in a freaking bathroom?"

His fingers flex and contract. He's serious. Unsmiling now. "I think, at the time, it was because I didn't want you to hate me. But thinking about it now, it was because I was so in love with you and the idea of hurting you and then admitting to it out loud was . . ."

"I don't hate you," I tell him quietly, filling the silence he's left. "I could never hate you."

I'm surprised by how much Dax's face goes soft with relief. Even his shoulders relax a little, as the weight lifts. Did he really think . . .

"Wil, I wish I could go back and do everything differently. I would tell you that I wanted to go to Yale. Before I got in, or even applied, I would've told you. And I would've said that you should come with me. I would've insisted. And we would've let the show, let Marnie and Dougie go, together, the way it should've been."

It's funny. A second ago, my heart was flat, barely beating.

But it's so loud now that someone could hear it from the back row.

My eyes fill with tears, and when I let out a laugh, they fall.

"If we're time-traveling here, can we go back and lock Katrina in a bathroom on the day she met my dad?"

Dax throws me a slow, building smile that crinkles at his eyes and flips my stomach. He licks his lip. "I Jell-O'd her car."

My eyes widen. "What?"

"Her vintage Aston Martin is currently full of strawberry Jell-O. Well, by now, it's definitely melted so it's full of strawberry . . . goop?"

Oh my god. I squint at him. "I'm sorry, what did you just say?"

Daxon's smile grows wide and boyish and excited, and the blood in my body rushes to my face. "It took forever. My hands are stained." He holds up his palms, and sure enough they're vaguely pink.

"Oh shit, you *committed*-committed." I laugh again and it feels good.

Dax laughs, too. "I go all-in, Wilhelmina." There's a long few seconds of silence between us. Not awkward, really, but not completely comfortable yet. "Listen, I told Greg that I'd try and convince you not to walk away from this. To come back and finish the movie. And I do want that to happen. I want you to come back and do this with me—with us—but I don't want you to think that's the only reason why I'm here."

The quiet in 7B is pressing and the weight of it is heavy. It sits between us for a little while until I can cook up the right thing to say.

What do I want?

I don't want to be known as a quitter or as unreliable or flaky. And as much as Marnie made me, as much as finding her here on this stage turned me from a hyperactive child to a performer, I don't want to be defined by one character.

I would so much rather be myself.

Lila is the best bet for getting there.

"You Jell-O pranked for me?" I ask him fondly.

He lets out a sigh, soft and easy. He gets bashful. "I'd Jell-O *kill* for you, Chase."

We laugh. We laugh so hard. And it's the most beautiful sound after so much fear and guilt. I hold my hand out to him and Daxon walks to me and takes it.

"Let's finish it."

"Yeah?" He's grinning.

"Yeah." I'm grinning back at him. We stand there for a long moment, holding each other. I press my face into his chest and breathe in the smell of home. "But we have to do something first."

Dax loosens his grip so he can look down into my face. I tip my chin up, meeting his eyes, and he stares back, quizzical.

"What's that?"

I untangle my arms from around him and then reach for his hand. Tug him along after me downstage towards the front row. Inadvertently, I hit a mark taped to the floor. It's like a second has passed since I was here last. But also a hundred years. Dax stands next to me, and we breathe in the familiarity of 7B.

"I love you, Marnie. Thank you for what you gave me. Goodbye."

I can feel Daxon's eyes on me, but I'm staring out into the dark audience seats one last time, taking in the stage lights above our heads, the way the air smells in here. Like a dream that came true.

"Thanks, Dougie, you smug little asshole, for everything. It's not you, it's me."

My hips pivot towards Dax, our hands still clasped. "Okay," I say, "I'm ready."

∽

TO THE STARS - OFFICIAL SCRIPT

EXT. BATTLEFIELD - NIGHT - 1944

The night air is quiet after a day of nonstop bullet-fire and the screams of young men leaving this world. Smoke rises weakly from the trenches dug through the French countryside. Voices are hushed. Cries are stifled.

There are small signs of life here and there: Two men crouch over a pot of coffee. Another nearby smokes a cigarette to the stub with a shaking hand, crying silently as he reads a letter from home.

INT. AMERICAN MEDICAL TENT - NIGHT

We follow at the shoulder of a nurse walking the length of cots lined against the side of the tent, each holding a man

more badly wounded than the last. She
stops at a new arrival. We pan up to
reveal that the nurse is . . .

LILA, now in her early twenties, still
beautiful, still with an air of upper-
class elegance despite showing the wear
of wartime.

LILA
(to another nurse beside her)

They just keep coming, don't they?
Let's clean and wrap that foot.
We'll check it again tomorrow at first
light. Is this the only new one?

NURSE

One more came in earlier.
Bullet wound to the shoulder.

LILA walks across the length of the tent.
She's consulting a chart of notes for each
patient, her eyes tired, her mind
somewhere else. She stops at the foot of

the new soldier's bed and she lowers
the notes. We see her face change from
sobriety to recognition.

                    LILA

                Nick?

Now

DAXON

Wil arrives back on set in South Carolina and right away requests the attention of cast and crew.

"I'm sorry," she tells them. "Truly, truly sorry. For holding this production up. I'd love to finish this with you as strong as we started it."

I get to watch, then, as she's embraced. Kissed on the cheek by the actress playing her sister. Given a noogie by our wig mistress from hair and makeup.

I catch Greg's eye and we know everything will be okay.

Once we wrap on South Carolina, we head back to Los Angeles to finish up, filming pick-ups. Little moments of scenes that need to be reshot or require additional camera angles. Wil and I get to race through Nick and Lila's lives as we revisit scenes we haven't dipped our feet into in over a month, this time on a soundstage.

My favorite to go back to is the first-date scene. Not the initial meeting on the pier where they ride the Ferris wheel, but something a little different. The first time they feel like more than polar opposites, more like magnets destined to come together.

TO THE STARS - OFFICIAL SCRIPT

EXT. THE PIER - NIGHT

NICK and LILA walk along the pier with AMY
and her FRAT BOY ahead of them, busy at a
game booth. Off the moonlit surf . . .

                    NICK

   I'm still not sure you aren't out here
   husband-hunting. That's what girls like
                you do, isn't it?

                    LILA

              Girls like me?

                    NICK
   (leading them to the rail of the boardwalk)

      Girls who get all gussied up and go
   searching for rich, eligible bachelors.
   Girls who spend all summer wishing after
   boys who could care less, 'cause they've
      got all the power. And that's not the

girls' fault, that's just how it is.
How it's been for years and how it'll be
for a long time, I'll bet.

LILA is extremely amused by this and drops
her guard long enough to throw a full-
bodied laugh into the sea air. The wind is
whipping. The ocean below them is choppy
and windswept. She gazes into the depths
and shakes her head, smiling slightly.

                    LILA

You think you're pretty smart, don'tcha?

                    NICK
                (lifting a brow)

            Not particularly.

                    LILA

But you've figured me out. You've got my
number. I'm a silly woman and the small
space in my head only has enough room for
planning weddings and tea parties. Looking

for a husband. Shopping. Getting . . .
what did you call it? Gussied.

                    NICK

Well, come on. Look at you.
        That's gussied.

                    LILA

    This isn't gussied.
I didn't gussy for you.

NICK smiles uncomfortably through a blush
and looks up at the stars so that she
might not see the break in his resolve.
LILA is so quick, so smart and funny.
Girls like LILA, well-bred, proper girls,
aren't supposed to be funny. He doesn't
know much, but he does know that.

                    NICK

        That so?

LILA

Mmhmm.

NICK

You wanna get your feet wet with me?

LILA
(aghast)

Do I . . . excuse me, what?

NICK
(off her bewildered expression)

Do you wanna walk with me?
Down on the sand. By the water.

LILA

Okay.

(a beat)

But I might push you in.

EXT. THE SHORELINE - NIGHT

NICK and LILA pull the shoes from their
feet and walk, barefoot, down the winding
coastline. We come into the shot from
above and slowly zoom until we're level
with them.

                    NICK

         So, you don't have any fun,
          is what you're telling me?

                    LILA

         What I'm telling you is that
          I don't have time. I'm busy.

                    NICK

              Busy with school?

                    LILA

    Busy preparing for college. My entire life
     is schoolwork. Tutors. And when I have a

break from that, it's paying calls and
dinners. Tea.

NICK

You made it to the pier.

LILA

Summer's a little different.

NICK

You know what I like about summer?

LILA

What's that?

NICK

Something about it feels infinite to me.
There's about a hundred different directions it could go.

LILA

Maybe your summers.

NICK

My summers. Yeah. But yours, too,
            if you wanted.

LILA

What do you mean?

NICK

I just mean that summer's like . . .
      the night sky. Like the stars.

We pan up slowly to the night sky, alive
with stars. Over LILA's next line, we stay
there, catching far-off twinkles of light,
like the stars themselves are talking to
each other.

LILA

How is summer like the night sky?

NICK

Just that it goes on and on and on.
You could stand here and look up there
and never see the same thing twice.
It's full of possibility.

LILA

And your summer is full of possibility,
that it?

We're back on LILA and NICK. There's something electric crackling between them.
LILA's beginning to realize she hasn't
really seen him all night until right now.
This moment. NICK's sure more than ever
that she's something he dreamed up that
was made real.

                    NICK

         Could be. Is yours?

They lean in close to each other, water
rushing around their ankles. NICK's hand
folds around her elbow. LILA's tucks its
way around his jaw, hesitating at first
before settling comfortably.

                    LILA
                 (whispered)

     I think mine is full of stars.

NICK closes the gap between them, his forehead touching down on LILA's. Her nose
brushes his, her eyes closing. He takes it
all in, the planes of her face, the curve
of her eyelashes. The softness of her skin.

                    NICK

         To the stars, then.

They kiss.

Since she came back to the project, things with Wil have been different. Not bad, just different. She has walls—always has—and they've been up and down all the years we've been friends, but they're higher than I've ever seen them. Rapunzel in the tower.

I would climb them in a second if she wanted me to.

The press picked up on Wil's temporary departure from the film and there's this bizarre haze around us in the media right now, like the skies in LA during fire season. Air that was cool and light before is heavy, smoky, toxic with rumors.

Between takes, Wil is glued to her phone, frowning as she scrolls endlessly.

"They don't think it's gonna be good," she says. "What if they don't think I can do this?"

"They don't think that."

Wil hands me her phone where a creator is giving a TikTok presentation on all the reasons why a film adaptation of *To the Stars* is a terrible idea, and why Wil and I are disastrously miscast.

"Okay, you gotta put this away. How is this helping?"

"I need the validation."

I laugh and my eyebrows crease together, pulling low. "This isn't validation. This is masochism."

She glares. "I *need* it. My *precioussss*," says Wil in her best Gollum impression, which is truly terrible, and if I wasn't twenty billion percent sure that I would love her endlessly before, this seals the deal.

Except that since we got back to filming, it hasn't been like that. And that's fine, that's cool, I can sit back and wait and give her all the space she needs to figure out her next steps.

But also, I have that heartsick feeling in my chest that reminds me of my fourteenth birthday when Wil wore a halter top to the (mostly boring adults) party my dads threw me, smiling at me over the rim of a Coke with her bare shoulders. My heart shot clean out of my chest and bounced around the room.

Core memory.

I haven't moved on, clearly.

I hand the phone back and, finally, she sets it aside.

"I don't wanna toot my own horn, Wilhelmina, but I would wager that you and I are better than any performers in the history of entertainment in this picture here, and, ultimately, we'll drown under the crushing weight of the solid gold award statues they'll be flinging at us."

"At least we'll be together," says Wil, off-handedly.

Together.

"Let TikTok and whoever else be mad," I tell her. "And when this movie comes out and you take over the world, watch them change their minds."

Maybe it's delusion talking, but I have a real feeling that no one is going to watch this movie and come away pissed. Greg's made our soundstage look incredible and real and it feels so lived-in when we're in the scene.

Hair and makeup are killing it, too. For the later scenes where time has passed, they've taken Wil from a long, late-thirties styled wig to something shorter and curled into forties victory rolls. Which she looks like she was born to wear. Where I'd grown my hair out a bit longer for younger-years Nick, now it's cut soldier-short.

I look at us on the dailies, and we *feel* like time has passed.

You see the history in our faces. Nick and Lila's, sure, but also ours, Daxon and Wilhelmina's. All the golden years, the brutal ones, too. I hope people watch this movie and feel the chemistry, the heartache, the loss and the gains, like they're their own lived experiences.

The lighting is locked. The set is ready. It's time to roll. Hair and makeup descend for a few touch-ups, then Greg calls for quiet and Wil and I shift into our places for the top of the scene.

I take this feeling coursing through me, this burning, wildfire feeling, and I set it loose when Greg calls action. Knowing us, Wil and I, where we've been and all the collision courses we've been on towards each other for most of our lives, it's only a matter of time before we collide.

TO THE STARS – OFFICIAL SCRIPT

INT. MEDICAL TENT – LATE NIGHT

It was a clean shot, the bullet in NICK's shoulder. Went right through. But the skin is flaming red with infection and it's spreading. If they can't get the infection to clear, NICK will die.

LILA
(to another nurse)

You're sure it didn't come in?

NURSE

I'm sure.

LILA

Check the bag again. Maybe we missed it.

NICK lies half-asleep with exhaustion,
pain and sickness on a cot, a hand stained
with dirt and blood tucked firmly into
LILA's where she perches at his feet.
We've seen him golden and vibrant. This is
that boy's ghost.

NURSE

Nothing.

                    LILA

Damn it. When I get my hands on whoever
packed these supplies, I swear.

           Nick, can you hear me?

                    NICK
        (mumbled, almost delirious)

                 Yes ma'am.

                    LILA

          Good. Don't go anywhere.

              (to the NURSE)

          Grab me a clean towel and
             hand me that dish.

LILA dunks the towel into the water,
wrings it out, then presses it gingerly to
NICK's wound. His body convulses with pain
and we see it all over his face. It's not
what he needs in order to cure the infection, but it's all she has.

                      LILA

        Shhh. You're alright. I'm here.

                      NICK

        I'm sorry.

                      LILA

        Quiet now. Rest.

NICK closes his eyes but his expression is
troubled, painted with all the terrible
ways they left things, and the horrors
he's laid eyes on these past years. They
could have had it all. A marriage that no
one but the two of them would've celebrated, but a life that was theirs.

Through NICK's eyes, we see a film reel of
memories. Waves crashing. LILA's laughter,
head thrown back, letting herself be carefree
for the first time in her life. The lights of
the boardwalk. The Ferris wheel. That first
kiss, that fumbled first time. The fights. The
make ups. All of this is light, airy,

softened by time. Then, with the distant
sound of bombs falling, men's desperate
voices crying out in warning of incoming fire,
of fear of death, the film fades.

                    NICK

                 Lila . . .

LILA will never love anyone like this
again. Her hand is tight on his, willing
him to pull through, to live, to breathe,
to suddenly sit up and smile and ask her
for a ride on that rickety old Ferris
wheel. But time is slipping away. If she
had better supplies, a real doctor, a
clean place and something to ebb that damn
infection, she could save him. But around
the wound the veins are dark and promi-
nent. And if the temperature of his hand
is any indicator, the fever has set in.

                    LILA

  Listen to me, don't you go anywhere. You
     hear me? Stay here with me. Stay here
          through the night, at least.

NICK

I can do that.

LILA

Shhh.

It's not proper, it's not allowed at all,
but LILA shifts to lay herself down next
to NICK on the cot, tucking her head into
his good shoulder.

NURSE

Nurse Patterson.

LILA

Leave us. Please.

They're alone now. Serenading them is a
chorus of the sleeping breaths of broken
men. Rasping, wheezing, snoring gently.
Farther off, someone is crying.

NICK

I like to imagine that we made it.
You and me.

LILA

Me, too. Farther than anyone wanted or
thought we could.

NICK

That you married me. I asked and you
jumped into my arms.

LILA

Mmhmm. Let's say we did. You asked, I
jumped. We had a life together.

NICK

Kids?

LILA

Course. Three. Two boys,
stubborn as you. Strong.

NICK

And one little girl. Even stronger,
just like her mama.

They whisper off and on like this into the
early-morning hours, the sun bleeding a
new day in through the torn places on the
medical tent. LILA stays awake the whole
night, counting his breaths. His heartbeats. Trying to remember them, the sound
of them, the feel of them against her
skin. She doesn't want to admit that
they're getting fainter, farther away each
minute that passes.

LILA

You awake?

NICK
(faintly, his eyes closed)

Mmhmm.

LILA

I decided something.

NICK

What's that?

LILA

We don't need a church or a gown
to be married.

NICK

How do you figure?

LILA

I figure we just need us. Us, right now.
Our memories will be our witnesses. I,
Eliza Patterson, take you, Nicholas
Greene, to be my husband.

NICK blinks open his tired eyes, shifting
them to LILA, whose head rests beside his.
When she catches his eye and sees how
little time is left, her face falls into
emotion, a sob racking her body. NICK
presses a kiss to the tear on her cheek.

NICK

I, Nicholas Greene, take you, Eliza
Patterson, angel on earth, to be my wife.
In this life, and the next.

LILA
(pressing a kiss to his lips)

Always.

Now

WILHELMINA

$\backsim$

We finally wrap *To the Stars* in October after a few weeks of coming in to re-record audio and trying on costumes for our last scene.

Typically, movies don't film scenes in order. But it was important to Greg that we make this scene the very last. The set is green screen with practical props, a Ferris wheel they've built just like the one we rode months ago in South Carolina.

Fall in LA is like that game The Floor is Lava, except it's also the air that's lava. Most of the rest of the country is pulling on sweaters, but on this last day of filming, I'm sweating my ass off every second we're outside our soundstage.

The stage is dressed like the South Carolina pier we spent so many summer nights on, and the scene is fucking gorgeous. It's not a dream sequence, it's not Heaven, it's . . . I don't know.

Peace, I guess.

Lila goes on to live a life that is full and adventurous. But she lives it without Nick, who dies in that tent in the middle of the war. This is the part that kept me up crying when I first read the script. Why does that feel like ten million years ago? Staying up through the night, clutching that fucking script like, if I wasn't careful, I'd fall in.

Knowing that the next morning, I'd be doing these scenes opposite Daxon.

I've never known a script to smack me in the face like that.

Lila learns to fly an airplane. Swims the English Channel. Protests for women's rights, among a hundred other incredible things. After Nick, she never marries. Never has any kids. And it isn't because she's sad about him being gone; it's because she feels like the life they imagined together was better than anything she could make for herself without him.

She passes from cancer in her late sixties. But at the end of the movie, Lila is young again. Seventeen. She walks the boardwalk alone, looking for something. It's not in the game booths. It's not down on the shoreline. It's at the top of the Ferris wheel. Descending slowly towards her. Seventeen and whole again.

Grinning, full of love, a hand extended out to her.

She climbs into the seat next to Nick, and they ascend to the stars, together . . .

"That's a wrap on *To the Stars*, everybody!" Greg's voice calls across the set into a megaphone. The cast, the crew, everyone packed into this soundstage screams with joy. I run up and hug him.

"Sorry for the hell I put you through," I say. There's still this boiling hot guilt in my stomach. I can't believe I walked away from this. Even for a short time. Here was a line so solid and clear and perfect and I bolted across it without looking where my feet were going.

Greg laughs. "Forget it," he says jovially. "We'll start post next week. Wil, you killed this. When I'm done with this thing? Get ready to launch."

On those words, I meet Dax's eyes.

He's holding back, his newsboy cap in his hands, hair a mess. And he's looking at me like I'm a priceless work of art. It makes my stomach drop. My heart flutters. *Stop*, I beg them. Because I can't. I can't feel that much for him, let it drown me the way I know it will.

I'll be auditioning, hopefully daily. Submitting tapes, taking meetings. When I'm not running around Los Angeles, I'll probably be learning lines or even doing photoshoots. Interviews. How do you squeeze a boyfriend into that?

Daxon smiles at me, and it's a victorious, happy, warm-as-the-sun smile. It's done. Our movie. This story. Something that started out seeming so unreal, so terrifying, but turned out to be exactly what I needed when I needed it, is over.

He takes a few steps forward. So do I. *Magnets*. We are magnets. We meet in the middle and hug, desperate at first, then sweet and rocking, laughing. We laugh so hard our eyes fill with tears.

"We did this," I say.

"We did," says Dax.

"Did we do this?"

"You did. I helped."

We laugh until we remember the world. Our hairdresser comes to remove my wig.

"What's next for you?" she asks me.

"No idea," I say. "How about you?" I turn the question on Dax.

"I'm gonna be in a play in New York. Off-Broadway."

"You mean you won't be singing?" I tease. Dax is without a doubt the most terrible singer I've ever heard in my life.

"You'll have to see for yourself," he teases.

My eyebrow quirks upwards as I'm freed of my wig and pull the cap from my head, beginning to fish for the pins. Feels like six minutes ago, we were right here. At the end of something huge. Me, pulling out my wig pins. I almost miss his words and have to replay them in my mind.

You'll have to see for yourself.

"What do you mean?" I ask.

"You've got a ticket. Fourth row, orchestra. Best in the house."

My heart is skipping. *New York.* An off-Broadway theater, small and intimate, Daxon Avery center-stage. Suddenly, my heart's tripping over its own feet. I won't survive it.

I can't go.

There's no way.

But I hear myself say, "I'm there!"

Now

WILHELMINA

⁓

The marquee is golden in the cool, evening air. Outside the small theater, crinkled leaves skitter across the pavement over the feet of the gathering crowd. I keep my head down. My sunglasses on—even though it's coming on night and they probably look ridiculous.

But I don't want any press. Not yet.

I'm handed a playbill at the door, and when I get to my seat, I open it. There's a square black-and-white headshot of Dax on top of a little paragraph about him that he's clearly written himself:

PLAYBILL

DARCY / DAXON AVERY

Daxon is thrilled to step into the epic, curmudgeonly boots of Darcy. He would like to thank his sister, Rainie, for constantly reminding him that he's "no Colin Firth or Matthew Macfadyen, but break a leg anyway. I mean, try not to actually break a leg. That would make those regency-style dance scenes really hard." Daxon would

---

also like to thank his long-suffering agent, Dolores, for sticking with him through thick and very, very thin. He comes to this production following *Kill Switch* (Amazon Prime) and *Son of a Gun* (Sony). Next summer, please enjoy Daxon in *To the Stars* (Edgeway)—though he's well aware you'll all be too mesmerized by Wilhelmina Chase to notice him.

I snort and laugh to myself, ignoring the looks from the people on either side of me. Inside my chest is that swelling feeling I'm used to getting with Daxon. Like the sun is rising inside my body. I love him in every way it's possible to love someone. A friend, more than a friend, a piece of myself.

And I'm about to spend the next few hours watching him be the literal picture of a romantic hero. Someone who acts without thinking, determined to be right. Only to find that, for all the hours he spent wishing it away, it was love all along. The bold kind, all-encompassing.

They'll probably have to scrape me off the floor once the curtain rises; there's no way I'm leaving this performance not having turned into a puddle of lovesick goo.

The lights in the theater dim and people dip into their seats. There's the uncomfortable scooting along full aisles for those that are late. Ushers bring an elderly couple to the end of my row who are dressed like this is the royal symphony, and I feel completely tacky and gross in my jeans and coat.

But when everything in the audience goes dark and the stage lights up, I don't feel anything but peace.

That's what it is to watch Daxon Avery perform—it's

peaceful. You feel safe. He'll carry you through the story easily, like it's nothing, across dialogue that would stumble on my tongue, but off of Dax's, it flows. It's easy. He's perfect as Darcy. Dismissive and shy, curt and terrible, until he's suddenly blooming and pining.

If I was any less spellbound, I'd probably feel a huge pang of jealousy for the woman playing Elizabeth. That she gets to spend a few hours dancing with him. *Dancing. Daxon.* Daxon who cannot dance at all, except for our little waltz. There he is. Light as air on his feet.

You have bewitched me, body and soul.

Yeah, no fucking kidding.

This, right here, this feeling, is what I want for myself. Forever. Tipping my cup, spilling a splash of my soul for an audience.

The next few months will be eaten up by press and excitement around *To the Stars*. And in so many ways, I'm ready. But in a thousand others, I'm trembling, terrified, looking for a good patch of sand to shove my head into.

You can't have it both ways, but fuck, I wish I could.

I wish I'd gone to Yale, too. That we'd gone together. That I'd had the foresight to know that I needed more time to learn real craft and understand that the juiciest roles come when you're ready for them. Not when you want them the most.

I wasn't ready then. That summer. Watching Dax's car drive into the morning sun.

I'm ready now.

My face is wet when the lights come up and the cast bows, but I can't remember when I started crying. I'm on my feet, clapping so hard my hands are numb. And then, outside, I follow a gaggle of teenage girls who are apoplectic with excitement and giddiness as they wait at the stage door.

Piece by piece, the cast comes out. But it's clear right away that Daxon is who everyone is waiting for. He's swarmed with playbills and cameras, and I watch, tucked into a dark square of sidewalk, as he patiently, exuberantly, signs everything and anything they push at him. Posters and shoes. An iPhone. One girl cries with excitement and joy as he signs her forearm.

I take a mental picture. There's a whole scrapbook inside my skull of good, precious memories that will live there forever. This is one.

And then the sidewalk is alive with flashing. Not from the phones of fans, but from paparazzi. Suddenly, two things happen. A fan negotiating the cramped sidewalk sidesteps onto my foot to avoid being trampled by a pap, looks into my face, and their eyes widen.

"Wil Chase?" they yell.

Next, the cameras pivot. Phones and tablets, but also the enormous flashes of paparazzi pushing in close.

By the time I turned fifteen, I had a bodyguard. He'd go most places with me when I was out in public—the mall, the movies, wherever, whenever. Not because I was vain and rolling around gleefully in being famous, but because I *needed* a bodyguard. *Marnie* was the biggest it ever was, and I couldn't go anywhere without drawing a crowd.

When I was seventeen and *Marnie* was canceled, I let him go. Didn't need him anymore. I could dodge people easily, and the number of interested fans was waning. New shows had premiered on Magicworks with shinier, newer stars. I was glad the day I went somewhere without him. Relieved.

But now, I get a rush of the same thing I used to get when I was in the middle of a store, trying on a sweater, and thirty excited, screaming—some even crying—teens, adults, whoever, pressed in close: fear.

I forgot this feeling.

My eyes hit the pavement, and there's nowhere to step. I can't move. Bodies push closer. I can't breathe.

Pieces of paper are shoved at me, some low from children, some high, from grown people who should know better. But they push and they cry out and there's flashing, constant flashing, so that every time I blink, all I can see is blinding green.

I want to cry out, but I can't take a breath. I'm drowning.

"Back up!"

I know his voice, but I've never heard it reach that pitch before. It's never been dangerous, the way it is now. Snarling. There's a small break in the wall of bodies and the night air hits me hard in the face, bitter and cold. I suck it in. A hand reaches for me, and I try to pull away, but it fastens around my forearm and yanks me forward.

"*Back up!*" It's feral, the sound of it. Desperate adrenaline.

Now

DAXON

∞

I can't see Wil out in the audience because the lights are so incredibly bright, but through every scene, every line, every time I'm second-guessing whether or not I look completely ridiculous in my period costume, I can feel her.

She's radiating pride, emotion, awe. All the things you want the girl you've loved since you understood what love is to feel for you.

Out at the back of the theater, where fans are stacked three rows deep hoping for an autograph, I can feel Wil, too. I glance up between signing a shoe and an arm—which, by the way, is never not supremely awesome, if not mega-surreal—and I can see her at the edge of the crowd, hanging back in the dark place between the streetlights.

My signature gets sloppier the more things I sign. Not because I have horrific handwriting, which I do, but because I'm rushing. I want to get to her.

We left everything so wide open. Once *To the Stars* comes out, I think our lives are going to get a lot crazier, a lot busier; we'll be everywhere. We won't have time for each other the way we'll want to. The way I want to, at least.

I can be okay with putting things aside for now. With being friends.

Except that the moment I hear a fan's voice cry out her

name, see heads turn and cameras raise, feel the manic electricity of bloodthirsty paparazzi closing in on her instead of me, a sudden instinct to help barrels through my veins.

"Back up!"

I didn't know my voice could come out like that. Not a jovial exclamation, but forceful. I'm shouldering through the crowd as Wil is eaten alive. She's always convinced her star has gone out, that no one cares anymore. But children's television shows inform so much of who we are for the rest of our lives. They nestle in deep, and when you're a key player in the emotional psyche of a generation of people, you'll never go forgotten.

That's Wil. Bigger, greater, more important than Marnie, but Marnie to the people that loved her, forever.

I get closer. I can almost reach her. The look on her face is enough to pluck my heart from my chest and send it flopping, sodden and cold to the pavement.

"*Back up!*" I yell again, and this time, enough paparazzi jerk out of my way that I'm able to reach my hand between their bodies and close my fingers around Wil's arm.

I give a pull and she comes with me, darting eyes flicking between unfamiliar faces until they hit mine, and I swear I can see her pupils dilate with relief, can see the air coming back into her lungs. Wil grabs for me and I lock my arm around her in a vise grip and steer us off down the dark sidewalk, away from the yells and flashes.

They don't stop. The paparazzi follow us excitedly, wolves with blood in the air. But I fling out my hand for a passing taxi, yank open the yellow door before it's even stopped at the curb, and all but push Wil inside, sliding in after her.

"Go, please," I tell the driver the moment I'm sitting down.

Next to me, in the quiet, I can hear how hard Wil is breathing. Air seems to be coming into her lungs, but it isn't coming back out again.

"Address?" the driver asks.

"Wil." I reach gently but firmly for her face, my fingers at her chin, and turn her head to me. Her hazel eyes are full of tears. "Breathe with me, okay? In, count to four. Out, count to six." I model the breathing and she tries. I know she's trying, but she's hiccuping now, falling apart.

"Address?" the driver tries again.

I forgot he was even here. "Oh, 64th and Riverside," I say without looking away from Wil's face.

"Sorry. I'm so sorry. Panic attack. I-I'll be okay. Just . . . forgot how it can be. Thank you," she says, "for jumping in like that."

I wrap her up and pull her in. Lean my head against the top of hers, the movement of the taxi rocking us. Her hair brushes my cheek, my lips, and I press a soft kiss to the top of her head. We're quiet for the rest of the ride, Wil regulating her breathing. Then the cab stops and I reach for my wallet, pay the driver, and guide Wil out into the night.

Arm around her, I walk us to the elevator and we ride up to my apartment's floor. I turn the key in the lock and forget for a moment to be embarrassed by what's sitting at the tiny breakfast table against the window.

"Is that—" Wil says.

"It's Lego Darth Vader. Yeah. Well, it's his head. Really, it's the mask, but it's not . . . important . . ." I trail off.

She sniffs, and then soft laughter that's all breath falls between us. Wil tucks hair behind her ear, looking down. I watch as her head lifts and she takes in the rest of the place.

"This is really nice—"

"You okay—?"

We say this at the same time, and for a second, I know we're both about to say *jinx!* but we don't, probably because last time ended with us making out against a refrigerator, which is absolute textbook non-just-friends behavior.

"Thanks—"

"I'm alright—"

Damn it. I laugh. Wil smiles.

If I loved her less, this would be so much harder, but because I have a lot of practice shoving down the leaping in my heart and trying to behave normally, I say, "Let me take your coat." Wil slips out of her brown coat and hands it to me. She wipes at her smudged eye makeup with her fingertips.

"You were so spectacular," says Wil after a moment.

My lips pick up in a grin, wider than I hoped it would be, and I can feel the heat rising in my face. I shake my head. "I'm a dorky dancer."

"I know," Wil says with a smile. "I lived it. But Dax, for real, you were incredible. Congratulations. You broke a thousand legs."

"Thank you," I tell her. "I'm really happy you came."

"Me, too." Wil crosses her arms across her chest. "I'm sorry about the . . . with the cameras and—"

"No, hey, it's completely okay. I'm sorry that happened."

She studies my face. "I've never seen you like that."

"Like what?"

But Wil shakes her head and laughs quietly as if to say
never mind.

"Wait, like what?" I ask again.

"I don't know," she says, after thirty seconds of looking into
my eyes and clearly trying to think of the right word. But it's
what she doesn't say that tells me everything I need to know.
I look down at my shoes and smile.

"Stay here tonight," I say. "I'll take the couch."

Wil nods. "You sure?"

"It's a really nice couch. My dads picked it out. Actually,
they did the whole place." Rather, their team did. Construction
workers, painters, design assistants. They came in one night
like cobbler elves while I was away, and when I came back,
the place was beautiful. Not my style at all, ironically, but
nice. Really nice.

"I can tell," Wil says. "Nice curtains."

They're gold. They shimmer. But they also tie the room
together and marry colors you wouldn't think would go
together, but do. And it looks so chic and masculine and
effortless, when, in fact, it took a lot of effort.

"Listen, they decorated against my will," I say.

"This is a total bachelor pad," Wil says, looking around.
"You sure you want me here cramping your style?"

"I'm sure. Chase, this is the nicest hotel in Manhattan. We
have, uh, Lego structures that were never meant to be seen
by human eyes, and an embarrassingly full laundry hamper.
Two-to-three socks laying around. Absolutely nothing in the
refrigerator. It's the height of luxury."

∽

Wil has a morning flight, so I hail her a taxi in the chilled autumn air and try not to memorize the feeling of her goodbye hug.

But I always do. The way her arms lock around my waist. The feel of her fingertips brushing my back. I watch her taxi get smaller and smaller until I can't see it anymore and I head to the theater for a new cast member's put-in rehearsal.

As I'm walking out the backstage door, sweaty and exhausted two hours later, my phone pings. I refuse to follow news about myself, but I must have set this alert and forgotten about it.

★ **BUILT TWO LAST *CANCELED*.**
HGTV WILL NOT RENEW ITS LONGEST-RUNNING
SERIES AFTER FOURTEEN SEASONS.

And it isn't the news itself that has me flagging a passing taxi, climbing in the back seat and saying, "JFK, please, fast as you can," but the fact that I'm hearing it from Google, and not from my dads' lips. They won't ask, but they need me.

∽

As I'm climbing out of the Uber in their driveway (nothing with me but the clothes on my back), I can feel a despair radiating off the house like someone's just died. In a way, that's kind of true. *Built Two Last* was my third parent, my second sibling, the family pet in one all-consuming package.

Between the four of us—Dad, Pop, Rainie, me—it was the most important—the Matriarch—always.

Did I ever fantasize about this day? About the show blowing up out of the blue like Alderaan? Yes. Yes, I did.

But now isn't the time for dancing gleefully on the grave of a home improvement TV show. It's about making sure my parents, who have built everything around this, are still standing.

Pop answers the door, and when he sees me, his dark eyes mist. He grabs for me, pulling me into his chest. My heart swells because these hugs are so few and far between. "Daxie," he says, nearly throttling me with grief. "You came."

Gently, I push him off and nod somberly. It's truly wild to me how two people so exuberant, with so much love for life, can forget how to be parents so often. Pop has no lack of enthusiasm for my existence. It's just the inner workings of my life, my separate interests, my friends—those are the things he breezes right past.

"Came as soon as I saw it. I didn't hear it from you guys, by the way."

"Come in, come in, Dad's ordering dinner, Rainie's here."

"*Ordering dinner?* Dad's version of ordering dinner is walking into the kitchen and telling the chef what to cook."

My twin, Rainie, appears at the doorway to the living room, rolling her eyes. "You'd think he was on DoorDash. Hey."

I pull her into a hug, messing up her hair as she whines and shoves me away.

"So, elephant in the room," Pop says, "the show is done. Dead. Six feet in the ground. And this is our funeral procession." He gestures grandly to Rainie and me, and we share a look.

"How're you holding up?" I ask.

Dad leans his head out of the kitchen. "Hey, sweets," he says. "We're spiraling just a little bit. But you know what? Everything will be *fine*. It'll be fine. Don't worry, okay?"

I am worried.

"You know what we need?" Pop asks.

"Booze," says Dad.

"Bingo."

"I'll get the wine glasses," Rainie offers.

"Shot glasses," Dad clarifies for her.

Rainie throws me a wide-eyed look of comic horror and I feel the tension in my chest slip. I don't know what I'd do if it was just me and them, no Rainie to keep things light.

We sit in the living room, Rainie and I beside each other on the sofa, Dad and Pop lounging on the plush carpeting, and we do shots. Well, Dad and Pop do shots. Rainie and I do one each and then nope out of there real quick.

This is bound to snowball into an avalanche of emotions, and we're on ski-patrol duty.

"So, what's next?" she asks them, mopping spilled tequila off the coffee table.

"Oh, god, honey, who knows?" Dad asks, laughing. He and Pop toast and down another shot.

"Okay, I'm officially cutting you two off," I say.

Rainie caps the bottle and hands it off to me so I can place it up high on the table beside the couch, out of their reach. "You have to have something lined up," she says. "You guys don't stop moving. Ever. It's freaky."

Pop and Dad look at each other, their expressions so fond, so sad, little smiles that grow then fall, then change into soft reassurance for the other. "Actually, we were talking about buying a house somewhere tropical and spending some time away," says Dad.

"Not putting together a new show?" I ask.

"Or a kitchenware collection?" Rainie adds.

They shake their heads. "I think we need a break," says Pop, "from everything."

"From everyone," Dad says. "We had sixteen sympathy boxes of roses show up this past week. *Sixteen*. We have too many friends."

Rainie snorts. I shake my head. I want to laugh at this, I want it to be something light and nice between us, but Dad said *this week* not *today*, which means that they've known about this for days and chose not to tell me.

After dinner, Rainie and I suggest our old family stand-by, charades, to see if it'll keep the mood light, but Pop falls asleep on the couch mid-game, snoring loudly, and Dad is distracted texting Kris Jenner about getting lunch this week, continually missing his turn to guess.

Eventually, it's just Rainie and me. We give up, yawning.

"They're going to crash," she warns when we drift from the living room into the kitchen to eat Oreos out of the box like we used to. "I don't know when, I don't know where, but I have a feeling it'll be soon and on top of us."

"They're buying a house somewhere tropical," I say doubtfully.

"Right? *Somewhere tropical*. So specific. Quick, spin a globe and I'll put a finger down, and wherever it stops, that's where we'll spend millions of dollars to avoid our responsibilities."

I laugh, looking around this kitchen. It's had about ten

face lifts since I've known it. The entire house has changed constantly over the years to where I barely recognize it or consider it particularly home-y; it doesn't have that childhood nostalgia thing going for it.

Wil's house, or rather her dad's house, is that for me.

"Did they tell you?" I ask Rainie.

"What?"

"That it was canceled? Did they ask you to come?"

"No," she says. "I saw it online this morning. Drove over."

"Yeah, same. I left as soon as I saw it. Got in a cab and got on a plane and . . . I don't know why."

Rainie offers me the cream side of her split Oreo. "Because in this family, we're the parents. They're the kids. Your kids needed you," she says.

I let that sink in.

In so many ways, I know it's true. But it clicks on a light for me that I didn't realize was switched off.

∾

In the morning, Dad and Pop bicker excitedly over whether they'd feel more relaxed in Greece or Bora Bora, and when I sit down at the table, reaching for the coffee, they want me to settle the debate.

"You don't speak Greek or French," I remind them.

"We'll learn," says Dad.

"I got Duolingo on my phone," Pop says, holding it up so I can see. He's so excited. They both are.

"What about somewhere where they speak Spanish?" I suggest to Pop, who's fluent.

But he shakes his head at me with a grin. "Where's the challenge in that?"

I laugh, but it comes out as a sigh. "Or what if you just stayed here?" I don't mean it to come out bitter, but I think maybe it does. Because Dad and Pop share a look and then Pop turns to me, frowning.

"Do you not think we should go?"

The second he says it, I feel bad. My stomach twists and sinks low with the special kind of shame that comes from hurting the feelings of someone you love. I set my coffee cup down and drop their concerned gazes.

"I think you should stay in LA. My movie's coming out. It'd mean a lot if you guys were around to come to the premiere, instead of in Bora Bora."

Both sets of eyes are trained on me, and slowly, I look up to meet them. I feel seventeen. I feel seven, begging them to make time for me.

Their expressions are soft and tender, maybe even apologetic. Dad stands up from his chair, walks around the table and hugs me to him. Pop reaches across for my hand and grabs hold. This might be the most attention they've ever given me in my entire life.

Dad kisses the top of my head. "You'd have to bring in a bulldozer to try and stop me from coming to that premiere."

"You know how proud of you we are? Christopher, do I ever shut up about this kid?" Pop asks Dad, happy tears in his eyes. He's not the only one.

"No, literally never," says Dad. "And who would? Our boy's a movie star. He's taking over the flipping world."

I wipe at my eyes and Dad holds me tighter. "We want to

hear all about the movie, the play, that series you did. Every detail. Go."

And it's like I'm a rusted latch on a gate, stuck for so long, feeling constantly forgotten, and they've just wiped away the years. I can swing wide open again.

∞

Wil stops by that evening with a bottle of vodka, and my dads lose their minds with excitement over seeing her again. It's been years.

"I saw it in the news. I came right over. You two okay?" Dad and Pop take turns smothering her with hugs.

"God, finally, someone sane." Rainie sighs dramatically and wedges her way between our dads to hug Wil, too. "I'm obsessed with this hair," she says.

Wil touches the short, blunt ends with her hand and grins, color in her cheeks.

"Thanks," she says. "It was annoying the shit out of me so I chopped it."

"Amen," says Rainie.

"Okay, so come in, come in, tell us everything about what you've been up to. How's your dad? God, I love that man. The funniest human being on this planet," Dad gushes. He and Pop usher Wil into the kitchen where wine has been poured and a charcuterie board waits.

Wil throws me a smile over her shoulder that I feel bursting inside me all the way from my scalp to my toes.

"Oh shit," Rainie says, once they've gone.

"What?" I ask.

"You're down *bad*-bad."

"What?"

"Daxon," she says, flicking me in the shoulder. I shove her gently away in response. "I knew you were obsessed with her and had your little summer fling thing, but holy shit. Somebody call a doctor."

"I don't know what you're talking about," I mumble, laughing to make it sound convincing, and head to the kitchen wondering if everyone around me can hear the hammering my heart's doing.

But Wil's hazel eyes jumping to mine over the top of her white wine, the sound of her laugh mixing with my family's, her genuine sadness at my dads losing their show, the feeling of her hug goodbye this morning. The fact that she's here at all—Rainie's right, I'm down bad.

"Did you change up Dax's room upstairs?" Wil asks Dad and Pop as dinner winds down. "I saw his New York place, and I gotta say, I'm impressed."

"You know what, that's the one room we haven't touched yet," says Pop. "We can't agree on what to make it."

"I vote Pilates studio," says Dad.

"See, okay, but what we really need is another closet," Pop argues.

"Actually, that's true," says Rainie. "These two have more shoes than anyone on this planet."

Pop tweaks her nose affectionately. Wil and I catch each other's eyes.

"Let's go see it," Wil says to the group at large, even though she's looking right at me.

I stand up right away. "Sure."

Wil follows as I head towards the staircase. Out of the corner of my eye, I watch Dad and Pop start to get up to come along, but Rainie drags them both back down to the couch by the elbows, shaking her head.

As far as sisters go, I have a good one.

Then

WILHELMINA

∽

On a Tuesday morning, my phone rings.

"Wil? Hulu loved you. You booked it!"

It was the last audition I submitted before my agent, Sherrie, suggested I take a break. I've been preparing myself to retire as some Hollywood has-been recluse, jumping out at passersby to yell about how I used to be on lunch boxes. But with Dax at Yale and nothing but club-hopping to keep me going, I let myself get excited about this chance to reinvent myself.

It's weird not having the warmth of studio-audience laughter in your ears after every funny thing you say once the cameras start rolling. Weird, and delicious.

No one peels me away from set to go to school. I'm not fussed over. I'm not babied. And the costumes? Holy shit. No more kindergartner-who-got-dressed-in-the-dark aesthetics. Hulu has me in fitted jeans and a crop top like a whole-ass adult woman. Filming this pilot, not even knowing if it'll go to series, but being here and trying and, as far as I can tell, succeeding, feels incredible.

The cast is sick. Talented, hilarious women. I watch the scenes I'm not in being filmed and take a thousand mental notes.

"You're funny," Katie Port tells me as we load up plates of catered lunch. Katie fucking Port, stand-up queen. "I didn't think you'd be funny because of the whole kids' show thing, but you're awesome."

"Oh my god, thank you," I say. "Please know this is going straight to my head." We laugh. It's easy here. Hair and makeup are kind and accommodating; the script is tight and funny with heart. I think it has legs to get picked up. Fuck, I hope it gets picked up.

"Wil, come meet our producers," says my director, Salma, on our last day. She guides me across our base camp lot where the trailers are parked towards the craft services table. "This is Chris Sherman, Gloria Lee and Harris Bastian. Everyone, this is Wilhelmina Chase."

No.

Fuck.

I force myself to smile. Be normal. Shake hands. Down the line I go, until I get to Harris, who reaches his hand out to shake mine, an overly familiar grin starting on his lips. My hand flops into his. Sweat starts at the back of my neck as his fingers tighten too hard around mine.

"I know Wil," he says, his eyes on me. Then he turns to Salma. "Known her since she was a kid. We worked on *Marnie, Maybe* together."

The way he says it, I get a chill like a thousand spider legs crawling down my spine. I smile and give a little laugh. I should keep the mood light. Nothing's set in stone here. If there's one person you keep happy in this business, it's your producer.

"We're thrilled to have her," says Salma.

"Thrilled to be here," I quip. Everyone laughs. Harris's eyes drop and linger at my chest. The pores on his red nose are huge, but I can't look away. "I'm gonna get back to my trailer," I hear myself say after what feels like an hour. "Prep for the next scene. Nice to meet you all. Thank you for this chance." I walk away gagging.

The inevitable knock an hour later sends a flush of ice through me. There are a dozen people it could be, I know that—an assistant, a costumer, anyone—and yet, I know that it's Harris.

I hesitate. He knocks again. I take a breath and count to five. Just answer the door, see what he wants, and move on.

"Yes?" I ask, the door half-open.

Harris takes in what he can see of my trailer behind me. "Nice digs. Mind if I come in?"

"I'm running through some lines. Maybe later . . ." Even though it's the only word in my head right now, audibly shouting *NO* is so fucking hard for some reason.

"Come on, just five minutes." He puts his foot on the first step up to the door, and it makes me back up.

"Um, I guess," I say. My heart is pounding in my ears. You want a long career? You don't throw an executive producer out of your trailer. I don't want to make a thing of this. I don't want to draw attention. I sit on the stool at my lighted vanity, facing him. "What's up?"

He runs his hand along the top of the leather sofa across from me. "I just got word that the show's going to series."

"Seriously?" My screaming heart leaps into my throat. "Oh my god. That's amazing." A series. A full season. Maybe more. I'm looking at job security, at a chance to break myself out as more than a kid actor. I get this flash of stage lights and glittering gowns. Someone hands me a tiny statue made of gold. Nobody remembers Marnie. No one looks at me and sees her.

This is going to change my life.

"Seriously," says Harris. "And I wanted to see if you'd like to come out and celebrate with me tonight."

Right about here is where my heart turns to coal and sinks. I get it now. This is practiced. Planned out. Checkmate.

I know what the career-focused person in my place should do here. Harris is laying out this ugly, messy thing as neat and pretty as he can. But when I look at his face, feel the burn of his eyes on me, I'm thirteen and doubling up on sports bras, ashamed of myself for a reason I can't even say out loud.

"No," I say, my voice suddenly hoarse. Quiet. Weak, maybe. "No, thanks."

Harris blinks at me. His mouth twitches. It turns into a smirk, but it isn't handsome or kind. "You sure?"

"I'm sure," I say to the wall beside his head.

The way the look in his eyes shifts from faux-friendly predator with a clear-cut agenda to dangerously bruised ego is enough to set off a dozen alarm bells in my brain. "Okay," he says, and the word is loaded. "Take care, Marnie." Harris slips out of my trailer, shutting the door too hard behind him.

I've fucked up. Even if I did the right thing, I've fucked up. Majorly.

∞

On Sunday, Margot and Cassie argue over how long to set the microwave for popcorn while I pull up the Emmys on the living-room TV. Katrina's nominated for her sitcom *Apart*

Together, which in my opinion is overly precious and hardly funny, but hey, I'm not in charge of the nominations.

I don't care about that, though. I'm watching for the red-carpet coverage. For my dad.

"I still think you're being paranoid," Cassie calls to me. "Like, this isn't a movie, Wil. People don't do crazy shit just because you turn them down."

Cassie, who has never lived in reality, likes to tread as uncarefully as she can on my last nerve. I would toss her out if she wasn't someone who means a lot to Margot.

That's when the knock on my door sounds.

"Did we actually order that pizza?" I ask, heading towards the foyer. But when I check the peephole, it's my agent, Sherrie. The hair at the back of my neck prickles. I undo the lock and turn the knob. "You making house calls now?"

"Hey, Wil," she says. The smile on her face is tight and too small, like the kind they paint on dolls. There's a secret behind her teeth. Something bad. "Can I come in a sec?"

I pull the door wide and she steps in. "What's up? You wanna sit down? We've got the Emmys on. Red-carpet stuff."

"I can't stay," says Sherrie. "But let's sit a minute."

So, I sweep her into the living room and mute the TV. Sherrie sits in the plush, vivid green armchair, and I perch on the edge of the magenta couch. If a room isn't violent with color and life, I don't want it.

"Everything okay?" I already know the answer. My lungs barely inflate as I take tiny, useless breaths.

"We've never had this happen before, you and me, so I'll just tell you upfront what the deal is."

My stomach, my kidneys, my heart, my everything turns upside down and inside out as the blood in my face drains. "What happened?"

"Hulu is letting you go. They're recasting your role."

And right as she says this, the camera pans the whole of the red carpet and lingers, just for a moment, on Harris and the far younger woman glued to his arm.

∽

"Wil, this is stupid," Cassie whines.

I pull over to the curb across the street. It's not a neat parking job. It's like if you gave your car keys to a kid and said *have fun*.

But in this moment, chaos thrumming through my veins, I don't give a shit about parking nicely. I don't give a shit about anything—except revenge.

Without answering her, I shove the gear into park and kill the engine. It's a dark street. Limited streetlights. Private driveways. The night is warm and the moon is low as Margot hands me the carton of eggs. The wind prickles across my throat and cheeks, and it's freeing knowing that there's no one, no Dax, here to stop me. Nobody's going to talk me out of this. This revenge is *mine*, and I get to decide how much or how little to take.

"Be careful," she says, but I don't answer her.

My feet carry me quickly across the black road, crickets calling. I open the carton, pluck an egg, and hurl it gleefully, giddily, grinning in the dark, at the black Tesla parked on the driveway.

It's one of those circle driveways with bushes for privacy but no fences. No gates. No gun towers or trolls or whatever really wealthy famous people have guarding their homes. Getting close is easy. I waste half the carton on the car, throwing like something mechanized. Slow and deliberate.

"That's good," Margot murmurs, appearing at my side. She touches my arm, my hand searching blindly for another egg. "That's enough."

I look at her. The way her eyes widen slightly tells me that the expression I must be wearing is carnivorous and fanged. Hungry.

"It really isn't," I hiss.

My fingers close around another egg and I pull my arm back and let it fly towards the house, splattering yellow, vomity yolk across a picture window. Again and again and again and again, egg after egg, windows and the front door and the siding, the shutters. I throw until my fingers search the carton and come up empty.

"Wil, you're shaking. Come on." Margot tugs softly at my elbow.

"No," I whisper. "No, it's not enough yet."

How hard would it be to open a window? I could climb the tree growing out of the patio space beside the front walk. I could get up there. Maybe a window's open. Maybe a lock is loose. I let the empty carton fall to the asphalt, and start circling the tree. It's all about finding your footing. Find a place to start and go from there.

"Wil, Jesus Christ. Come on." Margot jogs to the base of the tree when I'm five feet off the ground, fitting my boots into holds among the branches wherever I can find them. "This is stupid."

I don't answer her. I keep climbing. Up here, the branches thin out. But I'm a few feet from the ledge of a bedroom balcony. It's all wood, and the railing is short. I can make it if I stretch, if I really push.

The tile roof is close enough now that I can touch it. I can get a little bit of a grip. One hand on the roof, one hand locked around a thin branch, I hear the slow, deadly sound of splintering wood. This isn't a climbing tree.

Maybe that's what Harris was counting on when he planted it next to his house then left for the evening with the balcony doors ajar.

I can see the curtains blowing. Beckoning. Slowly, carefully, ignoring the hissing of Margot and the whining of Cassie, I get a good enough hold on the oval tile shingles and pull myself from the leaves onto the edge. Next is a deep breath and forward momentum to grab the wood balcony rail. I work myself to a standing position.

One leg over and I'm there.

No alarms, no attack dogs. Just the blackness of an empty house. The sharp, adrenaline smell of moving through a place you shouldn't be. Do I have a plan? Not at all. What I know is that this asshole took something from me that I can't replace—twice.

The first time was my dignity.

The second time was my livelihood.

All to serve what made him comfortable. What made him *rich*. What I need to do now is steal something precious from him, something he can't get back.

At the landing, outside of the room I came in through, framed and hanging on the wall, is a magazine. It's an old *Playboy*. The discoloration, the font and color choices, register as seventies to me. I reach up and pluck it slowly from the wall, carefully bringing it down to examine. The woman on the front is beautiful and young, blue eyes and mouse-brown hair with fluffy, straight-across bangs. *BARBI BENTON* it says in curly, yellow font. It's signed, too.

For Harris—
Happy Sweet Sixteen!
xo Barbi

I tuck the whole thing under my arm and take the stairs as fast as I can. My heartbeat squelches in my ears, my stomach swooping low. What I'm going to do with it, I have no idea.

Rip it up and leave it here in his foyer for him to come home to? No. There's no mystery in that. It's a question with an immediate answer. And as far as revenge goes, that's no fun.

I'll take it home with me. I'll burn it.

And Harris Bastian will wonder forever who took his precious autographed seventies porn.

He'll walk up and down those stairs and look at the empty wall where the paint is lighter in the shape of a missing frame, and feel that emptiness that comes with losing something you can't replace.

Like girlhood, tender and bright, so easily extinguished.

As I open the front door, prancing out to show off my loot to Cassie and Margot, all I hope is that, for years, whenever he's missing this once-in-a-lifetime gift, he thinks of me.

Now

WILHELMINA

⤮

Daxon's old room is pretty much how I left it a hundred years ago. Same bed, same comforter, same pillow.

"Jesus, Avery, talk about a time capsule."

Dax hangs back in the doorway, watching me look around. "Yeah, I should really get someone in here. Know any professional decorators?"

I laugh and walk to the window, looking out between the curtains.

"Remember that summer when we found binoculars on set and brought them up here?"

"Oh yeah, you don't forget that," he says in his dopey Midwestern accent. Dax's fingers lift to mess with his hair. My heart blooms from a bud to a full, perfect rose in the span of an instant, like some sped-up nature documentary footage, as I watch him.

"Oh no ya don't," I say back. "Mrs. Bangor in that lime-green velour sweatsuit?"

"How many cats did she have?"

"Eight thousand," I say.

"And they all had matching lime-green velour sweatsuits," says Dax.

I turn and cross to the bed, perching there before reaching for the bedside-table drawer. "Something embarrassing, something embarrassing, something embarrassing," I chant hopefully.

It's empty, except for a single cigarette smoked down to the filter.

Wrapped around it is a red lipstick kiss.

It rolls from the back of the drawer and I pluck it out, holding it in my palm.

I smoked this nine years ago at a Christmas party, after climbing out of that window right there and onto the roof of this beautiful house, Daxon by my side.

Something happens when you go from being a child star to a teen star. You catch eyes you didn't before. There's new media attention. More rogue cameras following you. Constant flashes and shouts, as you dive into your car and drive away as fast as you can just to get out alive. I hated it. I was coping however I could.

Not wanting my dad to catch me smoking, I tried to toss it, but Dax said he'd keep the cigarette here and then flush it when no one was looking.

Except, I guess he didn't.

It's so tiny. Trash to anyone else's eyes or heart. But sitting in my palm, painted in my mother's favorite lipstick, is a piece of time, frozen.

My blooming heart wilts a little.

"You . . . kept this?"

Dax looks at his shoes, then up at me and breathes out a laugh. "Weirdly enough, yes. Yes, I did."

"Why?" I ask. Even though I know.

"Um, to clone you should anything happen. That way *Marnie* would go on. It was for the children."

"Uh-huh," I say, my smile widening until my cheeks ache.

"Wilhelmina, if there's anything you should know about me, it's that I'm a great philanthropist and renowned advocate for our youths."

We smile at each other, eight feet apart. Close enough to easily close the distance but neither of us moving. I still feel New York on my skin. His arm around my shoulders, protective, strong, easy. So easy. Pressing my face into his neck and knowing, without a doubt, that I was safe. How it felt to sleep in his bed, Dax on the couch in the next room, and smell his good Daxon smell on the pillow.

I still feel seventeen in my skin. A parked car on a dark street, trust radiating between us like something nuclear. Laughing until we ran out of breath, trying to get dressed again in the back seat. Running around Los Angeles on borrowed time trying to slip past goodbye like it was a parent and we were sneaking home past curfew.

Beyond that, I feel the early years, too. Thirteen, bullying Dax into learning his lines faster. Fourteen, racing each other on set to see who could eat the most licorice in one sitting. Fifteen, feeling true fear as the crowds grew and the cameras closed in, but always having Daxon there to lean on, to prank with. Sixteen, Dad and Dax laughing over homemade dinners.

I miss those dinners. Dad's pot pie. Chicken placemats.

I realize that a huge part of me is still missing. I can't move on, can't grow, if I've cut my roots.

My eyes fall to my palm where the cigarette sits, looking up at me. I want to keep it. But when I look back up into his face to ask, I know it's not mine to keep. So I tuck it back into the drawer and close it gently.

And I know that, by leaving it with him, I've turned on a green light between us.

Except nobody hits the gas. We're happy to sit here, idling.

"I think this'll be a great Pilates closet," I tell him.

Dax nods seriously. "Oh, yeah. Absolutely."

∞

"Hey," I say into the phone when Margot, who's been in Paris for work, picks up. "It's lonely around here without you. Wanna come over for dinner? You and Cassie?"

I'm fucking awful at keeping in touch with people. They'll put that on my tombstone. But what's really happening is that I need another human to come over here and talk me out of all the things my floundering heart wants to throw itself at—Daxon. A life with Daxon.

I'm terrified. The timing's all wrong. How many things are supposed to begin at the same time? Shouldn't you space them out? A career resurrecting itself and a new relationship shouldn't begin simultaneously. They both need too much of your soul. Or, at least, they do for me.

An hour later, when I've paced a solid trench in the plush lavender rug in our living room, the doorbell rings. "If you brought a guillotine with that wine, that would be helpful," I say.

"Oh boy," says Cassie, "it's a crisis." She follows Margot in, carrying a pizza.

"I told you I was cooking," I say, my brow furrowing.

"Oh, we know," says Margot. I shoot her a glare. She glares back. Then we laugh.

"How are you?" I ask her.

"Exhausted." Her smile shows it, but her voice is full of its usual warmth. "So, what's the crisis, Wil?"

"Where is Gorgeous McMovie Star?" asks Cassie. She starts looking around, like Daxon might appear out of thin air to sign an autograph for her.

"Cass," Margot scolds, shaking her head. "*That's* the crisis." Cassie's eyes go wide and she pulls a face.

"Whoops."

Laughing with my teeth clenched so that my soul won't fly out of my mouth like a ghost, I take the pizza from Cassie and lead them into the kitchen. Margot heads for the cupboard and pulls down the wine glasses, filling one for each of us.

"Okay, so spill," she says.

The cigarette. All I can see in my mind is that cigarette rolling around in his bedside-table drawer. Nine years, it's been there. I poke at the soggy stew on the burner that I've been babysitting for the last hour. They were right to bring a backup. No sober person would trust me in the kitchen.

We're friends, Dax and I, best friends. With years of silly, glittering memories taped together into a living, breathing scrapbook that I can flip through any time I close my eyes. If I'm going to do this career thing and do it right, we can't be more. And that'll have to be okay.

So I tell them everything.

"I want to go all-in, you know? Jump and be fine with that. I've got this second chance now. A redo."

"On your career," Margot adds, nodding.

"Yeah." I sip from my very full wine glass. "I'm grown-up, I'm different. I want to put the past in a little box and push it to the back of my closet."

"Okay, Marie Kondo," Cassie says with a grin. "So, working's gonna bring you joy?"

I nod. "Yeah. It will. But only if I . . ." I don't know why, but I can't say it.

"Do it solo," Margot finishes for me. Again, I nod. But it's slower, sober.

We've just left *Stars* behind us and I'm still drunk on it. Lila and Nick still swim in my head. But Dax? He's on to the next. A real professional actor. Constantly moving, always focused. And he got there by putting work first.

It should be easy. So fucking easy. Walk away, make the choice, stick it out. But it's like digging to the core of the earth with a plastic spork. Cassie and Margot exchange glances when they think I'm not looking.

I down the rest of my wine in one go. Margot refills it for me without asking.

"You know what I think?" she asks. My eyes hit hers. "You're really good at what you do. That's never gonna change. If you want to go all-in and take over the world, do it. I'll help you. Cassie will, too. But that doesn't mean you have to be miserable."

I reach for the pizza and plunge a slice into my mouth. "Maybe it's like ripping off a bandage," I say, once I've chewed and swallowed. If I say this loud enough, maybe it'll be true. "It's gonna suck, and hurt, and be gross, probably, but it's what I have to do, right? Let him down easy?"

Margot and Cassie exchange a look. They don't agree with me, but likely because I'm shoving pizza and wine into my mouth at alarming speeds, they won't say it. I love them for not saying it.

"Hey, how's your dad?" Margot asks, pivoting. She's always been great at that, reads people better than I ever will.

"I don't know," I tell her. Because it's the truth. I don't. I should—god, I should. But we're not where we used to be, not by a mile. Really, I could say that Katrina fucked everything up. She didn't dip her toe, she full-on cannonballed her way into the middle of our family. Then decided *eh, you know what, I'm out.* She left us with most of the water gone and no way out of the pool.

But that would be half the truth.

When she came, I left. I chose to walk away, to isolate. I stopped calling. Stopped visiting. And then, when she left for someone else, slowly, I came back. Not because I forgave, but because I couldn't stomach the idea of my dad swimming alone with not even a shark for company.

But when I did come back, it wasn't the same as it was. I was bitter, he was hurting. Stealing back that ring had felt like the thing that might patch us up.

Fuck, I can really be wrong when I want to be.

"You should find out," Margot says. And I know as I walk around the kitchen island and hug her, thankful she's here and on my side, that she's right.

∽

Turn right. Pull up the drive. Park. I've done this eight thousand times, easy.

I'm out of the car, my key in my hand, about to slip it into the lock and turn, when my auto-pilot feature fails. Which, oh my god, sounds like something Dax would say with a long-winded argument about which would win in a galactic starship race: the Enterprise or the Millennium Falcon. I literally shake my head.

I used to be cool.

Daxon Avery has made me into a nerd-lover.

My hand forms a soft fist and I raise it to knock. Dusk is settling on another hot October day. Melted-butter sunset streaks the door and the walls around it, pouring through the trees along the front walk behind me. I wait a minute. I knock again. I don't bother to ring the bell. For years, you'd ring it and nothing would happen. Mom always said she'd fix it but never got around to it. Dad didn't know how.

Finally, the lock clicks open and in the doorway is my dad, exactly like I've always known him. Just a little more tired at the eyes.

"Wil," he says, clearly surprised to see me.

"Hey, Dad," I say. A hundred thoughts and feelings cross his face as we stand there. Apologies, arguments, memories. Closeness and separation. My stomach is tight. "You got a minute?"

He nods. "Yeah, I—" I watch his face fall. "Oh shit," he says and turns, hustling away into the house.

"What?" I ask, but he's gone. Through the foyer, down the hall, into the kitchen and out to the back patio. I follow the chain of open doors until I find him swearing at a smoking barbecue. "Oh shit," I say.

"Agh, fuck. I was making ribs. Hey, call Jim Cameron, would ya? Ask if he needs some charred bones for a *Terminator* sequel?"

I laugh. "I'll do that."

Dad closes the lid of the barbecue, turning the heat off and rubbing his brow. He grabs for the open beer bottle balanced on the grill and takes a sip. "Want one?"

"Yeah," I say. "I can get it."

"No, no, no, no, you sit, I'll get it."

Right, because I'm a guest here now. Even though it's the house that built me, it isn't mine anymore.

He gestures with the bottle to a patio set I've never seen before. Mom's was a white table and matching chairs with chicken cushions and a chicken runner. Katrina liked lifeless, minimalistic things in shades of beige and gray. She replaced the chickens as soon as she could with a muted rainbow.

But this is new entirely. It's turquoise chairs with cerulean cushions. The table is covered with a tile mosaic colored like the sea. It's the kind of ocean you want to swim in. Soft water. Calm water. Like my last day filming in South Carolina, when we held hands and ran into the ocean, then floated in the gentle water, full of hope.

"This is really nice," I tell him, running my hand over the tiles. He hands off the beer bottle and takes the chair opposite me. A pair of birds chase each other across the sky above our heads. He's strung lights out here. It's peaceful and pretty in a way I didn't know my dad knew how to be by himself.

"It's nothing," he says. "Just wanted a place to sit that wasn't . . . well, you know."

I nod. I do know. "That's why I moved out."

After Katrina was gone, I came back slowly. I cooked the dinners. Rebuilt everything that had been torn down. And then I had to try to get the ring back, and it was ruined again.

"I figured," he says. He's not mad. Not really bitter. Just quiet. "House is good? Need anything?"

"No, it's good. It's good. I had Cassie and Margot over last night."

"How are they?"

I love that he cares. He's always been like that with any friends I've brought around. Anyone important to me immediately became important to him. Especially Daxon. "Good, they're really good. We had pizza and wine and talked about the movie and . . . everything."

Does he know? Everything sifts through my head like an old photo album. The kind my mom would get out sometimes and flip through. Point out people that weren't here anymore. *To the Stars*, Katrina, the life we used to live together.

Dad's face softens. "I heard a bit about . . . everything."

"You did?" I want to breathe out the gulp of anxious air in my lungs but it won't leave, so I hold it in, waiting.

"Daxon filled me in."

I blink at him. "What?"

Dad takes a hit from the bottle and then sets it down, his eyes tracing the tile. "He came here looking for you. Told me about Katrina and Max Perry." A laugh leaves his lips but it's sad. Bob Chase the comedian has the best laugh in Hollywood. In the world. Big and barking and contagious.

This isn't that.

"When was he here? Why?" I lean forward in my chair.

"When you left set. He looked freaked. He told me what happened. Was looking for you to bring you back. I'm guessing you finished the film?"

I nod and the air in my lungs finally slips out. "Yeah, I went back and we finished it."

"How'd it turn out, ya think?"

"Really, really fucking good," I tell him honestly.

Dad considers this for a little while, nodding to himself. He's happy for me. I can tell. But there's more behind those eyes and I swallow nervously. Brace myself for whatever comes next.

"You know how proud of you I am," he says, and it's not a question. I nod. "Even way back, I mean, hell, from the moment you were *born*, but especially those years when Mom was so sick and . . . you were like rubber, Wil. Seemed like everything bounced off of you. I wished so hard that I was rubber, too."

It's instantaneous, the influx of tears that build and break down the length of my face. Dad rubs at his eye. He's crying, too.

"I'll never love anyone like I loved your mom," he says. "She was my best friend. She gave me you."

"Dad, I know, it's okay, you don't have to—"

"No, I do. I do. I thought maybe I could move on after so many years and be happy. Well, fuck me, that didn't pan out, did it?" He gives a wet-sounding laugh, hitting his fist lightly against the tabletop. "I didn't think, Wil. Didn't think that maybe you weren't made of rubber after all. You're an incredible actor. I was too thick to see it."

"Dad . . ."

"I'm sorry that I was careless with our life together. We had our own clubhouse, just the two of us, and I made it a three without making sure you were okay with it. Worse, I thought maybe, if at first you weren't okay with it, that you'd get over it. You didn't. That's okay. I lost you there for a while and I'll have to reckon with that forever."

My eyes stream and I wipe at them, coughing, sipping my beer just to try and calm my heart.

"I didn't want to be lost," I manage. "I don't want to be lost."

"I love you, kid. I'm right here. And, Wil?"

"Yeah?"

"I'm truly sorry."

It's a key turning in a lock I didn't know was there. I stand up. I walk around the table. Dad holds out his arms and I fall in.

And right there is where we rebuild our clubhouse—just us two.

Now

WILHELMINA

8 months later

∾

Margot's careful fingers zip up the back of my dress. Cassie does the grunt work of smushing my waist like a ripe banana to make sure it closes, because this thing is *fitted*. Margot takes the flowing bottom layer and gives it a practiced shake so that it lies clean and fanned behind me.

It's silver, the dress. A-line. Hand-beaded thoughtfully, intricately, expertly across my chest, and then open in wide expanses along my waist, across a hip, down my left thigh to the knee. Soft, fine mesh silver letting the skin beneath show. Avant-garde and classic Hollywood had a baby, and I'm wearing it.

The train is like a dream made real, silvery and fluttering. Fairy dust.

I've been growing my hair out. Tonight, it's slicked back and knotted at the base of my skull in a complicated twist. Braided pieces are tucked inconspicuously around a vintage silver brooch.

Looking at myself in the mirror, the way the beading catches the light, the way my skin complements the glowing fabric—I'm walking starlight.

Margot and Cassie stand back and do tiny victory claps. They're so excited. They're beaming. Even though my stomach is a black shriveled pit of nerves, I'm able to throw my head back and laugh. I'm excited, too. Or nauseous. It's really hard to say.

Tonight is the premiere of *To the Stars*, and in a lot of ways, it feels like the premiere of . . . me.

The moment the opening credits start, I'll be someone else.

Mostly, that makes me feel like lying down face-first on the floor and crying like a small child, out of anxiety and nervousness. But there's a tiny part of me that feels like punching my fists into the air and screaming in triumph.

I didn't think this day would come.

My phone buzzes from where I left it on my bed and Cassie grabs it for me because maneuvering in this dress is harder than it looks. It's so tight. And the train is so magnificent and long that even turning around is a freaking feat.

It's a text from Daxon:

> Pumpkin carriage en route

> ETA is right now because we're in your driveway

> Honk honk

It was his idea to go together. Well, not like together-together, but together. A united front. Which is what we've been the last six months when press began to swell. And what we will be, I'm sure, as it becomes this huge tidal wave over the next few weeks.

"Ready, Cinderella?" asks Margot, grinning wide.

I snort. "Does that make you my mice friends?"

"Um, we are your fairy godmothers, okay?" Cassie explains this like she's deeply offended. She's grown on me more and more as the years have peeled by. You don't break into someone's home, steal something priceless, get away with it together, and not wind up friends. I laugh.

"Okay," I say. "I think I'm ready. To vomit. And then, eventually, a week from now, to go to the premiere."

"The premiere of your own *movie*," says Margot. "That you're starring in. Because you worked really hard." Her eyes are welling. Her trembling lips are drawn into the widest smile I've ever seen there.

"Stop it, don't you dare," I say, jabbing a finger at her. "If you start, I'm fucking doomed." Already there's that familiar tightness behind my eyes.

"Wil, if you ruin that glam, I will smack you," Cassie says. She raises a hand for emphasis and we all laugh.

"Okay, alright, no crying. Maybe some light panicked running away, a little shrieking, sure, but no crying," I say. They roll their eyes at me and collectively push me towards the door, Margot scooping up the bottom of my gown.

Daxon is leaning against the limo, scrolling through his phone, when I open the front door and step out into golden hour.

At first, he doesn't see us.

Then Cassie calls out to him, waving excitedly, and he looks up. Everything on his face changes. Where he was squinting against the dying sun, his eyes go soft. The concentration frown he wears because his eyes suck and he doesn't have his glasses on goes slack.

He has the audacity to be wearing a dark blue suit that's cut close and clean across his shoulders. I have to have a stern conversation with my stomach to chill out and stop going all fork-in-the-garbage-disposal berserk.

Friends. We are friends. Best friends. That's it.

Dax waves weakly back to Cassie but he's not looking at her. His eyes are on me. On my dress. Traveling up from my hand-beaded silver heels to the soft glow of diamond dust Cassie brushed across my chest with a poufy pink brush minutes ago.

Finally, our eyes connect.

"I was standing out here thinking *shouldn't the moon be out by now?* And here's my answer," says Dax. He buries the tenderness, the nervousness, in his voice with a sudden laugh. Drops my eyes. Opens the limo door for me. "That's a . . . *dress,*" he adds.

I like the breathlessness there. It's like, for a moment, his brain short-circuited. And I think maybe I'm the lightning storm that caused it.

I like that even more.

"Pretty good, right?" I ask him, starting to climb in. Margot carefully folds the train in after me and I collect the soft silver bundle from her, tucking it gently beside me on the seat.

"Home by midnight, Cinderella," she says and winks my way. "Have fun, you two!"

"Pretty good," he agrees, nodding too much. He's still nodding when the door closes behind us and the driver pulls away from my house. What a dork.

"What's with you?" I say.

Daxon swallows hard. "Who? Nothing. No one. What?"

"Should I call 911?" I side-eye him.

"I'm good," he says quickly. "All good."

"Can I tell you something?" I say.

"Anything."

"I'm so fucking nervous." My hands tangle in my lap. "Okay if I throw up on you?"

"I would be honored," says Daxon without missing a beat. His fingers twitch up towards his hair like they're going to run through it—his go-to nervous tick—but they're stopped immediately by the gel and hairspray there. Whoever did his hair tonight is doing the lord's work. Somehow, they got it slicked back but not gross. It's relaxed and cool with this debonair edge.

Daxon Avery is not cool enough for this hair. But he's doing a really good job convincing otherwise.

"Wanna drink?" I ask, pointing out a bottle of champagne chilling on ice. Two glasses sit beside it, clinking gently with the movement of the car as we head across Los Angeles towards the Fonda Theatre.

"God, yes," Dax says, grabbing for the bottle.

We both yell excitedly as he works the cork. And, finally, it rockets into the padded ceiling, foam spilling from the bottle's mouth.

"Not on the dress!" I say, scooping the fabric out of the way.

"That's what she said."

"Get out." I point soberly towards the car door. Our eyes connect and we both break, laughing.

It's so natural, so easy. And it was like that in South Carolina, too. Until the real world tapped us on the shoulder.

This next phase of my life—my career—feels like it's walking one foot in front of the other, slow and wobbling, across a tightrope. If I take a wrong step, I'm done. That's it. No more movies. Or limited series or original streaming whatevers. No more chances. I need to put my head down and focus. Do the work. No distractions. I don't have time for a relationship.

The way Dax is looking at me, like I'm the moon rising, makes that so *fucking* difficult.

Now

THE PREMIERE

_"I_'m Paisley Hutton with _Entertainment Now_ and we are live outside of the _gorgeous_ Fonda Theatre in Hollywood, California, for the premiere of _To the Stars._"

The Fonda Theatre is lit so beautifully, it gives the impression, with all its vintage glamour, that it's living and breathing. Instead of a red carpet, this one is white and it stretches from the limousine drop-off all the way down the front of the theater, where the cameras are lined up, waiting.

"And coming down the carpet right now is Greg Edgeway, the film's director. Greg, so happy to see you tonight. Congrats on this, I can't wait to see it. How are you feeling?"

"We're thrilled with it, absolutely thrilled," he says into the microphone.

"This is a leading role for Daxon Avery," says Paisley, "who we've seen coming up over the years between film and a few things off-Broadway, but this is a major moment for Wilhelmina Chase, who we just haven't seen, period. What was it like casting her after so long away?"

"Daxon, I don't know if you know, was cast. Then it became, like, this thing of _who are we going to get for Lila?_ It was a lengthy audition process. Tons of people came in to read; we did several chemistry tests with Dax and some talented, very famous young women, but nothing was really feeling right."

"Until Wil."

Greg nods. "She walked in totally prepared. Didn't need to talk about the character, didn't need anything. I had her start off a scene with Dax and *boom*. That was it. Then we did another and another and another." He spins his finger for emphasis. "And when she left that day, Daxon and I looked at each other and we were, like, *this is it*."

"And you're pleased with her performance?" asks Paisley.

"Listen, I've been doing this forever. You know that. And it was one of the greatest pleasures of my life getting to direct this young woman, as well as Daxon. I mean, the two of them together are electric. As a director, you dream about this kind of chemistry. Once you see the film, you'll get it."

"Fantastic, I can't wait. Have fun tonight! Thanks so much."

Greg waves jovially into the camera, then continues down the carpet until he's disappeared into the theater.

It's then that the buzz of talking, laughing, calls for a pose in this direction, cameras clicking excitedly, drops off almost altogether, as though it's one collective, deep, anticipatory inhale.

A limo has just pulled up.

Its door is opened.

"Paisley, have we seen Daxon or Wil yet?" asks the voice of Delilah Beck, her co-host back at the studio.

"You know what, Delilah, I have a feeling that we're about to see Daxon or Wil coming down the carpet right now. Okay, yes, someone is getting out." Paisley touches her earpiece. "Yep, Delilah, they're telling me this is Daxon Avery."

Daxon climbs slowly out, adjusting his suit jacket before extending his hand back inside for another passenger.

"Is there someone else in the limo?" Delilah asks.

Carefully, Dax guides Wil out of the car and the buzz roars back to life.

"Oh! Gorgeous! Coming out of the limo right now is Wilhelmina Chase looking absolutely divine in what I believe is an Oscar de la Renta runway dress we've seen from this past Fashion Week. Unbelievable. Truly stunning."

The air is alive with shouts and whistles and screams of excited glee from the mob of fans just beyond the white carpet.

They have *Marnie, Maybe* posters and backpacks, dolls and pillowcases. But they also have *To the Stars* posters. The pens in their hands are uncapped and eagerly anticipating a signature from two people who brought something precious to their younger selves.

Something you never really lose with the years. Something magical.

"Paisley, she's an absolute vision in that dress. The way it complements her skin tone, the hair very underplayed but still giving this chic edge against the fairytale gown. I'm loving the red lip."

"I completely agree, Delilah. Daxon Avery is wearing a dark blue velvet suit jacket, bow tie, it's effortless, very movie-star glam. Which is a big difference to how we've seen these two come up together over the years. It's almost like a phoenix moment, rising from the ashes of children's television to a major movie."

"Paisley, I'm noticing that they're walking the carpet together."

"Absolutely right, Delilah, they are arm-in-arm, looking like a dream. I mean, get a look at the way he's looking at her when they stop for pictures. It's how we're all looking at her."

Dax presses a hand into Wil's back and guides her gently towards the cameras. He whispers something in her ear. Wil lets go of his arm and steps forward. A production assistant dressed in black slacks and a headset rushes forward to help pose the dress's train for photos, but Dax beats her to it.

With gentle, careful hands, he gathers the silver material and pulls it flat against the carpet so it's draping, fanned to its full breathtaking capacity.

"And this is the first time we've seen them on a carpet since their show was canceled, is that right?"

An audible hush falls over the white carpet. Another limo has pulled up, and a blazing red dress is climbing out.

"Hang on a minute, Delilah, I'm getting word that another star has arrived on the white carpet. Katrina Tyson-Taylor is in the building! And she looks like a million bucks."

"Is that custom Versace?"

"It is, and we're seeing a big change tonight from Katrina, who has gone platinum blonde! Oh my god, I can't believe how incredible she looks. Just a total movie star. This is a huge night for her. Following familial issues with Wil and Bob Chase, she is absolutely stunning. Completely reinventing herself here."

Her dress is one-shouldered and timeless, embellished with a diamond brooch at the hip.

Every camera on the carpet turns towards her.

Finally, Wil and Dax arrive in front of Paisley's camera.

"Wil, my *god*, you look incredible. Tell us about the dress," says Paisley.

"Hi, wow, thank you," says Wil, her hazel eyes lined delicately tonight, looking beyond the reporter to the sea of screaming fans. "The dress is Oscar de la Renta. I'm actually styled tonight by my very good friend, Margot Martinez, who is so much better at dressing me than I am." She laughs.

Paisley laughs, too. "How are you feeling being back out on a red carpet for the first time in years?"

"Nauseous," says Wil without skipping a beat. "No, but I'm excited. It's exciting. It'll be my first time seeing the movie, and usually I hate watching myself perform, but my buddy Daxon Avery is supposed to be really good so I'm stoked to see his performance."

"Daxon," Paisley gushes, "what can we expect from Wilhelmina in *To the Stars?*"

"Well, Wil has this really annoying habit of being great without trying, so you can expect to feel just incredibly bothered the entire time by how good she is," he says with a straight face, before breaking into a wide grin.

"I'm sorry, can I see your invitation?" Wil turns to Dax. There's faux-sternness on her face. A beat later, they're both laughing.

"You two are *so* cute!" Paisley is beside herself. "Wil, what can we expect from Daxon tonight?"

"Dax is the most honest actor I know. Everything he does on camera is so authentic and real. You will walk away tonight fully obsessed with him. I guarantee it."

Ahead, production assistants wave to those still on the

carpet, beckoning them towards the theater where the film is ready to start.

"Thank you both so much for stopping by! Have a wonderful time tonight and congratulations—this is huge!"

Dax bends his elbow and holds it out to Wil who takes it, and together, they walk inside, looking like a star and her night sky.

Now

DAXON

⌒∽

"Can you say Jell-O dress?" I whisper to Wil about Katrina as we wait in our seats, the darkened screen ahead of us about to light up any second now.

She snorts. "Having flashbacks?"

"Uh, yes. Yes, I am. Hours of scrubbing my hands clean, thank you."

"Think she got it out of the leather?"

I grin, picturing it. "Chase, I like to imagine that, to this day, that car is still Jell-O red inside, top to bottom."

"She drives around with the top down and people pass by, going *that is such a unique leather, what a fun color*, and she waves and smiles and then drives away furiously screaming."

"All the way to the salon," I add and we both stifle ugly laughter.

Of the thousands of things about Wil that I'd consider a favorite, this kind of stuff is near the top of the list. Truly, we're gremlins together. I don't know which sane person let us meet, let alone get to know each other and become friends.

I hope one day, thirty years from now, she's still next to me, cackling. And I realize for the hundredth time just how much I missed our friendship while it was broken. I won't let it get to that place again.

The lights dim, people settle into their seats, the talking dies to whispers and the screen ahead of us blazes to life.

Here we go.

This is it.

From this second onwards, everything will be different.

I clap, everyone in the place erupts into applause, but Wil is still and quiet beside me. It's like I can feel the air paused in her lungs. My eyes slide to my left where she sits and I can see her hands are holding on to either side of her chair for dear life. Like at any second it's going to catapult her into the ceiling.

The music, scored by an incredible composer we were lucky enough to get, is sweet but sweeping. Already, before a single line, you know what time period we're in. You know the stakes; you know there's no way in hell you're walking out of here with dry eyes.

Gently, slowly, I reach for Wil's hand. Not in that sly, seventeen-year-old way I would've done back then, but in a confident gesture of reassurance. My fingers brush the top of her hand, trying to pry it from the seat, but she isn't budging.

Her voice fills the room with Lila's first line: *For a girl from a family with more money than God, that summer cost me everything; but I'd live it over again a thousand times, given the chance.* Wil's fingers wrap around mine and hold fast and tight.

On-screen, we get a close-up of her face in an old, fancy car from the thirties, as the Patterson family pulls up to their new home.

I only filmed outside this place on location once or twice, and I'd forgotten how beautiful it was. Long-leafed, romantic willows drenched in sunshine guard that sloping front drive. The vibrancy of the greens and yellows mix with the endless blue summer sky against the glass like they're colors on a palette. And just behind them is Wil.

Her eyes on-screen are fiery, intelligent, guarded, gorgeous.

I squeeze her hand and she squeezes back. All the tension in her body slowly starts to ease and Wil turns to me from her seat. She's beaming in the dark. I grin back at her and flash a thumbs-up with my free hand.

By the time I have my entrance out on the pier, I'm so sucked into Lila's wealthy world and its rules and expectations that seeing myself looking like I slept the whole night outside is jarring.

But man, fucking Greg. He doesn't miss anything.

Every little movement I've worked into my face, every twitch of my lips or raise of an eyebrow, he's captured and highlighted so that when you step back, he's rendered this charming, golden kid who you'd follow into the sea if he asked.

Wil squeezes my hand twice in a row when Lila and Nick meet. And then she's still for a while, our hands still clasped in the cool darkness, watching months of hard work pay off. Across a summer of first love and bitter goodbyes with a war on the horizon, Nick and Lila are so unbelievably watchable. Greg's made sure of it.

They're bright, like shooting stars passing across the sky.

The big, epic kiss is a particular stand-out moment. Lila running across the pier for Nick, the sunset all sleepy oranges and wispy pinks. She's going to college. He's staying here. The breakup is inevitable, and comes after a bitter fight. But she's sorry and so is he.

She runs for him full-out, desperate for one last goodbye, then throws herself up into his arms. Her legs lock around his waist. His arms support her. Their lips crash together in a kiss Greg frames with the dying sun.

Holy shit. The chemistry between us in this movie is its own third character.

I wonder if it's like that in real life, too.

Wil turns to me, excitement and shock registering all over her face. "Remember how messy that was?" she whispers gleefully. "Literal hours. So much lipstick."

"It was the sweatiest, most choreographed anything ever," I whisper back, nodding.

"We killed it."

"Oh, there's no question. We crushed it."

She bounces our hands excitedly, and if it were possible for me to love her more, like if I had any real estate left in my heart or soul or kidney, maybe, this would be the moment that would've done it.

Instead, I force myself to look back at the screen, so I don't puke up the surge of butterflies rushing out of my stomach towards my esophagus.

You know what, I hate to admit it, given the shitshow parade she's been grand-marshaling lately, but Katrina is undeniably fantastic. She's so mean in this movie, so cruel and bitter and committed, which isn't exactly a stretch, but on camera, it's captivating. You love to hate her. It creates this feeling of adrenaline each time she pops up on-screen, and unfortunately, all that serves to do is make her iconic.

By the end, though, there's no doubting that this is Wil's movie.

Lila is alive and nuanced, even if her circumstances aren't particularly unique. During the last scene of the movie, as Nick's life fades away, around us we hear the sound of noses sniffling, of people digging in pockets and purses for tissues.

Even I feel a tight twisting in my throat watching Wil act her face off as Nick and Lila marry each other knowing they only have minutes left together.

I had it easy. I was half-dead.

And while I can see a lot of doors opening for me after this—romantic comedies, maybe some more serious dramas—I know for certain that it's airplane hangars that are going to open for Wil. And I wouldn't have it any other way.

Now

DAXON

∞

"Daxon, I don't want to inflate your ego, but I have some incredibly exciting news for you," says Wil two weeks later in between press interviews.

We've been locked in this room all day. Literally since the sun came up, one-by-one, every possible media outlet for entertainment has filed in, and asked us the same four questions:

1) *What made you want to work on this film?*
2) *How do you film a romantic scene like the big kiss between Nick and Lila?*
3) *What was it like working together after all these years?*
4) *You two briefly dated, is your love story anything like Nick and Lila's?*

And I don't know about Wil, but I'm about four seconds away from crawling into the nearest corner to rock back and forth and potentially eat my own hair as my sanity slips away. So this news, whatever it is, is life-giving.

"Tell me," I say.

"I know you've always wanted to win an Academy Award," Wil begins stoically, slowly, like she's building to some huge reveal. "And I'm here to tell you that you *and* I"—she pauses, eyebrows raised, staring me down; I can feel the grin at my lips struggling to break free, but I try to hold it back for the sake of the bit—"have been nominated for *Best Kiss* at the MTV Movie Awards."

I can't hold it in anymore—I laugh.

I laugh so hard, my entire body is shaking, my face flushed and cheeks aching. Wil laughs too.

"Should we practice a speech?" I barely manage to ask.

"Absolutely," she agrees, comically breathless with import-ance. "This is once-in-a-lifetime—there's no room for error. The highest accomplishment."

We both snort, clapping our hands and folding in half as a producer calls for quiet and the next interviewer settles themselves into the chair before us.

Finally, in the late afternoon, we're done.

"Wanna grab something to eat?" I ask her as we head towards the elevators that'll carry us down into the parking garage.

Wil stifles a yawn and leans her head against my shoulder, shutting her eyes. "I'm gonna head home, I think. Vegetate. I'm shooting a magazine cover tomorrow."

I can't blame her. We've been up late and up again early for the two weeks since the premiere, doing interviews, photoshoots and random press events nonstop. The elevator dings. Wil drags herself off my shoulder to walk inside, settling herself back into a slumped-over, half-asleep position against the elevator wall.

It's just us.

I press the button for the garage, stand back beside her against the wall, and we start descending.

I have a choice here, a chance, and either way I look at it, I'm terrified of what's going to happen next. Not with the movie, not with my career, but with Wil and I.

On the one hand, we make fantastic friends. She's the first person I want to tell about anything that happens to me. I trust her with my life. Really, there's no one on this earth who knows what it's like to be us, who's lived through what we've lived through together, shared what we've shared.

On the other hand, my soul will love her forever. Friends or otherwise. And if I don't take a chance on this now, I don't know when I'll work up the courage again.

"Hey," I say quietly, turning to her as the doors open, "I just have to tell you . . ."

Wil looks up into my face, her eyes big, waiting, maybe a little scared. "Yeah?"

"I'm in love with you."

"Dax," Wil starts.

"It never stopped for me."

She shakes her head, her eyes darting away from mine. There's no smile on her lips. When her eyes find their way back to me, my heart starts sinking to a lower depth than I've ever felt it.

"This next step is really crucial for me. Now that *Stars* is out, I need to . . . be my own person, make my own way," she says. The elevator doors start to shut and she lurches forward, pressing her hand to the edge so that they stay open. "You've already done that, now it's my turn."

The thing is, I know she's right. She has a huge alter-ego to shed. This is her moment to claim something on her own, without me attached. I know this. But the air in my lungs comes in too quickly and leaves too soon and I can't get a good deep breath to calm the whirling panic inside my brain.

"Okay," I manage. You don't ever think that heartbreak is going to be like it is in cartoons, with your heart cracking into literal halves, but I think in this moment, mine does. It splits in a jagged line and falls away to crumbling dust. "I'm sorry, I should've . . . I'm sorry."

"No," Wil says quickly, shaking her head. She's touching my arm, I think, but my entire body is numb. "It's okay, it's . . . Daxon, you know how much I love you. I just—I don't know. I need to do this on my own."

I nod. The elevator doors start to close again and it's my turn to slap my hand against the frame, making them reopen. It would be so much easier to have this conversation out in the garage, or better yet, truly alone somewhere private. But that would mean someone has to make the first step to leave, and I don't think either of us wants to be the first to walk away.

There's a script sitting on my bedside table, waiting for me, and the first thing I'll do, when I'm done drowning myself in my shower tonight, is settle in and read it. On to the next. Forward momentum.

When you start building something out of Lego, especially something intricate like the Falcon, sometimes you screw up and knock it over, the pieces flying in a million directions. Even if it's supposed to be this unbeatable, iconic thing that never loses a fight, never really goes down—sometimes off-screen, in your own hands, it does.

I think I need a new hobby. There are too many scattered pieces this time.

"Right," I say, nodding. "No, yeah, of course. Of course.

Yeah. You're—it's . . . you'll be great. I'll see you, uh, what? Wednesday? Whenever our next press thing is. Get home safe, okay?"

I take the first step out and I don't stop walking until I'm at my car. Even then I get in quickly and shut the door, starting the ignition and shoving the gear into reverse like I'm being timed.

This is it. Minute one of the version of my life where Wil is a friend, of course, but also a memory, the best memory.

A ghost inside of me that years won't fade.

It takes me a few seconds to register why my vision has blurred, but then I get it. The road clears as I blink, a cool tear rolling towards my jaw, dripping onto my T-shirt, and I understand that it's dive headlong into the work for a distraction, for some semblance of a life fulfilled, or die slowly, piece by piece, of a broken heart.

Now

WILHELMINA

I have four auditions this week. Four more next week. I'm on the cover of this month's *Cosmopolitan*, *Teen Vogue* and *People Magazine*. There's a billboard three blocks from my house that's just Daxon and I smoldering at passersby as Nick and Lila.

I don't know who my fairy godmother is but she's been bibbidi-bobbidi-boo-ing the shit out of my life lately.

Everything is how I dreamed it.

But there is a cavernous hole in my chest. No matter how many morning-show interviews I do, how many photographers take my picture, I can't fucking fill it. Because of course that's how it is. I take one tiny stand and try to do this shit on my own and look at me. I'm a *mess*.

Riding around the layers of my brain, circling like he's riding a fucking monorail, is Daxon. Daxon in that elevator, telling me he's in love with me. The look on his face. The hope in his eyes. *Nope*. My self-control is going to win. I'm determined.

Between auditions and photoshoots, talk shows and events, Dax and I are side-by-side, elbow-to-elbow, for hours at a time all week. We answer the same questions. Over and over. Sometimes even in the same order. It's horrific. But Daxon makes it fun, because he makes everything in this life fun.

Tonight, we're doing a late-night show appearance together and we take bets backstage on what question's going to be first.

We agree that the loser has to stuff eleven Red Vines from the craft services table into their mouth at the same time and try to eat them without puking. I bet that first up is the question about us having worked together before and what that was like. Daxon says it'll be the one about why we wanted to do this movie, what attracted us to the project.

We're both wrong.

Our names are announced. A cool, jazz-style band plays us in. The audience lights up with applause and whistles. Benjy Preston, a *Saturday Night Live* vet turned talk show host, waves us down into the two seats beside his fake desk. Motions with his hands for the crowd to quiet. The drums hit, the symbols crash, and then it's quiet.

Benjy does this bit where he doesn't say anything at first. There's this huge, hilarious silence as Dax and I stare blankly at him and the audience giggles. Benjy's glaring calculatingly at us, looking from me to Dax, Dax to me, before he says, "You two, it's real, isn't it?"

The room explodes. Cheers and applause. Somebody catcalls. People are on their feet.

The anxiety monster inside of me wants to laugh and blush and hide my face. Maybe slip off this chair and huddle up under Benjy's desk like a small, terrified woodland creature. But press, especially late-night shows, is all about the bits. Commit. Say yes.

Next to me, Dax's shoulders are getting tight with discomfort. But he's playing it off like a pro. He pulls a face and looks at me like I'm a slug. I do the same thing, sticking my tongue out and pretending to vomit. The crowd *loves* it. Benjy can barely get them back, they're screaming so excitedly with laughter.

"Come on," he whines, drawing the word out and pressing his palms together, "tell me you love each other."

"I've never met this woman in my life," Daxon says, completely straight-faced. And I burst out in ugly laughter, the crowd joining me.

"Actually, yeah, I was wondering who this is?" I say to Benjy, pointing at Dax. "Jack Something?"

We play like that a while until Benjy goes into a bit about introducing us to each other with less-than-flattering facts like *Wilhelmina Chase has a lot of great skills, I think you'll really like her, for instance she's extremely neat,* while a paparazzi photo of me stabbing trash on the side of the road, looking miserable, pops up on the monitors to another round of raucous laughter and applause.

I go to bed that night, grinning in the dark like a freak. No idea why. Just smiling. Silly, weirdo smiling. My chest feels light and fluffy and pink. Like I'm human cotton candy.

Over and over, I replay that interview. How Benjy introduced Daxon to me by showing a still from *To the Stars* where Dax as Nick is shirtless, dirty, bloody and dying in the medical tent, and saying *Daxon Avery is really just the picture of health. Total health nut.*

Every minute twitch of Daxon's face from my vantage point beside him in that interview is funnier and funnier as I play it on loop in my memories. He's so good. Hilarious. Smart. Kind to everyone. And so pretty. Prettier than I'll ever be.

You two, it's real, isn't it?

I'm up most of the night with the idea of it.

You know when something hits you going a hundred miles an hour and you know you're a goner? That's me all day. Through a breakfast I can't remember eating, to a workout I'm not even sure I went to. And all the way through getting my hair and makeup done for the MTV Movie Awards.

It's real, isn't it?

Getting dressed, I'm a zombie. Which is wild to me, because this outfit is an *outfit*. It's a *look*-look. It needs grounded confidence and attitude and sexuality and I am currently in outer space, orbiting another sun.

All press tour, I've been in dresses. Sparkling, gorgeous dresses. Long for the premieres, with old Hollywood glamour for effect. Short romantic dresses for interviews, talk shows, appearances, whatevers.

This is not a dress.

This is trousers. High-waisted, black, velvet, relaxed down the leg. On top is a lot of nothing. If you called it a bikini, you wouldn't technically be wrong. But it's a *fashion* bikini. Beautiful, supple black velvet kissing each end of a thin golden bar in the center of my chest to keep itself together. It frames my shoulders like a vest might, with thicker straps.

This look is not glamorous or romantic. Standing in the mirror, looking at myself, at my hair blown out around my shoulders, at my cleavage showing up for once, I feel sexy.

Until I get there, and I feel small. Extremely alone. Overwhelmed to the point of having to convince myself not to climb back into the limo and tell them to gun it and take me to In-N-Out instead.

This is my first red carpet without Dax next to me. He's running late tonight, shooting a commercial on the other side of town. He might not even make the carpet. The crowd behind the photographers, fans with posters and phones in the air, scream as the cameras flash. My stomach is tangled inside me, wishing I had Daxon's familiar height beside me. His shoulder occasionally brushing my arm. Posing with him is easy.

Everything with him is easy.

It's real, isn't it?

My hands clammy, I turn away from the shouts and the flashes once I've made myself stand still before them for a good five minutes.

When I went to bed last night, I thought I had my mind made up. But when I woke up this morning, something else had taken over. I was feverish with it. Stomach-plunging, hair-on-arms-prickling, might-vomit *excited* about it.

I turn and head for the theater.

"Wil!"

It's Dax, jogging away from the cameras towards me, photographers calling at him as he skips them altogether.

My free-falling stomach catches itself, mid-air. "Jesus, Avery, buy a watch," I say, rolling my eyes at him. But my lips tug into a smile I can't push away.

"Doesn't go with this outfit," he explains. He's in light-colored, high-waisted, wide-legged trousers, a vintage, short-sleeved collared shirt with a wild pattern tucked into them. The whole aesthetic is grandpa chic—and it's working for him.

The tangled anxiety knot that my organs formed on the red carpet loosens.

"You've really sold out," I tell him.

What I don't tell him is how *good* he looks. Sharp. Grown-up. Confident. A book flipped to the first page, full of promise.

"That's Hollywood, doll," says Dax in a transatlantic, movie-star accent. I give him a shove. He laughs. "Is it weird if I tell you that you look amazing? I don't wanna be weird. But, Chase . . ." Dax doesn't have words. He just gapes in a goofy way where I feel all the blood in my body racing to my face.

I think my heart is going to explode.

"Mister Avery, you forget yourself," I say in an over-the-top old-timey movie-star accent of my own.

Emotionally, I have never been so sweaty in my life. Literally, I think it's fair to say that I have never been so sweaty in my entire fucking life. Which is insane, really, because I *don't* get like this. Not with anyone else.

We laugh and shoot off phrases like, "You see here," and "Well, I for one," in our silly, affected accents the entire way inside the theater, looking for our seats.

Conveniently, at least for what I'm planning, they're right next to each other.

Award shows are a lot of sit and wait. Somebody wins something, then you sit and wait some more. And between all that sitting and waiting, I keep looking at Dax. Not obviously. Not like I'm trying to get his attention. I'm full-on side-eyeing him. Pretending to scratch my cheek. Turning my head a fraction of an inch so that I can sneak a look, my heart pounding. It's so high school.

But I don't want him to catch me. I don't want him to have an idea of what's going to happen if everything goes according to plan.

It's just that, with us, it's real. Like Benjy said. Like you can see plain as day in *To the Stars*. Maybe we're good actors, but we aren't that good.

And I've been fooling myself thinking I could plunge myself into work and put blinders on like a fucking racehorse so as not to distract myself from the prize. But work isn't life. It isn't what's real. I can see that now.

We sit through a handful of awards for Best Duo, Best Sidekick, Best Action Star. And then the screens behind the presenters shift to five different kisses. Dax and I as Nick and Lila are second from the right. Production teases little clips of each nominated kiss and my heart is rising like a kite in a hurricane.

I was a dramatic little monster child who turned into a dramatic adult, and if I ever do anything half-assed, kindly kick me. I'm going all-in on this.

Please let us win. Please. Please.

"And . . . Best Kiss goes to . . ." The envelope is opened. The presenter grins excitedly at the result then looks into camera. "Daxon Avery and Wilhelmina Chase, *To the Stars*."

The crowd erupts. Music is playing, but I can barely hear it. Dax and I laugh as the cameras push in on us, and before he can stand up, I whisper in his ear, "Let's give them a show. Go stand stage left by the wings."

Daxon gets up, his face confused, but I mime for him to get moving and he does. Jogs amiably for the stage steps. Then, doing exactly what I've said, he parks it all the way across one side of the stage.

If he knows what I'm about to do, you can't tell.

He's making a show of it, shrugging at the audience as I make my way casually, slowly, like it's no big deal, towards the opposite end of the stage.

From the stage steps, I stop and I point at him. Then I turn my hand around and motion with my finger for him to *come here*. I'm close enough that I can see the shift in his face. The jovial, game-for-a-joke expression he's been wearing for the cameras drops, and underneath it is exhilarated hope.

He starts walking.

I start walking.

The audience is thundering now. Screaming. Wild. Up out of their seats. The music is louder on stage, sweeping and propulsive. As Dax approaches center-stage, I start to run.

Six feet apart.

Four.

Two.

His arms extend and we crash together, me flinging myself up into his embrace. My legs lock around his waist. Daxon holds my weight comfortably, hungrily, against him. The music crescendos.

And then we kiss.

Now

DAXON

⌒⌒

In the history of great kisses, of the kind directors have carefully curated on camera for decades in all your favorite movies, this one is the best.

The crowd, the music, the lights, all of it goes away.

Gently, we break, and Wil presses her forehead to mine.

The look on her face is undeniable, clear as day, strong and confident—she's in love with me. And it doesn't scare her anymore.

The howling of the audience is reaching such a breaking point that we can't ignore it. I carry Wil over to the podium and she takes our golden popcorn bucket in one hand, the other around my neck. Gently, I set her down.

"You guys are gluttons for punishment," she says into the mic. All I can do is watch her glowing under the stage lights, the way they illuminate the bareness of her shoulders, the curve of her neck. There's lipstick all over my face, I know it. I can feel it. I couldn't care less.

Comfortably, because I need something to hold on to, to stop myself from passing out with excitement, I take hold of Wil's semi-bare waist and lean in to the mic. I've got no idea what the hell I'm going to say, or if I can actually speak anymore, so I stare out at the audience, who are howling with laughter— probably at my lipstick-stained face and mussed hair.

"*Thank you*," I say finally, grinning.

And then I stop and hoist her back into my arms, where she locks her ankles around me, and I stride backstage to the holding place before the press line where I finally set her down.

"Come here," Wil says, and takes my hand, leading me not towards the waiting photographers but to a small, empty green room.

Alone, she reaches up with her free hand and rubs her thumb across the places on my face where lipstick has smeared.

"I think you're stuck like this," she says, grinning.

"Hey, no complaints here."

Her hand moves to rest against my jaw, cradling my face, and I know that my pulse is jumping against her fingers like I've just been running for my life.

"Let's make a pact," says Wil softly. "You and me? We're not gonna be just friends ever again."

My eyes jump around her beautiful face, almost frantic to memorize it, and this moment, and the way her voice sounds so confident and sure and *sexy*.

"No?" I ask, but it's redundant. My voice is low, wanting, and my hands slip around her hips, pulling her in.

"Not even close," says Wil, and we're kissing. Kissing like we're not trespassing in the green room of this theater, like this is our house and we can break any rule we like. "I love you," she breathes between kisses.

I nod frantically, then lift my hands to catch her face and hold her there a moment before my lips break into a huge smile.

"You sure?" I ask.

"Well, Avery," says Wil, pulling a face like she's really mulling it over, "I'm mad with power. I want it all. But I want you most."

I kiss her. I put a lot of years into that kiss. The sparkling beginning ones, the long-suffering middle ones, and these ones, right now, where we're exactly where we wanted to be.

And all the golden ones to come.

I pull back, beaming. "I love you, too. Like, you have no idea how much."

There's a firm knock on the door.

"Press are waiting," comes a nervous PA's voice.

Wil and I look at each other and laugh. The silent kind, where all we can do is clutch each other and try not to pee our pants. Then, her hand in mine, and the golden popcorn bucket along for the ride, we walk out into the press room where a hundred voices start shouting at once, flashbulbs blinding.

"Wil!" a photographer calls clearly through the din. "This is such a departure from your earlier work. Do you miss *Marnie, Maybe?*"

"Not anymore," she says, gazing up at me.

I know it's true, because the best thing about *Marnie*, that summer we were seventeen, was always me and her. My eyes meet hers and we grin at each other, fingers tangled. The best thing about Hollywood, this movie, our lives together from here on, will always be me and her.

And I think, this time, the pact's gonna stick.

ACKNOWLEDGMENTS

To begin with, I want to thank you, my readers. Thank you from the bottom of my heart for taking time to read my words. I'm forever grateful.

I and this book would be nowhere without a supporting cast of brilliant, wonderful people!

Enormous thank you to Allison Moore, my editor, for loving and championing this book through each draft. Thank you to Renata Sweeney and the team at 8th Note Press for all of your hard work and stellar ideas.

Michelle Kwon, thank you thank you thank you for designing and illustrating the cover of my dreams! You brought Dax and Wil to life flawlessly.

My incredible agent, Rachel Beck, thank you for your unwavering support and encouragement throughout this journey. I am so very thankful that our paths crossed! Cheers!

To my family, thank you for supporting me through the rollercoaster that is publishing a book and always knowing I could do this. To my husband, Andrew, the love we share will be woven into the words I write forever. Thank you for everything. I couldn't have done this (or anything, honestly) without you!

For the sweet, incredible friends that read early drafts of this book, who selflessly shared wisdom, laughs, and ideas, screamed with me over the wins and losses, and championed Wil and Dax across social media and beyond: Kalie Holford, Audrey Goldberg Ruoff, Hadley Leggett, Jordan Kelly, DJ Caddy, Hana Gibson, Michelle Hazen, Isamar Ariana, Kasee Bailey, and Janni Sparks—THANK YOU!!!

To the writing community, to Author Mentor Match R7, thank you for giving me a place to belong, grow, and bloom. All of you inspire me constantly with your brilliance and passion.

Special thanks to Eva Scalzo and Speilburg Literary for brokering this deal and being my very first yes in publishing.

And to Taylor Swift, thank you for providing the forever soundtrack to my books, my dreams, and my life.

AUTHOR BIOGRAPHY

Caitlin Cross grew up in Los Angeles on the sets of the TV shows her father wrote, directed, and executive produced. She spent her early twenties as an auditioning actor before realizing that writing about Hollywood was her passion. She now resides in the Pacific Northwest. *On Screen & Off Again* is her first novel.